Amy Myers was born in Kent. After taking a degree in English literature, she was director of a London publishing company, and is now a freelance editor and writer. She is married to an American, and they live in a Kentish village on the North Downs. She also writes under the name of Harriet Hudson.

Murder at the Masque

Amy Myers

HEADLINE

First published in Great Britain in 1991
by HEADLINE BOOK PUBLISHING PLC

First published in paperback in 1991
by HEADLINE BOOK PUBLISHING PLC

10 9 8 7 6 5 4 3 2 1

ISBN 0 7472 3674 7

Printed and bound in Great Britain by
HarperCollins Manufacturing, Glasgow

HEADLINE BOOK PUBLISHING PLC
Headline House
79 Great Titchfield Street
London W1P 7FN

Author's Note

For the purposes of this story the Tsar Alexander II has been credited with an additional son, the Grand Duke Igor. He, his household and the Villa Russe are fictitious, as are the other active participants in the plot. For information on the Cannes Cricket Club I am indebted to Patrick Howarth's fascinating *When the Riviera was Ours* (Routledge & Kegan Paul Ltd, 1977); the pavilion, however, is my own invention. *La Fabuleuse Histoire de Cannes* by Jean Bresson (Editions du Rocher, Monaco, 1981) provided much information on the history of the grand villas of the town; *The Man Behind the Iron Mask* by John Noone (Alan Sutton, 1988) provided comprehensive details of the mysterious prisoner kept on the Ile Ste Marguérite, and in particular an epilogue concerning rumours of the ghost recently seen near the old town in Le Suquet. It is a fictitious extension on my part to cast this apparition back nearly a century, but with stories about Iron Mask circulating in the town ever since the masked prisoner arrived, it did not seem to me far-fetched.

I am, as ever, grateful to my agent Dorothy Lumley for her constant support, and to Jane Morpeth and all at Headline for making the path to publication so pleasant; to Rodney Burton; and to the Bibliothèque Municipale in Cannes, situated so appropriately in the former Villa Rothschild on the route de Fréjus. A special thank-you to the artist Natalie Greenwood, who so expertly interpreted Inspector Rose's sketch of the Cannes Cricket Pavilion.

The Cannes Cricket Club Pavilion

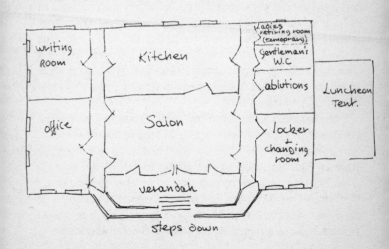

office

writing ROOM

Kitchen

Salon

ladies retiring room (temporary)

Gentleman's W.C.

ablutions

locker & changing room

Luncheon Tent.

verandah

steps down

Chapter One

Auguste Didier stepped off the Calais–Mediterranean Express and sniffed. He gave a deep sigh of satisfaction. Ah, the perfume of the air. The scents of the pines of the Esterel mountains and the hillside flowers still filled the air of his native village with their warm magic. Some said Cannes belonged only to the English, that it had become the new battleground of Europe with the Romanovs to the east on the hill of la Californie and the English to the west on the route de Fréjus. But to those who really knew it, Cannes was still Cannes, the small fishing village that over the centuries had seen invaders come and go, Romans, Greeks, Saracens, Italians. Here he had been born in a small house on the hillside of Mont Chevalier, gone to the small school in the Rue du Barri. Here he had been apprenticed to *Le Maître*, the great Auguste Escoffier. Cannes was in his blood, a village blessed by the heavens.

'Murder! It's murder, I say.'

Auguste spun round at the shrill sound of an undoubtedly English aristocratic voice disturbing the peace of the south. He smiled with relief when, peering curiously outside into the Place de la Gare, he saw a familiar scene. Skirts rustling in indignation, an English lady was waving her lace-edged pink parasol threateningly at an uncomprehending cabbie who was merely persuading his bored horse by time-honoured means to begin yet another journey to the Hôtel du Parc. Or perhaps to the Hôtel Gonnet, though with the seaside front position the latter

1

was not so popular. It would not suffice for this stiffly corseted martinet with her fashionable trained carriage dress.

Murder indeed. Auguste laughed at himself. He must have murder on the brain.

'A holiday,' the secretary of Plum's Club for Gentlemen had said to its *maître* chef reproachfully. 'You need a holiday, Monsieur Didier. It isn't like you to forget the truffles in the Chicken Bayonnaise.'

There had been A Complaint. About *his* food. And moreover it had been justified. Auguste had been appalled. How could it have happened? He had briefly contemplated suicide, and had decided against it. Honour could be restored another way. After his holiday, they would be waiting for him with open arms – or rather mouths – after six weeks of Monsieur Archibald Binks's efforts. Pah! Trained in the Marshall School. The school gave excellent training for cooking treacle pudding no doubt. But the gentlemen of Plum's required *la vrai cuisine*. Auguste gloated with satisfaction. He would return and cook them delicacies such as they had never imagined, inspired by the perfumes and tastes of his native land.

The smell of the coffee from the café tabac in the railway station recalled him from theorising on how to transform Alexis Soyer's turkey *à la Nelson* into something edible – the sauce, he wondered, was that the mistake? Omit the tomato perhaps? He found his *billet de baggage*, exchanged ritual imprecations with a porter who tried to relieve him of his hand luggage with the practised ease of the French, bypassed the crowd of English *hiverneurs*, arranged for the delivery of his modest suitcases to his parents' home and walked out into the Place de la Gare, a happy man. He was home.

'Fiacre, monsieur?'

A cab? No. He would walk. Absorb the smell of the south. His mother had once told him that when the Empress

2

Marie-Alexandrovna of Russia had come to Cannes nineteen years ago in 1879, her last words on leaving were, 'Let me smell once more that perfumed air . . .' The warmth was in his nostrils, beguiling his senses, for all it was only the beginning of March, as he crossed the Place into the Rue de la Gare, heading for Le Suquet, the small house in the Rue du Barri and six weeks of pure bliss.

For Cannes had one other blessing that London, delightful though it was, seemed to lack, at least as far as he was concerned. For Auguste, London was inextricably bound up with murder, which seemed to stalk him as inexorably as Jack the Ripper his victims.

Not long after he had been instrumental (he tried to put it modestly even to himself) in solving the murders at Stockbery Towers in Kent, he had become the chef at the restaurant of the Galaxy Theatre in the Strand – and murder came too. Delightful though Plum's was, he felt that at the age of thirty-eight he should consider his future carefully. That dream, the dream of every *maître*, to own his own restaurant, even a hotel, was but a dream yet. As seemingly unobtainable as that other dream of Tatiana, his beautiful Russian princess in Paris. His, he thought ruefully. But she could never be his. He was a cook, albeit a *maître*, and she a princess.

But, he had told himself firmly, one cannot produce a dish for a Grimod jury without peeling a potato. And Plum's in St James's Square was a potato *très sympathique*. Alas, incredibly, in that place of quiet gentlemanly retreat from the world, murder followed once more. True, all these melancholy events had brought him into contact with *cher* Egbert, Inspector Egbert Rose of Scotland Yard, but murder was murder; it tore at the emotions. He needed a holiday.

And no cold hand of murder could possibly touch this delightful place of sun and warmth.

* * *

3

Early March in London was not a time of beautiful perfumes and scented air. It was a time when the skies were grey, even when they could be glimpsed through the smoke from chimneys that failed to disperse but hung loweringly over the blackened buildings. Muddy pavements were cluttered with equally unsunny Londoners – at least in this part of London – as the hansom continued its journey towards Wapping.

Pulling his greatcoat firmly around him, as the hansom arrived at his destination, Inspector Egbert Rose paid the driver his two shillings, having successfully won the battle of whether or not the journey was within the four-mile radius, by demanding to see his Book of Distances. He ignored the look of distaste at the customary meagre Scotland Yard allowance for tipping and picked his way along the river front. Accustomed to this street from his days on the beat, now thankfully well over twenty years behind him, the filth and smells were no surprise to him; the Thames looked an evil thoroughfare on this bleak day. Peabody could have spent some of his millions building a few new homes round here all right. Place hadn't changed in a century, if that.

A swarming den of thieving villains, thought Rose grimly, as he pushed open the door of The Seamen's Rest and surveyed the assembled company. A riverside pub would obviously be packed with seamen, and it looked like the scum of the earth had gravitated to this flash-house. Every villain on the Thames Police's books – together with Lascars, Arabs, Chinese – all stopped in mid-talk as he entered. They all knew a crusher when they saw one. Especially a jack.

Only the publican, a middle-aged gentleman with impressive Newgate-knockers sidewhiskers, seemed unperturbed as he carefully inspected a glass, whistling 'The Man Who Broke the Bank at Monte Carlo' in a thoughtful manner.

'Ah, Higgins,' Rose said blandly. 'I've come about those Fabergé Easter Eggs again.' He believed in the direct approach.

4

The publican dropped the glass, then fielded it as expertly as the great W. G. Grace himself. 'Now now, Inspector. I've got my reputation to think of,' he said indulgently. 'Don't want my customers to think I'm running a swells' dolly-shop—' His voice swelled in righteous indignation. 'You will have your little jokes, Inspector. If it's about that licence, you'd best come in here.' A broad hand firmly ushered Rose behind the scenes, after its owner's stentorian shout for 'Ma!' They were followed by interested and wary eyes.

'It ain't all perlice I'd invite into my home,' Higgins pointed out.

Rose believed him, glancing round. The room was plentifully though not ostentatiously adorned with the benefits of Higgins's trade as the biggest fence in London – 'international trade welcomed' (the pub conveniently near the docks for overseas business).

'Muriel,' Higgins yelled – this time to his wife.

So there was going to be business, Rose thought. Muriel was only summoned when something big was on. The lady appeared, simpering as if Rose were royalty. It was a misleading façade. Were it not for the fact that Rose had once viewed Muriel in full combat bargaining with the toughest cracksman in London, he would have put her down as an unlikely mate for the shrewd James Higgins. Since then, closer attention on his part had revealed her to be if not the brains behind the business, at least the treasurer.

'Any news for me on those eggs?' inquired Rose, pushing aside the leaves of an over-excited aspidistra, to sit in a chair surrounded by photographs of all the little Higginses framed in interestingly high-quality silver frames. It had been a long shot, but Higgins had been known to part with information if it suited his book. And Rose's usual channels of information had yielded nothing.

Higgins shook his head regretfully. 'Nah. 'Ad you asked me about Lady Becker's ruby suspenders, or the old Duke's

5

cuff-links with the naughty cameos, I might 've obliged. But eggs? Nah. Out of my class.'

'You, Higgins? Nothing too hot to handle, that's your line.'

Muriel interposed on behalf of her husband.

'Inspector, 'oo wants an egg everyone is going to recognise?' Her hands resting in her lap, she could have been presiding at an At Home.

'Abroad?'

'The Continong? Nah. Mind you, as one pal to another . . .' Higgins paused, a beaming smile extending almost as far as the sidewhiskers.

'No pal of yours, Higgins,' Rose reminded him blandly.

'Working mates, then. Nah, this 'ere cat burglar of yours. 'Igh-society lad, seems to me. Don't see 'im in the Ratcliffe 'Ighway pinching old Ma Thomas's tea caddy. And where does 'Igh Society hang out this time of year?'

Rose looked blank. 'Hunting?' he ventured.

'Nah.' Higgins tapped his pipe on the table impressively. 'Cannes, that's where they go. Down to the old Riviera.' An enormous wink impressed on Rose that something of importance was being conveyed to him.

Half London society seemed to own one of these Fabergé eggs, thought Rose gloomily as he left, and certainly over-pessimistically. Someone had decided to scoop the pool. Why?

He'd been on the case for weeks now and was getting no nearer to presenting the Chief with any kind of solution. Meanwhile the thefts continued. Six in all now. He felt rather as he had done in Hampton Court Maze when he and Mrs Rose took his sister Ethel's two youngest. All very interesting, but how do you reach the middle? The middle of this case, if the interviews he'd had so far were anything to go by, was very securely hidden . . .

*   *   *

Rose, assumed to have knowledge of the mysterious ways of the aristocracy after his successful solving of the cases at Stockbery Towers and Plum's Club for Gentlemen, had with some relief on the part of his superiors been handed the task of discovering who had been carrying out a series of outrageous jewel thefts. The husbands were decidedly well placed in society, and Lord Westbourne in particular had made his views plain. The jewels must be found: and quickly. Seemed straightforward enough, Rose had thought – until he had begun his usual inquiries. Nothing. Not a whisper on the villains' network.

'And you know what that means, Stitch.'

His subordinate, known privately as Twitch, was eager to shine.

'They're all in it together?' he suggested eagerly.

Rose regarded him sourly, and Stitch's overdue promotion went back a few months. 'Ever known any case where the lads stick together? All of them? Remember the Great Jewel Robbery in 'ninety-four? Princess Soltykoff out at Slough. The whispers came through then all right.'

Stitch fell into offended silence.

'No,' Rose meditated. 'We've got an amateur on the job. Or a newcomer.'

'Still got to get rid of the swag,' Stitch pointed out, his interest revived.

'Very true, Stitch. Very true. I think our friend Higgins might be the man . . .'

James Higgins had on Rose's first visit to Wapping presented the face of a man with no more on his mind than the pouring of the next glass of porter. It had taken all Rose's powers of persuasion, followed by threats, to extract an offer of 'keeping a lug open' on the subject of missing rubies. A second, hasty, visit to Wapping was required, however after Rose's conversation with the sixth and latest victim . . .

Natalia Kallinkova, former supreme dancer of the

St Petersburg Imperial Ballet, having now taken her ten-year benefit performance rewards and acquired a London residence, was taking the theft with more equanimity than her sisters in sorrow. A slight woman in her late twenties, she had sparkled round the room as she danced from one side to the other, pointing out the wreckage wrought by the intruder. Rose, dispatched by the Yard on a now familiar journey, leaned out of the third-floor window overlooking the garden far beneath, noting the drainpipe and small balconies up which the burglar had climbed to gain entry. His head began to swim and he thankfully drew it in. Must have a head for heights, this gentleman.

'What is missing, Miss – um – Mrs—'

'I am just addressed as Kallinkova, Inspector.' She smiled, her accent charming, her eyes lively. 'It is a greater tribute, you see.'

Rose didn't, but accepted it. He always moved cautiously with Russians. Never knew when they might burst into tears.

'I should like to meet this man,' said Kallinkova, a little wistfully.

'So would I, Miss – Kallinkova.'

She laughed, a rich chuckle. 'Ah, *mon cher Inspecteur*, it is my egg he really wanted, this burglar.'

'Egg, miss? Did you say egg?' Visions of stolen breakfasts had at first floated before Rose's startled eyes.

Kallinkova laughed. 'My *Fabergé* egg. A gift of His Imperial Highness the Grand Duke Igor. You understand?'

Inspector Rose did at once. That case at Stockbery Towers had given him insight into the ways of the aristocracy in England; he had little doubt that these Russians were much the same. Moreover, he had had dealings with the Grand Duke Igor on many occasions, summoned to the Mayfair home with relentless frequency.

'He gave it to me when we – ah – parted a year ago. He knows I am discreet. Of course he did not want to part, you understand, but the Tsar insisted. So did the Grand Duchess Anna,' she added more realistically.

Rose tried to maintain a straight face before her twinkling eyes, inviting him to share the joke. He failed, and let out a guffaw.

'Each egg, Inspector, opens to reveal a precious object inside. Outside it is the craftsmanship, you understand, which gives it its value. Inside, however, there is – in the case of the Imperial eggs – the precious stones or gold, fashioned in the likeness of some object, the Imperial coach for example. But my egg, Inspector, and' – she paused – 'each of those of the Grand Duke's other – er – lady friends contains a ruby.'

'The love of a good woman, eh?' said Rose incautiously, wrapped up in the story.

'Exactly, *mon cher Inspecteur*.' She gurgled with laughter, then continued thoughtfully, 'And I think you might find, dear Inspector, that those other ladies also have had eggs stolen. You told me there had been several burglaries of jewels, did you not? Rubies perhaps? If you ask them – tactfully of course. They have husbands . . .' She gave a little shrug.

After he had left, Rose mentally scanned his list, brows furrowed. Tactful inquiries had followed and elicited that a further five Fabergé eggs from a further five mistresses, all, like Kallinkova, now past, and all eggs containing rubies, had been stolen one by one from the great houses of Britain. In each case entrance had been gained by a drainpipe, balconies, or in one case a nearby tree provided access. Five re-interviews had followed. Rose shuddered at the memory of two of them. He wouldn't like to sit through Rachel Gray's (Mrs Cyril Tucker) tragic outburst again. He'd felt he was at a performance of one of Mr Pinero's plays. As befitting her position as one of London's leading tragedy queens, Mrs Tucker had tottered blindly across the room – though not too blindly to find the chaise longue and collapse gracefully upon it – moaning at intervals, 'My husband must not know.' Or Lady Westbourne, a very different kettle of cod. Cool as a cucumber, he had to prise the information out of her, like a whelk. In all five cases, husbands were to be barred from knowledge of the complete facts.

There was, Rose grudgingly admitted, good reason for this. The gift of a Fabergé egg could only come from one source, if not the Tsar himself: a Grand Duke of Imperial Russia. And Grand Dukes were not noted for handing out such prized gifts unless the relationship with the recipient was close. Moreover since even these eggs, which coming merely from a Grand Duke to a past mistress were somewhat less elaborate than those from the Tsar to the Tsarina, were a year at least in the making, it followed that the friendship with the lady was or had been no mere passing whim. Therefore Mrs Rachel Tucker, Lady Westbourne and three other ladies of equally impeccable social standing, if not morals, conveniently overlooked the theft of the egg itself, when reporting, albeit reluctantly, the theft of the ruby. Husbands, unaware of Fabergé eggs secreted in their households, would not be unaware of the disappearance of a ruby which in each case the lady concerned had been unable to resist wearing. They were exceptionally fine rubies.

Kallinkova being single and having no husband to wonder why his wife should be the recipient of a Fabergé egg, had entered into the spirit of the chase with relish, and gave Rose details of the London ladies' calling-hour gossip concerning the other five victims.

'I should like to meet this man,' repeated Kallinkova when in late February Rose had duly interviewed her again and confirmed her suspicions regarding her fellow victims. 'What an artist. As I am myself.' She pirouetted despite the confines of the tight heavy silk skirt. 'To steal from a collection and take only the supreme jewel. My ruby is beautiful, but it is nothing compared with the egg itself. He wants only the thing of beauty, the work of a master craftsman. Ah yes. He is an artist in himself, is he not, Inspector?'

'He's a thief, Miss Kallinkova,' said Rose glumly. 'And it's my job to catch him.' A job that was getting more difficult by the minute. A jewel thief was one thing, a stealer of Fabergé eggs smacked of something different. International art collectors for example. And that meant the Commissioner would be breathing down his neck, as well as the Chief Constable.

He sighed, and Kallinkova laughed at his lugubrious face. He looked like a bloodhound, she decided, summing him up. A reliable friend – and a relentless hunter, with his watchful grey eyes.

'You'd better give me a full description, miss,' he said, resolutely refusing to share the joke.

Kallinkova put her hands meekly in her lap.

'The Imperial eggs that his Imperial Majesty the Tsar gives to the Tsaritsa and Dowager Tsaritsa are naturally larger, more elaborate and the gifts inside works of art in themselves. This Igor could not do. It would not be *comme il faut*. But they are beautiful all the same. On the outside' – she smiled, inviting Rose to share her joke at male expense – 'a portrait of Igor himself surrounded by tiny diamonds. The egg – my egg is pale green enamel and criss-crossed in gold. And inside all the eggs, so Igor says, are the rubies. But a woman's value is high above rubies, is it not, Inspector?' Her eyes twinkled. 'Igor should know this before he takes another lover,' she added obscurely.

'Besides those we know about, did the Grand Duke have any other – um—?'

'Lovers? Ah, Inspector,' she smiled deliciously, 'how could I know? Igor is a very' – she paused, head on one side – '*enthusiastic* man.'

Rose blenched at the thought of tracking down a cat

11

burglar on the trail of an enthusiastic man. Why did these Grand Dukes have to live in London? Why didn't they stay in Russia? Somewhere off his beat.

'There is one thing, Inspector,' she added helpfully. 'I have a feeling there was one other egg – you understand I am a *femme du monde* and Igor talked to me as not to the others – that is bigger, more splendid than the rest, not because the lady was more prized, but because it is her profession, yes? Naturally she required more money. But she chose not money, but an egg that must be better than the others, she said. He was not happy, Igor, but he granted it to gain her favours. This lady does not live in England, so I think either it has not yet been stolen or you have not heard about it.'

'If it's not in England, it's not my concern,' Rose said swiftly. Other countries could take care of their own burglars.

'Perhaps your burglar has not heard of the egg, if he is a London person, just listening to gossip. As I do,' she laughed.

'Who is this lady?' Rose was curious despite himself.

She spread her hands regretfully. 'I do not know, Inspector.' She laughed as she saw his face fall, and relented. 'Yes, Inspector, I do. Her name is La Belle Mimosa.'

'What?'

'The beautiful Mimosa.'

'Mimosa what?'

'Not what. *La Belle* Mimosa. She is always known thus, and addressed so. As I am Kallinkova. It tells our professions. Mine, the greatest ballerina in the world; hers the most famous courtesan. During the summer she dwells in Paris and Biarritz; in the autumn in Mentone, and the winter in Cannes.'

'Cannes?' Rose pricked up his ears.

'But yes. *Everyone* must be in Cannes for February and March. I too. I leave tomorrow. Last year I dance for the

12

Tsar in St Petersburg, and at the summer palace at Tsarkoie Selo. This year I dance in London, in Paris and now in Monte Carlo. You come to see me, yes? I will dance my Odette just for you, dear Inspector.'

Cannes? That's where Auguste was going. Rose dispelled the undutiful thoughts that entered his head, as he left Kallinkova's house and went out into the biting cold of London's Mayfair.

That had been two weeks ago. Since when there had been no further burglaries of Fabergé eggs or their contents – and precious little progress on solving the six that had already taken place. Higgins had been his best bet; a frown crossed Rose's face as he clambered into the hansom outside The Seamen's Rest to return to the Yard. There was something odd there somewhere, that he couldn't quite put his finger on. Higgins knew something all right. And why did the South of France keep cropping up in the conversation?

This promised to be an excellent holiday. Auguste stared out at the blue sky through the window. The smell of the Mediterranean wafted in, or rather the smell of the fish in the busy port below them. And above all the smell of his mother's cooking coming from the tiny old-fashioned kitchen, the smell of the luncheon they were about to begin. Here he was merely a son, not a *maître* chef, and his mother had been hurt when he suggested helping her cook the luncheon. It had been a *faux pas* of the first order.

'No, my son,' she had said, firmly, 'you recall, you cannot even make a *brandade*. Goodness only knows how you look after yourself in London.' Useless to point out that the unfortunate episode of the *brandade* had taken place twenty-three years ago when he was fifteen. And so he had accepted his role as incompetent son gratefully. It would also have been useless to point out that *brandade* had hardly been a speciality of her own, before she married *Papa* and came to Provence. *Brandade* had hardly been a common dish in Lewisham where she had been born, nor even of Climpton Castle where she had been in service when she met Papa.

He had been dismayed, even if pleased for himself, to find his parents returned to this small house after he had bought them an attractive and rather more spacious villa on the fashionable route de Fréjus.

They had been apologetic. '*Mon fils*, we did not know anyone there.' His father, still as tall and upright as Auguste himself, had shrugged apologetically. 'They were English lords and ladies.'

'And not one of them could make a *sauce d'ail*,' chimed in his mother scornfully. 'Let alone an Albert pudding. Fancy that! And when I asked our neighbour how she made a sauce for the *gigot* she did not know.' Passionately convinced of the superiority of English food when she married Papa, she wavered between the two according to her mood. It was during her sporadic outbursts of patriotism that she had inspired Auguste with his love of the true English art of cooking.

'*Maman*, does the Grand Duchess Anna know how to make a *sauce d'ail*?' asked Auguste, lovingly exasperated. This was his other cause of concern. They refused to stop working. They did not go every day, explained his father, but when called upon they would make their way to the kitchens (*Maman*) and gardens (*Papa*) of the Villa Russe during the months when the Grand Duke Igor was in residence.

'She is a Grand Duchess, my son,' reproached his father unanswerably. 'And moreover Russian. Our neighbours are English.'

'But why don't they realise the thrill of stirring the hollandaise, the excitement of achieving a true *brandade*?' demanded his mother, returning to the heart of the matter – food. The ways of the gentry had always been a mystery to her, even after working for them for most of her life.

So his parents had returned to the house overlooking the port in the shadow of the fortress of Mont Chevalier, beneath the church of Notre Dame d'Espérance. Selfishly Auguste was glad, for he loved this house, full of memories, decorated with brightly painted plates and pots and redolent of Provence itself; he had been born in this house and as long as he could remember the old *chocolatière* had stood on the dresser, the *petits santons* lain in the drawer ready for Christmas, and the chipped jug with A Present from Margate emblazoned on it, *Papa*'s first gift to *Maman*, had been on the mantelpiece.

The villa had been let, his father explained, full of pride at his financial management. To make money, so they did not have to work.

'But you did not need to work,' exclaimed Auguste.

Seeing they had upset him, they tumbled over themselves to explain. They did not wish to miss the excitement of the Villa Russe. And the little villa in the route de Fréjus was let to *une grande dame Russe*. Madame Kallinkova.'

'Kal—' Auguste was spellbound. Suddenly this promised not only to be a good holiday, but the holiday of his dreams.

'She dances at the Monte Carlo ballet,' his mother explained in vicarious pride. 'In the casino theatre. But it is fifteen francs to enter, so we do not go.'

'*Maman*.' Auguste threw his arms around his mother, as she stood so tall and stiffly, as if afraid she might betray how much she loved him. He kissed her enthusiastically. 'You shall go *every* night. She is here now?'

'She arrived two weeks ago, *mon fils*.'

'Ah. Today,' Auguste said casually, as he began the fish soup, 'I shall return late.' A tiny frown. Something was different – surely there used not to be so much fennel? '*Maman*—' He changed his mind. No word of criticism should mar this perfect day.

15

He had met Natalia Kallinkova at Gwynne's, the hotel in Jermyn Street famous for its food and informal atmosphere, run by the redoubtable Emma Pryde. He admired Kallinkova, liked the way she moved her hands, liked the gusto with which she attacked her salmon, liked the twinkle in her eye, the way she walked – and most of all he liked her. She had been dining with a famous politician, but he seemed to play no important part in her life, either politically or romantically. She invited Auguste to call and he found a warm welcome. He smiled in happy remembrance. Many happy days (and nights) followed; he saw her dance Odette, wept at her Giselle, laughed at her Coppelia – and loved her at night. But she was elusive. When would he see her again? Ah, that she did not know. There were always engagements to dance in this country or that country, and when she was not dancing, then dining here, there, everywhere. And now she was in Cannes.

With a sense of anticipation he announced himself at the small elegant villa on the route de Fréjus. Built somewhat later than the first flurry of expressions of early Victorian grandeur by the British, the Villa Lavendre had opted for classical Greek pillars and porticos, and white stone, and large windows. It was through one of them that Kallinkova saw him coming.

'*Bonjour, Auguste.*' She greeted him as enthusiastically as if it had been yesterday, not three months since they had met.

'You are not surprised to see me?'

She sat down gracefully, then rose again as if she could not bear to be still. 'I am delighted to see you, *chéri*. You want I should be like the tragic Madame Gray—' She executed a neat impression of Rachel Gray as Mrs Tanqueray.

Auguste laughed, and that pleased her. She liked Auguste. Very much indeed. She liked his sense of humour, she liked his seriousness, his wholeheartedness, his tall slim figure (considering his profession) and his dark soulful eyes.

'*Eh bien*, and what are you doing here, Auguste? Now tell

16

me. Your Inspector Rose that you tell me about so often – he sent you here?'

'Egbert?' As always Kallinkova had the power to startle him. 'Why should Egbert send me here?' He watched her moving round the room, her cherry-coloured silk dress gently rustling.

'You like it?' She noticed his glance. 'The new colour. My maid is horrified. It is Lent she tells me. In France they dress so dully at such times, but me, I worship *le Bon Seigneur* in my own way, not with a dull, dull, dress.' She pirouetted, and the cherry-coloured skirts flared around her, revealing frothy lace beneath.

Auguste nodded, mesmerised.

'Good. *Eh bien*, Inspector Rose is working on a case. I thought he might be sending you to Cannes in his place, perhaps to visit La Belle Mimosa.'

'What case? And what is La Belle Mimosa? It is a new restaurant? You have tried it?'

'*Non, chéri*, it is not a restaurant. It is a lady.' She pirouetted again. 'Well, a sort of a lady,' she added laughing. 'La Belle Mimosa is *une poule de luxe*.'

'And why should Egbert send me to see this courtesan?' asked Auguste suspiciously. 'This is one of your jests, *chérie*? And do stop moving, *ma mie*.' In romantic mood, he had once likened her restless grace to the waves of the blue sea, constantly, gently undulating on their timeless path. Today it was merely irritating.

'*Oui, Auguste*.' Uncharacteristically meekly, she returned to her chair and sat down in a manner befitting the Tsaritsa herself.

'It is not jest. This,' she paused impressively, 'is the case of the—' she stopped. 'No, I will wait for the inspector to tell you,' taking her revenge.

'It is not murder, is it?' asked Auguste anxiously.

'No,' she laughed. 'It is not murder.'

'Then Egbert will not come,' he said rather regretfully.

17

'They would only send him for a murder.' What a pity. He would have enjoyed showing Egbert what a real *bourride* tasted like.

'Ah, but I think he *will* come,' she said conclusively.

Inspector Rose climbed up the last flight of stairs to his small office in the Factory. There, in the little room overlooking the Thames, he found two things awaiting him. A letter, and a sulking Sergeant Stitch. Twitch was full of ill-concealed huff that he had not been trusted with the contents of the letter, which was sealed with a coat of arms that impressed even Rose.

'He wouldn't wait, Inspector.'

'Who wouldn't, Stitch?' asked Rose patiently.

'Lord Westbourne,' said Stitch with reverent anticipation. Say what you like about old Rose; he had the knack of gathering interesting cases about him. Lords and ladies, chorus girls – Stitch approved of that. It was one of the things that made him stick by Rose.

With no sign that he was grateful for this devotion, Rose opened the letter with some interest. Lady Westbourne, the elegant fair-haired wife of this somewhat fearsome politician, was one of the victims of the theft of the Fabergé eggs. This fact still appeared to be unknown to her husband, who in his letter merely referred to the theft of a ruby; it also stated that he had positive information on the identity of the cat burglar, gleaned in London. Unfortunately he had to leave immediately for the afternoon train for Paris, where a sudden crisis had blown up. He was a member of the current, and it appeared lifelong, conference on the Niger, an issue vital to the future relations between London and Paris. War between the two countries might well erupt over Africa, if Lord Westbourne were not able to sway his fellow committee members into seeing sense. War between England and France. Shades of Napoleon all over again. Didn't seem likely, Rose thought, but then you never knew

18

with these hot-headed Frenchies! All except Mr Auguste, of course. Auguste had brains: he reasoned things out, almost like an Englishman – but then, come to think of it, his mother had been English. That must explain it.

'I can see you in Cannes.' Rose read his instructions again with mixed feelings. 'I shall be entertaining His Royal Highness the Prince of Wales on the 10th, but expect to see you in the Pavilion on the 11th at 7 p.m., after the match.'

What match? What Pavilion? Cannes? What on earth was the Chief going to say? It was a rhetorical question now, thought Rose with some pleasure. Now Lord Westbourne had summoned, he knew just what the Chief would say.

Vague mentions of cat burglars, 'hidden depths' to the case and hints from Higgins had done nothing to persuade the Chief to let his top detective depart on a jaunt down to the Côte d'Azur. The last time one had gone, he had discovered the delights of the Monte Carlo casino and had never returned. Now there was no question. Lord Westbourne had summoned and he'd be going. A rare smile of content crossed his lugubrious face. He'd be able to have some of those Provençal meals Auguste was always on about, and a nice easy case to solve as well. Then he had a sudden, belated thought. What was Mrs Rose going to say about this? In their twenty-five years of marriage they had rarely been separated, and now he was going to have to tell her he was going to the Côte d'Azur, and didn't know when he'd be back. He was not looking forward to going home at all.

Auguste strolled back along the Boulevard de la Croisette, admiring the red-pinks of the sun sinking behind the Esterel. Was there anything more beautiful in the world than sunset in Cannes? Possibly the sunrise over the Croisette peninsula with its pink-grey light and blinding golden promise. As he crossed in front of the Hôtel de Ville to mount the street up to the Rue du Barri, the sun made its final plunge behind the mountains, leaving gloomy dusk, and by the time he had reached the watchtower below the fortress of Mont Chevalier, he had to strain his eyes to see as the tall houses either side of the road cut out the remaining light. As he turned the corner, an odd shiver went up his spine, as the warm and welcoming Provence of the daytime suddenly gave way to a hint of the savagery of its wild past. A stillness in the air, vague shapes forming and unforming in the darkness. A flitting figure or a waving branch – or nothing? Surely a figure? Yes – he strained his eyes, and it swirled into the gloom, almost seeming to glow. He could have sworn it was a man wearing an old-fashioned cloak and hat, for all the world like something out of Dumas. He was half impelled to run after it to see; half inclined to stay just where he was. Curiosity won and he ran, his footsteps echoing in the stillness. There was the figure ahead, surely, hurrying on, soundless, silently; always the same distance ahead. A corner in the road – and nothing. Nothing but the empty road stretching upwards, tall walls on one side, a steep drop on the other.

Laughing at himself somewhat uneasily for chasing shadows, Auguste was glad when he entered the haven of his small home, and it was only some hours later, after a *rouget au safran* and a marc of the region, that he casually mentioned his strange experience.

His parents turned to each other and nodded sagely. 'Do not alarm yourself, my son,' said his father comfortingly. 'It is only the ghost.'

Auguste blenched. 'Ghost? What ghost?' he almost squeaked.

'The ghost of the Man in the Iron Mask, my son. You remember the old stories? He has begun to walk again.'

'He is not seen very often,' put in his mother comfortingly.

'But I don't remember any ghosts,' said Auguste.

'Because it is only recently he has begun again,' his father

20

explained. 'There were always stories, then they died out. Only the old people remembered those stories, and began to talk of them when the ghost was seen again. Only this week *la mère Peyret* saw it.'

Iron Mask had haunted Auguste's boyhood dreams. Days when he looked out from his window at the Ile Ste Marguérite, lying beyond the Croisette peninsula. He could just see the fortress where the Man in the Iron Mask was imprisoned until he was taken to the Bastille – or, if you believed local gossip, escaped to Cannes and hid here in secret. He had devoured Dumas's *The Viscount of Bragelonne*. He had seen himself as d'Artagnan, the fourth Musketeer. But now he saw things a little differently! Dead heroes were safest. Walking ghosts were distinctly disturbing.

'It is said he escaped from the Ile Ste Marguérite,' said his father excitedly, 'that he came to Cannes with his wife, the governor's daughter. And her name was Bonpart. He died here but she escaped to Corsica with their son. And this son was the forebear of Napoleon. And there is a young man who has come to Cannes who is a descendant of the Comte de Bonifacio, and he says he is the rightful king of France. Is history not exciting, *mon fils*? And it is *true* about the Iron Mask. After all, Voltaire quotes the soldier Rioffe as saying that he saw Iron Mask in Cannes.'

Auguste was determined, if only for his own mounting unease, to quash all talk of ghosts. 'But *why* should he haunt the place?'

'For justice, my son,' said his mother impressively.

'And why does he only want justice sometimes?' asked Auguste.

'This is odd,' admitted his father. 'Before now, he has not been seen for nearly fifty years.'

'So why on my holiday?' Auguste muttered resentfully.

'He was the brother of the great Louis the fourteenth,' said his mother importantly. 'Monsieur Dumas says so.'

'They are only stories, not truth, *Maman*,' Auguste insisted.

'Not to the Cannois, Auguste. He is very real,' his father said reproachfully.

'Yes, *Papa*, the man. But not the ghost. There are no such things. There must be a real person behind it. Am I not a detective? Very well,' he said bravely, 'I will find out what lies behind this so-called ghost of yours.'

After all, it would provide a nice gentle mystery for his holiday. He would not tell Natalia. Being a lady, she might be nervous at the idea of ghosts. If only Egbert Rose were in Cannes they might investigate together. That would be most pleasant. For ghost-hunting would have nothing to do with murder.

Chapter Two

The Villa Russe perched in all its white gleaming glory on the chemin de Montrouge on the hill of La Californie to the east of Cannes. It overlooked the Mediterranean, below its gardens, with a view over the whole bay of Cannes from the promontory of the Croisette, with Ile Ste Marguérite beyond it, to the Esterel in the west. Below, over the roofs of comparatively less ostentatious villas, lay the Croisette and the Gardens of the Hesperides, where 10,000 orange trees had been planted over forty years ago for the delight of any *hiverneur* who cared to pay fifty centimes.

During the dangerously hot summers, La Californie was almost deserted, but this was the height of the social season. During the bleak months of November to January Mentone pleased most, but for February, March and this year April there was no place other than Cannes. Although the English had encroached from their enclave to the east of Cannes on to the higher reaches of La Californie (indeed a prince of the royal blood had died at the Villa Nevada) and were making a determined onslaught on the eastern slopes of the hillside, Russian nobility remained firmly entrenched in the centre and south. Here during the season those unfortunate – or fortunate – enough to have incurred Imperial displeasure by marrying morganatically or not at all, advanced from England, Paris and Vienna to spend the winter season, often joined for holidays by those still basking in Imperial favour but seeking brief respite from the intrigues of the Russian court, by travelling in grand style on the

St Petersburg–Vienna–Nice–Cannes Express. A hundred yards away from the Villa Russe, the Grand Duke Michael and his morganatic wife the Countess Torby lived magnificently in the Villa Kasbeck (in the winter of course) and two hundred yards or so to the east, his sister the Grand Duchess Anastasia. In a few weeks the Russian church would celebrate the marriage of her daughter to Prince Christian of Denmark, thus inconsiderately extending the season unfashionably far into April.

The Villa Russe was built in the 1860s, when La Californie was still largely a barren hillside, by the enterprising gardener who had turned estate agent, and was now British vice-consul: John Taylor. Under the patronage of Sir Thomas Woolfield, he had created the gardens of Cannes, full of flowers, palms and eucalyptus trees, for which the town was now famed. The arrival of an earlier Romanov had been followed by the addition of some Russian statuary on the roof and porticos to remind him of the Winter Palace. Its present name had also followed, it being thought that the Villa Palmerston was no tactful appellation for a Romanov. The Grand Duke had also added a spectacular belvedere in the gardens overlooking the Bay of Cannes. Determined to go one better, and to rival that of the Grand Duke Michael at the Villa Kasbeck, he had rendered the ironwork golden, where it gleamed over the hillside as if in tribute to the old Russian sun-god Yarilo.

The villa still stood in splendid isolation, but its walls grew higher as the surrounding land sprouted more villas, churches and doctors. Admittedly there were now five British doctors in Cannes to the Russian one, and several English to the sole Russian church, but the lifestyle of the flamboyant Russians evened up the score.

'Cricket, cricket,' shouted the Grand Duke Igor jovially at the French local police inspector summoned to the Villa Russe at the un-French hour of 7 a.m. The Romanovs were brought up in Spartan fashion.

24

'But, Your Imperial Highness, who would possibly wish to kill you?' Inspector Fouchard asked rhetorically. He knew the answer.

The Grand Duke looked quickly round the room as though the samovars might hide an intruder.

'Nihilists,' he hissed conspiratorially.

The inspector sighed. He had heard it all before. 'I regret, *Votre Altesse Imperiale*, it is not possible to provide a permanent guard.'

The Grand Duke's eyes bulged. *Not* was not a word to use to princes, let alone to Grand Dukes. Jovial smile was replaced by Jove's thunder.

'Not! You want an assassination of a Romanov in your midst?'

The inspector did not. Even less did he want a repetition of the unfortunate incident some years ago when another Russian nobleman had killed a police guard under the impression he was a Nihilist. The incident had been brushed aside as an allowable mistake, for after all, these Nihilists were cunning. Nevertheless Fouchard did not intend it should happen again, least of all to him. He wavered.

'If the Prince of Wales has a guard, the Romanovs have a guard,' said the Grand Duke belligerently.

The inspector's brow cleared. 'Ah, the *match*. But that is different. Naturally we will be there. We do not want the Prince de Galles assassinated.' Too late he realised this could have been more tactfully phrased.

The whole six foot five inches of offended Romanov was concentrated on him, then unexpectedly roars of laughter filled the room as the Grand Duke slapped the unfortunate Fouchard on the back. 'Only one Prince of Wales, but plenty more Grand Dukes, eh?'

Another roar of laughter and thankful at his escape the inspector slipped out, mopping his forehead. He was not looking forward to this week at all. First, guarding the Prince of Wales as he laid the first stone of the new jetty on

Thursday; then trying to keep up with His Royal Highness's movements in and out of various clubs and/or beds for the rest of the day; then on Friday this cricket match, to guard both a Wales and a Grand Duke. Cricket? Sometimes he wondered who ran this town. That Lord Brougham had a lot to answer for – or rather that *salaud* who prevented his lordship from progressing into Italy in 1834 as he had intended, with the result that he was forced to stop in a dirty little fishing village that was quite happy looking after itself. On top of that, Paris had informed him that an inspector from the English Scotland Yard was coming here. The English. *Pah!*

One of the many sons of the assassinated Emperor Alexander II, sandwiched unimportantly between the eldest and the youngest, the Grand Duke Igor had earned the displeasure of his father by marrying the divorced wife of a remote relative, and while his father could hardly therefore deny her the status of Grand Duchess he could, and did, refuse permission for the Grand Duke to live in Russia. Indeed he leapt at the chance. Igor was not of sufficiently serious disposition to please his austere father, and as the requisite number of sons remained to fill key army posts, Igor was altogether too volatile to be left to his own devices. Cheerfully Igor had taken his new duchess, 120,000 roubles in lieu of a court allowance for his wife, his cook Boris and his small cat Misha to whom he was most attached, and departed to join his Imperial relatives in Paris. Here they lived a carefree life until the assassination of his father in 1881.

After the funeral Igor departed from Russia convinced the Nihilists lurked behind every tree. He was proved right when in 1890 a small group of émigré Russians in Paris turned out to be Nihilists lying low as was their wont, patiently waiting for their opportunity to exterminate more Romanovs. Despite the assertion of the Sûreté that they had been disposed of, Igor remained deeply suspicious and when Anarchists terrorised Paris with bombs during 1893 and '94 he packed his bags, and those of his Grand Duchess, and accompanied by Boris, though not by Misha, he departed for London where Anarchists had not yet publicly reared their revolutionary heads. The small group that existed, he was informed by Special Branch at Scotland Yard, was under careful watch, and the bomb-minded Fenians had nothing, but nothing against the Russian aristocracy. Whoever they blew up it would not be the Romanovs – not on purpose anyway. But the Grand Duke Igor remained deeply suspicious. The English translation of Mr Kropotkin's book on anarchy had done nothing to reassure him, and Scotland Yard was left in no doubt about the pleasures of having the Grand Duke Igor as a resident of London. His open-hearted warmth and zest for other aspects of life they were not in a position to appreciate. His impulsive generosity of purse as well as person, when it came to ladies, made him a popular figure in society, and if he sometimes repented of the former, he made no apologies for the latter. Life in London during the summer and in the Villa Russe during the winter was lived with few expenses spared. Unfortunately those that were, though minor, were unpredictable and he was thus a figure of awe to his staff, who treated him gingerly since the beneficent Grand Duke could turn at a moment's notice into a pettifogging tyrant. True, he swiftly metamorphosed back into his more usual self, but the interims were apt to be uncomfortable. Particularly in the regions where the work of the house was carried on.

Auguste looked approvingly round the kitchen. It was not what he himself would have chosen. The huge range was not to be compared with his own Sugg's gas kitcheners, though it was true for some dishes the range was to be preferred. The Jones smoke-jack installed on the chimney breast was admirable, as were the rows of small refrigerators. Certainly this light, airy place was a paradise compared with the small, antiquated basement kitchens of Plum's Club for Gentlemen. Tradition was all very well, but modern comfort was occasionally desirable. How he envied Alexis Soyer's chance to design the kitchens at the Reform Club himself. How would Soyer have fared at Plum's? Very well, he was forced to admit. A master chef could cook anywhere, and no one could have proved this more resoundingly than Soyer, cooking in the Crimean War, on top of the Pyramids, in the soup kitchens of Ireland. Auguste gritted his teeth. A showman, that's what Soyer was. Just a showman.

A massive figure lurched into the kitchen, dark-haired, dark-eyed, dark-bearded, white-aproned. Madame Didier grew pink-cheeked with barely suppressed pride.

'This is my son, Monsieur Boris. He's a cook in London.'

Auguste closed his eyes. How without honour was a prophet in the eyes of his mother. A cook in London indeed. Would Escoffier's *maman* describe her son so?

'So, London.' A bleary eye fastened on him. 'Vere in London?'

Auguste patiently told him, and was rewarded. 'You are *zat* Monsieur Didier. *Eh bien. The* Monsieur Didier.' He was enveloped in two brawny arms, kissed enthusiastically on both cheeks twice and released, feeling as if he had just been embraced by a bear.

'I understand you require advice for a buffet luncheon for the Prince of Wales at a cricket match on Friday. I have some experience,' Auguste began modestly – and cautiously. Instinct was telling him not to get in too deep here.

'*Katushki!*' cried Boris enthusiastically. '*Katushki* on black bread. Wonderful. *Katushki* for everyone. Meatballs.'

Horror of the first degree overcame Auguste. If this was the standard of cuisine at the Villa Russe, what was he, a *maître* chef, doing here? He had been misinformed. He understood Monsieur Boris had spent some years in Paris with the Grand Duke. Surely there he had been forced to progress in his culinary ambitions? Court circles in Russia were highly refined. The great Gouffet had been chef to Tsar Alexander. *Katushki* indeed. Peasant food. He had some knowledge of the gastronomic preferences of the Prince of Wales, and they did not include meatballs.

'Mr Boris, you are drunk again,' said Madame Didier robustly. 'He can never think of anything else but meatballs when he's drunk,' she explained to her son.

'It is true, it is true,' said Boris sadly, tears rolling down his cheeks. 'I think of Mother Russia, then I drink. And I think of Mother Russia *often*.'

Auguste braced himself. Was this not a fellow countryman of his beloved Tatiana, his lost princess in Paris? He firmly put his only true beloved out of his mind. There was little in common between Tatiana and Boris. Not that he could ever recall Tatiana speaking lovingly of meatballs. Nevertheless, how could he in honour let food be less than perfect when he had the means to put it right? The Mystery of the Ghost of the Man in the Iron Mask must wait a while.

'If I might suggest,' he murmured, 'um, meatballs for your Russian guests, perhaps, with *blinis* and *piroshki*, and for your other guests, perhaps *saumon froid avec beurre de Montpellier*. For His Royal Highness the Prince of Wales, I suggest a hot *plat*, *Poularde Derby*, created by *le maître Escoffier* for His Royal Highness at the Grand Hotel in Monaco. And perhaps also some Provençal dishes – *une tapenade, naturellement* – adapted for English tastes.'

'Yes, yes,' said Boris eagerly. 'This is good. What more?'

'Perhaps,' said Auguste, waxing over-enthusiastic under this unexpected and wholehearted approval, 'a *sanglier* in aspic, if you have one brined, with "Edouard" upon it in gum-paste – ah, *non*, perhaps not – and His Royal

Highness is particularly fond of lamb cutlets. Perhaps cold *à la Belle-vue*? And of course truffles.'

'Yes, yes,' interposed Boris, hanging on his every word. 'What then? The puddings. Blanc-mange?'

'*Non* – charlotte, soufflés, *une pêche Melba – une vrai*, with a cullis *de framboise* and a *Bombe Skobeleff*—'

'No,' thundered Boris. 'The Grand Duke no like bombs.'

'Quite,' said Auguste hastily. 'The savouries then.' He reeled off a list of His Royal Highness's likes and dislikes. 'And then there is tea to consider. This is most important at a cricket match.' He knew from overhearing conversations at Plum's that tea could stiffen the wearying sinew, and strengthen the frailest bat for the fray.

'Yes, yes, this is good. My friend, this is good. Mother Russia thanks you.' Boris took it upon himself to act as Mother Russia's emissary and fell upon Auguste again with open arms. Unfortunately, being short-sighted, he fell upon Mrs Didier first, a thing she stoically endured and obviously not for the first time.

'But I have my *katushki*, yes?' Boris looked threatening.

'By all means, Monsieur Boris. Please serve your *katushki*.'

Inspector Egbert Rose was travelling by the Express railway train. Inspector of Police Chesnais of the Sûreté Générale, pausing a moment from the continuous discussion of the trial of Monsieur Zola that was gripping the whole of the country, had tried hard to get him to travel by the de luxe train, but he was adamant in his desire for speedy travel, only to discover that the Express took some seven hours longer. It was therefore somewhat late when he arrived in Cannes, unappreciative of the air, and desiring only a bed and a sandwich.

'Those requiring to study economy will find the most reasonable hotels and pensions at the east end of town . . .' his guidebook had helpfully suggested. Gloomily convinced that Scotland Yard would indeed expect him to study this fine art, Rose had little distance to go to seek his bed. The Hôtel Paradis was very near the railway station, looking down upon it but hiding from this unfortunate neighbour in a large garden. The garden did little to prevent the rumbustious noise of the railway disturbing his slumbers, already light because of the substitute for his desired sandwich.

Service had finished by the time he arrived at the pension, but when it was understood Monsieur had not eaten, great concern was expressed. A sandwich? *Mais non*. The unfortunate Rose had met his first Provençal meal head-on. Some fish soup, some morsels of pigeon *à la provençale*, *une confiture de figues*. But was that enough? Madame inquired anxiously. It was, it was. Lying awake in the middle of the night, Rose remembered Auguste waxing lyrical about *la bonne soupe*. The well-beloved of the stomach, someone or other had said of it. He had news for Auguste. His stomach had a serious quarrel going on with its well-beloved. Finally he fell into tortured sleep, dreaming longingly of Mrs Rose's boiled beef and plain, plain carrots.

He woke the next morning, hating all things foreign, and the breakfast of stale bread did little to reconcile him.

Tomorrow, 10 March, everyone who was anyone would be gathered at the port to watch the Prince of Wales lay the foundation stone for the new jetty. His appointment with Lord Westbourne at the cricket match was not until the day after, Friday. Just like England, the only place you can be sure of catching these johnnies was watching – or in this case playing – cricket. The ladies would be there too, Lady Westbourne, Rachel Gray, perhaps that pretty ballerina – he wondered how the Grand Duke liked being surrounded by all his ex-mistresses?

Rose knew the Grand Duke Igor of old and he knew the Grand Duchess Anna even better. In London they held no fears for him. But they were not in London now. They were in France, albeit with the number of English around you could easily think yourself mistaken. Rose glanced around him. The number of English accents on this broad road by the sea, bordered by palm trees, made it just like Torquay. What was it his guide book had said? A Continental Bournemouth, but the better air would be found away from the sea. Well, this was good enough for him. Nice, bracing walk along the seashore. His spirits rose and he wished Mrs Rose were here. Perhaps he'd bring her one day. He thought he'd detected quite a wistful look when he'd announced where he was going. He'd always thought she was happy having her holidays at Ramsgate every year. Perhaps he'd have to think about bringing her here instead. He couldn't see her taking to the fish soup though. His stomach gave a slight lurch at the thought of it.

Perhaps he'd been wrong to walk; it was a fair old step to the Villa Russe. Rose puffed slightly, as he climbed the Californie hill. Still, it was clearing his brain nicely. He had to get this right. Couldn't go upsetting Grand Dukes with the wrong sort of question.

It was hard to take the case seriously, what with all these eggs and so on. But there was no doubt he had to solve it, and double quick too if he wasn't to find Twitch sitting at his desk on his return. So he had to find out about that Seventh Egg. Did it really exist? And were there any more? He devoutly hoped not. Where did this Mimosa live? Ten to one, his villain was in Cannes right now. What better time for a snatch than the ceremony tomorrow, or better still the match on Friday, when the whole of society would be away from their villas.

The Villa Russe, surrounded by its eucalyptus and aloes, reminded him of something out of the Arabian Nights. He was bemusedly studying one of the more naked of Cézanne's nudes (the Grand Duchess had modern tastes) when the door of the morning room flew open with a crash and the Grand Duke filled the gap it left, towering a good eight inches over Rose.

'Yes, yes, yes, you have come to tell me of Nihilists, Inspector,' he roared. It was not a question.

'Nihilists, Your Imperial Highness?' queried Rose resignedly. He had heard all this before from the Grand Duke in London. 'Here? No.'

'No Nihilists? Then why are you here?' asked the Grand Duke blankly. 'On Friday is the match. Tomorrow is the ceremony. So you come to guard me against the Nihilists, as I ordered.'

'I didn't know there were any around,' said Rose, side-tracked.

'They are *always* around,' said the Grand Duke sadly. 'Always. One must be on guard.' He advanced cautiously into the room, then leapt in the air and spun around. No Nihilist emerged, only the Grand Duchess entering through the door into the salon.

In her late forties, a few years younger than her husband, the Grand Duchess Anna was a beautiful woman. Her pale oval face, surrounded by dark hair drawn back to set off her fine features, gave her classic Russian beauty; she was as contained as her husband was ebullient. Rose had never warmed to her although she had never been other than charming to him – and to everyone so far as he could gather. If she were as charming as all that, he asked himself, why did the Grand Duke need so many mistresses?

'Ah, Anna, the man from the Préfecture has come to guard us against Nihilists,' the Grand Duke announced happily. He had a habit of mentally transplanting familiar faces to suit his own convenience, pawns in his imaginary chessboard of Romanovs versus Nihilists.

'No,' said Rose, pulling his thoughts away from his irreverent thoughts on the Imperial love life.

'Yes, yes,' insisted the Duke, going off into a stream of French, thus to prove that Rose was a Frenchman.

'Look here, Your Highness, it's about that—' Rose began desperately. Then he broke off. He could hardly mention eggs, neither Nos 1 to 6 nor No 7, in the presence of the Duchess.

'Yes?' Two pairs of imperious grand-ducal eyes were on him.

'Possible theft,' he ended weakly.

A startled pause, then the Grand Duchess said composedly: 'The Petrov Diamond, Igor. Of course.'

Another pause as the Grand Duke thought this over. Then he gave a shout.

'They're after the Petrov Diamond. Of course, my dear. That's why the inspector's come to guard us.' An unblinking eye dared Rose to contradict him. He was too well aware of a recent anonymous conversation. 'They sent us a letter threatening us. Saying they'd get it one way or another.'

'Indeed, sir, may I see it?'

The Grand Duke reddened. 'Burned,' he said fiercely. 'I dare say,' he added in a hurry, to forestall comment, 'you've never heard of the Petrov Diamond?'

'No, sir.'

'The Petrov Diamond is the second largest diamond in Russia,' the Grand Duchess told him informatively. 'Given – or some say lent – to the Tsar Anne in the seventeenth century by Count Petrov in the hope that he might become her consort. His hope was in vain, but she graciously kept the diamond. Unlike other Imperial jewels, the Petrov Diamond is not kept in the Hermitage in the Winter Palace under the guardianship of the Tsar, but is bequeathed by the current owner to whichever Romanov they choose. Igor was given it by his great-uncle Constantin. Unfortunately from time to time someone thinks they would like to acquire it, usually a descendant of the Petrovs, convinced that the jewel was lent, not given. No doubt the time has come to try again. At the cricket match, perhaps.'

'Because the house will be less guarded then?'

'*Non*,' said the Grand Duchess Anna coolly. 'Because I shall be wearing it.'

Head reeling, Rose began to trudge back down the hill, hardly noticing in his gloom the blue Mediterranean and the warmth of the sun. What he did notice just ahead of him was a familiar figure. He quickened his step.

'Morning, Auguste!'

Auguste spun round, dark eyes lighting up with pleasure. 'Ah, Egbert. What pleasure. What delight to see you.'

'You don't seem surprised though. Heard I was coming, did you?'

Auguste paused. 'I heard a rumour,' he said diplomatically, not knowing the conditions under which Natalia had acquired her information. 'A case, perhaps?'

'I see you're not on holiday either,' Rose said meaningfully.

Auguste blushed. 'A quick visit to the kitchen of the Villa Russe,' he admitted reluctantly. 'Just to give advice, you understand.'

'Of course.' Something in his tone told Auguste that Rose was not convinced.

'How could I let the Prince of Wales dine on meatballs?' he cried. 'A luncheon for His Royal Highness at the cricket match cannot serve meatballs.'

'Cricket,' remarked Rose disgustedly. 'I come all the way to France and hear about nothing but cricket. What's it all about? *What* match?'

'The Gentlemen versus the Players. There is coffee, then there is luncheon, then there is tea, then there is apefitifs. In between there is cricket,' Auguste explained simply. 'Everyone will be there.'

'Including my cat burglar perhaps?'

'The Grand Duke thinks someone will take Misha?' (This was not the original Misha naturally, but Imperial Grand Cat Misha IV to give her full title.)

Rose grinned. 'No, Auguste. The sort of burglar that runs up drainpipes.'

'And this is your case?'

'I'm blowed if I know *what* my case is,' said Rose.

'Then you may help me solve mine,' said Auguste generously. 'Mine is The Mystery of the Man in the Iron Mask.'

'I thought they solved that long ago,' said Rose. He'd been reading about it in his guidebook on the railway train. 'Not the brother of Louis the fourteenth, but an Italian gentleman by name of Matthioli, sort of messenger between the French ambassador to Venice and some Italian duke, while the ambassador was trying to get on the good side of Louis the fourteenth. Friend Matthioli was stupid enough to sell out to Louis's enemies and landed up over there—' He nodded towards the Ile Ste Marguérite lying peacefully in the blue sea.

'And you are right. There is his prison – you see. He was kept in a room overlooking the sea, forced to wear an iron mask all the time, even to *eat*, his face never to be seen by anybody. There are many stories as to who he was, the English Duke of Monmouth some said, others a Dutchman who planned to kill *le roi* Louis the fourteenth, some say even the great Molière. Recently a new one – Eustache Dauger. Oh, there are many. But what *I* want to know is: why does his *ghost* still walk?' Auguste paused impressively.

'Ghost?' Rose started to laugh. 'You a ghost-hunter, Auguste? That's your case, is it?'

'It is all very well to laugh, Egbert. But I have *seen* this ghost.'

'Too much fish soup,' chortled Rose, unable to control his mirth.

'Fish soup. Do not speak slightingly of fish soup,' Auguste replied indignantly, ghosts forgotten. 'Ah, Egbert, now you are here, I will cook for you the *real* fish soup.'

'No, you won't,' said Rose hastily. 'I've had quite

enough of fish soup, thank you,' and related his gastronomic experience.

It was Auguste's turn to laugh. 'Ah, Egbert, I will woo your appetite back. I will take you to the Faisan Doré in the Rue d'Antibes where I was apprenticed to *le maître* Escoffier, you will taste of the wild hillsides and perfumes of Provence, dishes that are a song of which the troubadours would have been proud, you will feast as the gods. The honour of Provence is at stake here.'

'And mine too, if I don't crack my case.' Rose turned to the matter in hand. He related the story of the Fabergé eggs, concluding with the Petrov Diamond. 'Whatever that may have to do with it, if anything. *Wearing it!* I ask you,' he added glumly. 'Now you just tell me, Auguste, why anyone should want to steal *just* Fabergé eggs? And should I warn the Princess of Wales to keep hers locked up? Is he going to make for Sandringham next? Her egg came from the Tsar, of course,' he added hastily, suddenly aware of his own implied *lèse majesté*.

'Perhaps he steals for blackmail?' offered Auguste diffidently. 'If all these ladies are worried about their husbands knowing.'

Rose considered this. 'It's a thought,' he said at last. 'But why just the Grand Duke's ladies? Why not any jewels from any former lovers?'

'Because,' Auguste thought carefully, 'these are the ones he *knows* about. He has heard gossip . . . perhaps he will move on to other things.'

'Perhaps,' said Rose. 'All the same, I'm going to find La Belle Mimosa.'

'Who?' asked Auguste slowly.

'Silly name, isn't it? She's the owner of the Seventh Egg, so Miss Kallinkova says.'

'*Who?*' repeated Auguste in awe-filled tones.

'Kallinkova. A ballerina. She lost an egg.' Rose laughed. 'Makes her sound like a chicken.'

37

Auguste had stopped in his tracks. Kallinkova! The lovely Natalia who had held him in her arms yesterday afternoon the mistress of the Grand Duke . . . The brute must have ravaged her. She was too pure, too good, to have yielded otherwise. Carefully, he asked himself if he minded. Was it not hypocritical of him to mind Natalia having other lovers, when always in his own heart he held the memory of his beloved Tatiana?

'You know the lady, do you, Auguste? What a lad you are. What about Princess Tatiana?'

'There are dreams in this world, Egbert, and there are today and tomorrow to be lived. They are different things,' answered Auguste with dignity. 'I do not think of her. I cannot. It makes me too sad, being in the Villa Russe. Tatiana too is Russian. I cannot help wondering—'

'So there really *is* a Princess Tatiana?'

'Ah, she is real. But not for a cook.'

'You're a *maître*,' Rose reminded him gently.

'The Tsar Alexander much admired *le maître* Fabergé. But he admired the artist in him. To him Fabergé was not a man. And it is the man one must marry, not the artist – or the *maître* chef. So what have I to offer a princess?'

'Fabergé,' said Rose, changing the subject tactfully. 'And the Case of the Seventh Egg. You help me solve it, Auguste – and I tell you what – I'll help you track down your ghost. How's that?'

Auguste smiled. 'Very good. At least here there is no murder, *hein*?'

'Tomorrow I dance for His Royal Highness. Come, you dance with me now.' Natalia seized Auguste and danced him round the room. Her blue chiffon teagown billowed round them, entwining his legs, a lacy feather from the white trimmings flew up his nose and made him sneeze. But he remained in heaven. 'There, you are Prince Florizel,

38

my Harlequin. How do you like dancing in the ballet?'

'*Mon ange*, I want you to myself, not share you with all those people out there.' He waved a hand towards the flowers adorning the balcony.

'And what will you tell me when we are alone?' She whirled him dexterously round a chaise longue. 'There, that is the end of the *Casse-Noisette* – the *Nutcracker*.'

'I will tell you that—' he began solemnly, only to find her laughing at him. 'I cannot be serious while you laugh,' he complained, kissing her.

'Then let us speak of solemn things,' she said.

'Eggs for example,' said Auguste severely. 'Fabergé eggs.'

'Now you make me laugh again. So your Inspector Rose has come after all. I told you he would.'

'Do you still see the Grand Duke?' asked Auguste jealously.

'Yes of course. Why not? But we are no longer *amoureux*.' She planted a kiss behind his ear. 'So I will help you find this burglar,' she told him. 'I would like to see my beautiful egg again.'

'How will you help?'

'I know all these people. I think, you see,' she frowned, 'this burglar is of society himself – he knows the ways. I know these people. You do not,' she pointed out. '*Voilà*, I help.' She sprang up. 'And now—'

'And now I will thank you,' said Auguste firmly, pulling her down once more on to the chaise longue. The gratitude took a considerable time to express in fitting manner.

Chapter Three

Lord Westbourne, envoy to the Niger Conference on behalf of Her Majesty Queen Victoria, stomped round the Villa des Roses in impotent displeasure. Impotent, because he could give no vent to his feelings; displeasure because he would personally far rather be either at Monte Carlo or at Pratt's where a fellow could at least relax. He was too old to enjoy playing cricket and Cannes didn't even have a decent casino; be damned if he was going to pay through the nose to join the Cercle Nautique just for the sake of one game. Thirty francs? Outrageous. Besides, they played baccarat there, still unacceptable in England, and the less, as Her Majesty's Envoy, he knew about that the better, if His Royal Highness was going to play. His relations with the Prince were sufficiently strained already, thanks to Her Gracious Majesty's trust in him, and he didn't fancy being cast in the Prince's eyes as his mother's spy in Cannes. Ten to one, the Prince would oppose his membership anyway.

'Darling.' Lady Westbourne swept into the room, dressed by Worth and half a dozen maidservants, ready for the drive to the port for the foundation-stone ceremony. Dora Westbourne, fair-haired, and steely-eyed, looked superbly beautiful, and utterly uninterested in her 'darling'. The fair hair was helped by dye to the Lillie Langtry *de rigueur* shade, and marcel-waved. The dress was rock-pigeon grey silk, the latest Paris fashion for Lent. She was no Kallinkova.

Her husband regarded her dispassionately. He wondered

if that small, almost feline, face lit up when she met her lover, whoever he was – although he had a shrewd idea whom she had her eye on now. Now that he was away half the time on this damned conference, he'd noticed she hardly seemed as eager to see him on his return as two months' chastity might suggest. Fortunately there had been La Belle Mimosa in Paris – until their last meeting, that is. He cringed at the memory of her screams and threats to kill him if he didn't provide more money . . . But he'd put a stop to that, and, thank heavens, he was sure he'd seen the last of her.

Dora's lover was another matter. He suspected the devil must be in Cannes now, hence her sudden enthusiasm for renting a villa down here – so that 'I'll be here when you can take time off from your boring conference, darling'. And *that* had meant they'd had to pay £1,000 for a whole season although they needed only two months. Dora had even agreed to attend the match – highly suspicious. A sudden alarming thought struck him. Her lover couldn't be H.R.H. himself, could it? His passion for Lady Warwick was fading at long last. No, Dora wasn't his type – though she had a fancy for princes, of course.

He'd have to face her with it, though, after the revealing conversation he'd had with the Russian ambassador in London about Fabergé eggs. The ambassador was a friend of the Grand Duke Igor's, and the fellow had told him about the Grand Duke's extra-marital enthusiasms (carefully edited, had Lord Westbourne then appreciated it) and his method of their termination with a Fabergé egg. Lord Westbourne, guffawing with all the satisfaction of a husband with nothing to worry about, had noticed a remarkable similarity between the ladies named by the ambassador and the victims of the jewel thefts that were the talk of London society. Thereupon two nail-heads had been more squarely hit than he intended. Firstly, with a startling dexterity that would have amazed the Niger Conference, he

42

juxtaposed information gathered from two quite different social circles and reached a conclusion about the identity of the cat-burglar, a conclusion he felt impelled to pass on to Scotland Yard if only to clear the matter from his mind.

The second nail-head had led him to think further about that odd ruby theft of their own. Now he knew all these Fabergé eggs had rubies in too, it had made him not only wonder, but pretty certain. If Dora, who had behaved very oddly about the theft, had had one of those eggs, that meant she'd not only known the Grand Duke, but known him rather well. Not that Igor was her lover now. He sighed, as the depressing truth of her current amour swept over him again. He was going to have a word with her about that.

The landau progressed down the Rue du Fréjus and onto the Quai de St Pierre. They bowed to the inhabitants of carriages on either side of them, all bound in the same direction. This wasn't the time or place for frank discussion. Still, he had to do it before he spoke to the inspector tomorrow.

'Who will be at this silly old match?' Dora inquired, twiddling her parasol carelessly.

'Gentlemen or Players?' he grunted.

'Which are which?'

Lord Westbourne was apoplectic. Dammit, the woman was a fool. Or was she? He shot a sharp glance at her. 'The English are the Gentlemen, of course, the foreign johnnies the Players. We've got Harry Washington for us, naturally.'

Naturally England's famous amateur cricketer would be playing at Cannes. Wherever society was, there was Harry Washington, tall, slim, handsome and, above all, eligible.

'Then there's that johnny in the Colonial Office, Tucker, Rachel Gray's husband, and that poet fellow and of course H.R.H. himself.' And a fat lot of use he'd be to the side. Westbourne knew he wasn't much of a bat himself, but he was W. G. Grace himself compared to H.R.H. He related the other members of the team, keeping a careful eye on an apparently fascinated Dora.

'And on the other side?'

'The Grand Duke Igor, of course. That stuffed shirt, Trepolov, and some other foreign count or other.'

He still watched her narrowly. Occasionally he remembered the time when he used to call her puss and he was her great big roaring lion. Unfortunately the puss had grown into something uncommonly like a cat – and at the moment one who had licked the cream. The cream? Surely not. The dreadful possibility that it was indeed H.R.H. raised itself again. After all, he flattered himself, he resembled the Prince of Wales, and Dora had a penchant for beards, as well as princes.

'Now, Dora,' he said casually, as the landau rattled over the cobbles into the Allées de la Liberté, which on this March morning was thronged with crowds come to see the heir to the British throne lay the foundation stone for their new jetty. 'I'm meeting a fellow from Scotland Yard tomorrow afternoon after the match. I've got some information on who took your . . . ruby.'

There was an infinitesimal pause before the last word as he caught himself at the last moment. It did not go unnoticed, and the correct inference was made. A parasol snapped shut abruptly, as Dora thought through all the consequent ramifications. She would have preferred her husband knew nothing about the affair with dear Igor. Indeed, she hardly remembered it herself. It was as boring as her current amour. The time had come to tell the latter so too. It had upset all her plans to find he was coming to Cannes. After all, the other *he* would be here too. The last thing she wanted was an inquisition by her husband on the past, when the present was so much more on her mind. She could not speak to *him* today, but tomorrow at the match she . . .

*   *   *

44

Natalia Kallinkova danced a pirouette of pleasure in the small (by Cannes' standards) Villa Lavendre on the route de Fréjus and glided sensuously into *The Awakening of Flora*. Enough of dull old practice for today. Now, regaled in sober gunmetal grey, albeit enlivened with bright pink trimmings, and pearls, and a pink hat with matching feathers that the Ladies Page of the *Illustrated London News* would undoubtedly classify as provocative, she was waiting for Auguste, to escort her to the opening ceremony. She was happy, oh how happy she was. It had been a good idea to give her ten-year benefit performance at the Hermitage Theatre and receive the usual hideous Imperial brooch from the Tsar as a reward. Now she could please herself, for her reputation was assured. She had danced in London, in Paris, now Monte Carlo, next Vienna, and then, perhaps, back to Russia. How pleased Igor would be to hear that. She laughed to herself.

Poor Igor. She was still fond of him, despite everything – she recalled the first time he had invited her along the corridor from the theatre to the Winter Palace for late supper. He had seemed so big, so devoted, and the most generous man in the world. Of course, as with many other generous people, she had noticed small acts of incredible meanness even then. Still, ballerinas needed the patronage of a Grand Duke, even an exiled one. Indeed, his exile had been a positive advantage, while she was still with the Imperial Ballet. Dear Igor. For now, with everything going right for her, he was her *dear* Igor again. She remembered the small *dacha* at Tsarkoie Selo during his visit to Russia one summer, their meetings in London and occasionally in Cannes. Here it had been more difficult since discretion was necessary. How nervous he'd been to see her yesterday, as her carriage had passed his on his way to the Golf Links. She smiled. She enjoyed being here in Cannes, oh how she was enjoying it.

And one of her pleasures was Auguste. He might not be

a Grand Duke, but he was infinitely more subtle – in every way. Ah, those eloquent dark eyes. How seriously he took himself, until she mocked him gently and then he would laugh at himself, take her in his arms . . . Ah. Such a pity he remained devoted to some mysterious lady in Paris. Perhaps one day she'd try to help . . . when love had passed.

'*Mon chéri, ma galantine, mon foie gras,*' she cried as Auguste was shown into the morning room by her maid. She hurtled towards him and he caught her slim body against him in his arms, rejoicing at its lack of need for artificial support beneath the silk dress.

'I am not a *foie gras*, dearest,' he murmured lovingly, but reproachfully. 'All that *fat*. I am' – he paused for reflection – '*une truffe de Provence* and your beloved.' He kissed her somewhat unrestrainedly after his enthusiastic welcome, and then hurriedly remembering etiquette, glanced round for the maid.

'You need not worry about Marie. She is used to me. *Alors*, Auguste, you have a look on your face as if you wish to partake of one of Carter's Little Liver Pills – you have found a murder?'

'Murder? *Mais non*. But two mysteries. One is that of Inspector Rose and the six Fabergé eggs. About which you know. Dearest, do stop dancing around,' he complained, his attention diverted to the beautiful instep fleetingly on view. Only last night, he'd caressed it – 'As one of them is yours,' he continued reproachfully.

'Yes.' She flashed him a smile as she picked up her parasol. He opened his mouth, but realised there was nothing more to say on the subject.

'So what have you discovered so far?' she said brightly.

'I—' Auguste was checkmated. No wonder Russians were so good at chess. It was unfair. How could he have found out anything so quickly?

'To find things out, *ma chérie*, one must first have

decided the recipe and ingredients. And even more important – the *reason* for the recipe.'

'Ah yes,' she said meekly.

'*Chérie*, do not flutter your eyelids at me. I am *right*.'

'Ah, but I know,' she laughed. 'Now, have you discovered the reason for our burglar's recipe?'

'I thought perhaps blackmail, but that cannot be as the ladies could simply deny the eggs belonged to them. It is not like incriminating letters. So, it has to be for the sake of the rubies – which is the most likely as the Petrov Diamond has also been threatened, so Inspector Rose tells me.'

'The what?' she inquired.

'The Petrov Diamond. The Grand Duke had a letter threatening that it would be stolen. And tomorrow the Grand Duchess wears it – darling, you do not listen.'

'I am sorry, Auguste. I was thinking of the burglar,' she said contritely. 'He knows very much about us all, does he not? I think we will find it is someone known well to us all.'

'Not necessarily,' said Auguste eagerly, determined not to lose the status of superior investigator. 'It could be a valet or maid chatting indiscreetly to a tradesman.'

'Ah, but I do not tell Marie about my egg. I tell no one. So it must be Igor who talks. *Voilà*, someone in society.' She paused. 'Someone here *now*.'

'And there is the Seventh Egg also. You can tell me where La Belle Mimosa lives?' he asked eagerly.

She laughed. 'Better than that, *mon chéri*, I will show you the lady herself. She will be there at the ceremony, of course. I will introduce you.'

'You *know* her?' Auguste was scandalised, using the word with its full social import.

'Of course,' she laughed. 'She and I, we are alike – we are in society, but not of it. She is exquisite, La Belle Mimosa. There is a fountain here, erected last year; it is sculpted into interesting and beautiful shapes – mostly

47

those of La Belle Mimosa; I will introduce you, but I will watch you carefully, Auguste.'

'You need not fear,' he replied devotedly. He hesitated as she stepped gracefully into the carriage. 'You are sure you wish me to ride at your side?' he inquired awkwardly.

She reached out her hand. 'Yes,' she answered simply. 'Why not?'

Why not? Auguste thought of the complex laws of society, of her reputation as one of the greatest ballerinas of the day, and his respect for her grew. He climbed up beside her.

'And now, *chéri*,' she announced happily, 'you will tell me of your other case.'

'Ah, the ghost.'

Ghost? A smile came to her lips. 'You are a *ghost*-hunter. Bravo, *mon héro*.'

'I have *seen* it,' retorted Auguste huffily. 'It is the Man in the Iron Mask.'

'Ah, my friend, you read too many romances. I let you hunt your ghost, while I dance, I think.'

'You may laugh, *chérie*,' said Auguste with dignity. 'But until I have laid this ghost to rest, I shall not rest. No matter where the quest might lead me,' he perorated in a manner of which Rachel Gray would have approved.

Rachel Gray waved a languid hand towards her husband, a cold compress clutched to her brow with the other.

Cyril Tucker sighed. He supposed he should have expected trouble, renting the Villa Sardou where her namesake, the famous tragedienne Rachel, had died. He should have foreseen his wife would metamorphose herself. Really, it was much easier to live with her on her occasional forays into comedy.

'Fetch me—' Rachel paused. What could she ask for? Nothing came to mind, 'Ah, it is too much,' she said, defeated. 'I cannot go. I lack the strength.'

She did not look as if she lacked strength, her Junoesque

figure stretched out on the chaise longue, black hair floating round her.

'My dear,' murmured Tucker on cue, but coming in with the wrong line. 'It is the Prince of Wales we are to honour after all.'

A savage look was his reward. 'What have I to do with princes?' Rachel demanded feebly. 'Art is my only mistress.'

Belatedly Cyril remembered the correct line, privately thinking a mistress of any kind might not be a bad idea. 'My dear,' he cried obediently, 'you have a duty to the public.'

'True.'

Rachel rose briskly to her feet, suddenly all practicality. 'Have you summoned the carriage? Is the *mistral* blowing? Shall I wear this' – putting an ornate confection of blue on her head – 'or this?' The blue was replaced by an even more elaborate red hat. 'And where is Mephistopheles?'

'Here, my angel.' Tucker was on cue this time, handing over the sullen bulldog gladly. It had been acquired nearly four years previously, not out of a great love for dogs, but in a bid to even up the score with her rival Mrs Patrick Campbell, and partly in a bid to pay tribute to Mr Jones's poetic drama *Saints and Sinners* in the hope of a summons for his next play. Both bids had failed, and Mephistopheles returned with relief to the servants' room where he now remained except on state occasions. This was one.

Rachel was very cautious where the *mistral* was concerned. She had once come to stay at the Grand Hotel in March, ignorant of the wind's frequency in that month, and sallied out to an unaccountably deserted Boulevard de la Croisette in rose-pink chiffon. She had ended up looking as if she were auditioning for a mad Ophelia, and spent the following week with an audience consisting solely of Dr Gordon Sanders of the Villa Nina, and a nose as pink as the chiffon she had so unwisely donned. After that, she had followed the guidebooks' advice, eschewed the simulating and bracing air of the seafront and repaired to climes more suited to her supposedly fragile health in the village of Le Cannet. Where better than the Villa Sardou where *she* had come to die? Not that Rachel Gray had any intention of dying. Life was far too interesting. Soon she would see him, and tomorrow at the match he would undoubtedly require an answer to his ultimatum. Would she or would she not yield to his embraces? Really, he was becoming uncomfortably persistent.

The Honourable Harry Washington, gentleman cricketer and man-about-town, gazed into a gilt-framed mirror in the Villa Esterel, to ensure that thanks to Rowland's Macassar Oil not a hair was out of place. He was right to have rented this villa. It might not be so grand as those of his neighbours, but it was on the right side of town, and suited his purpose admirably. It was good to be in Cannes for the season before returning to the new cricket season at Lord's and his comfortable bachelor flat in Albany. It promised to be an exciting year. Grace's fiftieth birthday. Surely not even the great W. G. could go on much longer? And when he retired the field, so to speak, would be open. This upstart Ranjitsinhji would disappear as quickly as he'd arrived. All the more reason for him to enjoy this last break here. In the match tomorrow he would be playing in the same team as the Prince of Wales. That would permanently ensure his social right to play with the Gentlemen at Lord's, without delving too far into his background. He'd arrange to be batting with him, to ensure the Prince faced the easy bowling and not that madman Bonifacio, for example. Yes, he flicked at his cuffs, tomorrow would be beneficial in many, many ways. A smile came to his lips.

'Basty.'

Miss Emmeline Vanderville bounced joyously through the doors of the salon in the family suite in the Hôtel du

Parc. She'd much rather have been down on the seafront in the Grand Hotel but her parents had insisted on the Hôtel du Parc. She might meet a real live prince here, they reasoned. But it looked so like something built by the Pilgrim Fathers. All these towers, and dull old folk. That is, until *he* had appeared.

Bastide, Comte de Bonifacio, twenty-five-year-old pretender to the throne of France by virtue of his descent, via Napoleon, from the Man in the Iron Mask, upholder of the Honour of France, particularly where the English were concerned, flinched. American heiresses were all very well and desirable in his present impecunious state, useful to The Cause, but they had no grace, no mystique.

Emmeline flung her arms round her wild-eyed hero. This was romance. True Love. A real live French prince – well, almost French and almost a prince. True, he had little money, but what a pedigree. Napoleon, the Man in the Iron Mask, Louis XIV, so Basty had told her (whoever they were). Surely her parents would approve.

'*Mon petit chou—*'

'I love it when you call me that,' she sighed. 'Kiss me, Basty.'

He obliged without undue difficulty, for Emmeline was eighteen years old and a very pretty girl, in the full vigour of American youth. 'Do let's go,' she pleaded. 'I've never seen a real prince,' she explained tactlessly.

'*Non,*' decreed Bastide, in the true French manner when faced with an Anglo-Saxon problem. 'It is enough I have to play in this 'orrible cricket match tomorrow. I do not wish to stand and cheer *le Prince de Galles* this morning. *Moi,* I am the rightful king of France and you expect me to cheer Wales?' he asked rhetorically.

'You don't have to cheer. Besides, I'm going anyway.'

'Very well,' said Bastide through gritted teeth. 'To please you, *ma chère*, I go. But do not blame me if – if anything happens.'

51

'Oooh, Basty, you aren't going to throw a bomb, are you? Like those Anarchists?'

'Never forget, *chérie*, that I am a dangerous man.'

With his wild look and romantic profile, Emmeline was impressed. She hadn't met a dangerous man since Buffalo Bill brought round his Red Indians Wild West Show. And now she had one all of her own.

'One day my countrymen will rise up against the aggressor. Perhaps soon. And I, *I* will lead them.' He paced the room, hands clasped behind his back. 'The English. Imperialists, all of them. Only France can stop their greed for land. *Now*. We must make a stand in Africa. All this talk in Paris at the conference gets nowhere. It is action that is needed. This Lord Westbourne, he thinks he is so clever, the English diplomatist. He stands in my path. But I, the Comte of Bonifacio, will show him. I shall rise, like Napoleon—'

Emmeline giggled.

He stopped in his tracks, and glared. 'You laugh. You doubt me. See if you doubt me after this.'

He swooped on her, as with a delighted giggle she threw her arms round his neck and they tumbled together in a flurry of skirts and arms and legs on to a nearby sofa. Only the arrival of an astonished Mr and Mrs Vanderville, back from their visit to the English chemist in the Rue d'Antibes in search of a remedy for the griping pains that had so mysteriously seized Mr Vanderville after his third helping of *civet de porcelet*, prevented the full honour of La France from being pursued.

Count Nicholas Trepolov of the Russian Chevalier Guards, member of one of the oldest boyar families in Russia, adjusted his uniform. Descended from one of the conspirators in the December mutiny, a follower of the Grand Duke Constantin, his family had spent much of the century living it down; they had succeeded, although one or two murmurs had been heard at the time of the assassination of the Tsar in 1881, and Nicholas now had the honour to guard the Tsar himself. He was therefore conscious of the need to prove his loyalty and adherence to the Romanovs at every opportunity.

Tomorrow's match would certainly be one. The honour of the Romanovs had to be upheld against these English gentlemen. The Dowager Tsarina might be the sister of the future Queen of England, but that did not make the English any more enticing. Today he must salute this Prince of Wales, but tomorrow the blood of Mother Russia would metaphorically be spilled in defence of her honour at the cricket match.

A young man of thirty, his blood was fiery and his path clear. Tomorrow would be a fight to the death between the two sides.

Meanwhile he was on leave in his family's villa, for two reasons: firstly at the behest of his lady. Not the true object of his desire who was in Paris, but the one who served to pass the time. Like the troubadours of old Provence, it was as necessary to pay court to a lady as it was to sing and to eat. He began to sing an old Russian ballad of love and death until tears of emotion filled his eyes.

There were two passions in his life. One was the Romanovs; the other was—

'The bees, the bees.' A distraught manservant rushed in, after the manner of Mr Irving in *The Bells*.

'I come.' The Prince of Wales could wait. So could love and death. Seizing his bee hat and veil, donning leather gauntlets, as fully armed as against a Saracen mob, he rushed eagerly into the garden of the Villa Melliflora where his beloved hives were placed. Bees in Cannes made the *best* honey, the food of the gods, and he pitied everyone who did not understand what absorbing playmates they made. It took his mind off other matters.

*   *   *

'It's a change not to be on duty,' Rose remarked to Inspector Fouchard. His English was not good, but he understood. Scotland Yard was taking no responsibility if the Prince of Wales should be shot.

In fact this hadn't been what Rose intended at all. He was simply pleased that he had a morning 'off'; that shortly Auguste would be joining him with news of La Belle Mimosa, whose whereabouts were apparently a closely guarded secret from all except the favoured few, and a secret to which the Préfecture de Police in particular was not a party, and that until then he had nothing to do but await the arrival of the Prince of Wales on this fortunately warm March morning. He couldn't count the number of foundation stones he'd watched the Prince lay, in almost as many variations of weather. Fishing boats and pleasure boats crowded the sea, adorned with flags. Yes, it was a nice place for a holiday all right, even if they did all speak French. He was aware that Fouchard was trying to speak to him, but his eyes were suddenly riveted by a couple at the back of the gathered crowd clinging to the statue of Lord Brougham for a good view. 'Well I'll be blowed,' he said slowly. 'Just fancy.'

Rose moved purposefully across the Allées de la Liberté towards the two familiar figures.

'If it ain't Inspector Rose,' said James Higgins jovially. 'Look 'oo's 'ere, Muriel.'

'Pleased to meet you again, I'm sure,' murmured Muriel, appearing from behind a parasol and holding on to her beribboned boater.

'What are you up to, Higgins,' inquired Rose resignedly.

'Doing the season, Inspector. What else? 'Eard that the POW was dropping in 'ere and I turned to Muriel and said, "What's good enough for Albert Edward, God bless 'im, is good enough for us." Didn't I say that?'

'Yes,' affirmed Muriel demurely. They exchanged pleased glances.

'If it so be that on this holiday of yours you bump into anything resembling a Fabergé egg,' said Rose meaningfully, 'I'll hear from you, no doubt.'

'No doubt at all, Inspector,' Higgins offered cheerily.

'I'm at the Hôtel Paradis, by the railway station. Where can I find you?'

Higgins jerked his umbrella nonchalantly in the vague direction of Italy. 'Villa Russe will find us, Inspector.'

Rose goggled. 'And *what* are you doing there, Higgins?'

'What's wrong?' Higgins looked pained. 'Quite a nice little place, the villa.'

'I'll nab you one day, Higgins, one day,' Rose warned him.

Higgins smiled blandly. 'Looks as if it'll keep fine for the match, don't it?'

At the villa under discussion the Grand Duchess descended the central staircase with the easy grace of a panther. Her husband stopped pacing round the vast entrance hall and with complete disregard of their presence announced:

'The froggie police have turned up.'

The Grand Duchess bestowed a hostess's smile on the three gendarmes standing somewhat nervously under the portico. Rumours abounded about the Villa Russe and its inhabitants.

'But the cow hasn't,' went on the Grand Duke, disgruntled.

The Duchess replied patiently: 'The cow is for tomorrow, Igor. We cannot take a cow to an official opening ceremony. Nor to the Cercle Nautique for luncheon.'

'I am not,' the Grand Duke's face turned the colour of Bortsch, 'drinking any froggie milk.'

'Today we drink only champagne,' soothed the Grand Duchess.

'Ah,' said the Grand Duke, mollified. Then he scowled. 'They can poison champagne, perhaps.'

'Who, Igor?'

'Nihilists, of course.'

'Igor, don't be ridiculous. There will be no Nihilists there today.'

'With all of us there in one place? They are everywhere. Did not my mother, the Empress Marie Alexandrovna, demand a full police guard when she visited Cannes? Was not my father assassinated? Were there not bombs in Paris from morning till night?'

'That was Anarchists,' the Grand Duchess pointed out.

'They are the same.'

'No,' said the Grand Duchess, who was of an exact turn of mind. 'Actually they are not. Nihilists believe in nothing, not even in society which is based on lies. Government and society must therefore be disobeyed so that truth may be exposed. Anarchists hold to the general principle that government is evil and has corrupted society and should therefore be abolished.' She smiled sweetly.

The Grand Duke understood not a word, but if Anna said so, he was prepared to consider it.

Nevertheless he announced with pride: 'At the match tomorrow, I shall have Scotland Yard. They will come if only to guard the Petrov Diamond,' he added realistically, darting a look at her. 'Nothing must spoil tomorrow. It is a great occasion. For the first time the English here have allowed us to challenge them at their national game, and moreover they acknowledge the superiority of the Romanovs. It is a great thing – and unusual,' he admitted. 'I am told we have the privilege of being named the Players, the supreme artists of the game. I had not realised we were so good,' he added ingenuously.

'No, Igor. The *Gentlemen* are the privileged team in this game of cricket. In England the Players are the peasants who play only for money?'

'What?' His face went white. 'They do not mean a compliment—?'

'No, Igor. So it is necessary that you win.'

The full horror of the situation hit the Grand Duke. The three gendarmes shrank back as the heavy Romanov charged in frustration round the marbled columns of the Villa Russe, bellowing, 'I shall kill them all. *And* the Prince of Wales. The English are dogs, *dogs*. Gentlemen? They do not know the meaning of the word. They do not play fair. They do not play cricket. And—' He stopped, still in mid-flow, then continued, moaning faintly, 'And they have Harry Washington on their side. I shall be ill. I shall avoid battle. I shall send in the servants to bat. This is an insult to Russia.'

The Grand Duchess smiled grimly. 'There are ways for revenge, Igor. Do not distress yourself.'

A short while before and a few hundred yards away, a poet had feebly raised himself from his couch and looked depressedly at the scene outside. Blue skies, sun, mountains and sea. There was nothing, but nothing that could honourably prevent his attending the laying of the inaugural stone of the new jetty by His Royal Highness Prince Albert Edward. He tried an experimental cough. Nothing. There was no doubt about it. Alfred Hathaway was getting better.

This was alarming. *She* would never, but never look on him with favour again if he recovered his health.

He had told her – and the world – that he had come to Cannes as a last attempt to save his life. Death was a necessary step in the aesthetic life of a poet which would give him a claim to be numbered amongst the greats. Keats, Dowson, Beardsley – seeing himself already immortal, he announced he would seek the sun in a vain attempt at life. The moment he did so, Smith and Elder, his publishers, told him to his pleasure that his sales had suddenly shot up. Alfred had found rooms, as instructed by doctors and guidebooks, in the gentler air at the back of the town. The improvement in his health proved far too rapid, so he had promptly found lodgings near the unhealthy seashore, with its air so charged with dangerous electricity, and retired to await the end. But it refused to come.

Near to tears and extremely cross, Alfred left the house. Now he might even have to play in that wretched cricket match tomorrow instead of watching with the ladies from the Pavilion terrace with a rug over his knees. That pink in his cheeks could not be disguised as a feverish flush; it was all too obviously good health. All his plans would have to be changed. *She* would have been all solicitude and concern, and now it was all spoiled. Pettishly he changed his mind about riding the steed hired from Mr Grenier's livery stables. Perhaps if he walked to the port, he would be sufficiently out of breath to arouse concern . . .

In the kitchens of the Villa Russe, Boris Bashevksy thumped the dough for the *piroshki*. The news had travelled by means of the gendarmes to the footman, from the footman to the parlourmaid, from the parlourmaid to the housekeeper and then to Boris. Tomorrow the honour of Mother Russia would be at stake. The English must be beaten. The Romanovs ruled Russia, and their honour must be supported at all costs. Soon, very soon, the people would come into their own, but until then the Romanovs *were* Mother Russia's honour. Thump. He reached for the vodka.

Madame Didier watched with horror as his hand went perilously near Auguste's *sanglier* in aspic. Thump. The boar's head's eyes jumped out in protest, and lodged halfway down its nose.

Thump. The broad sweep of his hand caught the unfortunate *sanglier* which flew through the air and landed upside down in its squashed and mutilated aspic.

Boris regarded Madame Didier guiltily. 'Is all right,' he assured her, seeing her appalled face, and hurrying to the scene of the tragedy. 'Is all right,' he repeated, rearing up from the floor some minutes later.

Madame Didier grimly regarded the results.

'Is all right,' said Boris again doubtfully, regarding the catastrophe on the plate. He reached for the vodka bottle.

Auguste carefully handed Natalia Kallinkova down from the carriage, full of pride to be seen doing so, and escorted her to their seats. Egbert Rose rose to his feet to greet them.

Her eyes danced. 'Ah, Inspector, you are here, you see. Just as I said. All the players are gathered; we await only the Prince . . .'

A disturbance in the crowd, and a sibilant hush ran through its ranks. Someone was coming. But it wasn't the Prince of Wales. This was an open carriage. Auguste craned his neck to see . . . In the carriage, dressed in a bright yellow silk dress with a matching pleated lace hat and parasol, and rouge on her face, was a pretty, doll-like figure, so dainty in form she could have been Japanese save for the tawny eyes and hair as golden as the Empress Eugénie's, knotted in curls high on the back of her head. All eyes were on her as she sat without moving, accepting the homage to her beauty.

'Yes,' said Kallinkova matter-of-factly. 'That is La Belle Mimosa.'

One other person in the reserved seats reacted strongly. Lord Westbourne shrank back, hoping to pass unnoticed. As the lady gracefully unfurled herself and descended from the carriage, slowly she turned her gaze and stared right at him. No smile passed her lips.

Off the coast of Cannes, the destroyer *Cosmao* let off a salvo, and a stir ran through the crowd. A little off-key, the 12th Regiment of the Line struck up with 'The Marseillaise', the men of the 7th Regiment of Chasseurs Alpins stood to attention. Albert Edward, Prince of Wales, heir to the throne of the British Empire, was on his way.

An elderly Cannois, walking by the rows of seats where

Auguste was sitting, spat. '*Les anglais*,' he muttered.

'*Oui, mon ami*,' Auguste said placatingly, and hearing this expression of sympathy the Cannois stopped and spat again.

'Look at the place,' the elderly resident expostulated. 'Ruined by the English. It's never been the same since that Lord Broogam' (as he pronounced it) 'came here, matter of sixty years ago. Then the others, building houses all over the place. Why, I remember this road' – he pointed to the glory of Cannes, the Boulevard de la Croisette – 'when it didn't have all these fancy palms and sugar canes. Nor this fancy sand either. Just a nice old lane and seashore, as *le Bon Seigneur* made it. Now look at it. *Les hiverneurs, pah!* Ruined,' he spluttered indignantly. 'Now they come and build new ports. What's wrong with the old one? The modern world, *monsieur*, the modern world!' Shaking his head sadly, he was about to continue on his way, when Auguste remember his second quest.

'You remember Cannes in the old days, *monsieur*? You have heard of the Man in the Iron Mask?'

'*Mais oui, mon fils*, and I remember you. The small boy of Monsieur Didier—'

'Yes, *monsieur*. But tell me, have you heard of the ghost?'

'Ah yes, *monsieur*. Rumour has it that when he walks, there is danger.'

'For whom?'

'For those who see it – or for Cannes herself.'

'But I have seen it,' cried Auguste in alarm.

The old man shook his head regretfully. 'Then, *monsieur*, beware. Old Madame Briard saw it and the next day she was dead. *Murdered*,' he said with gusto. 'And Monsieur Pintard, too, and' – remembering his grievance – 'many people saw him the day before Lord Broogam arrived, and see what happened to our beautiful village! Pah – *les hiverneurs*.'

Danger . . . Auguste frowned. There were no such things as ghosts. He would prove it, wouldn't he?

The portly man in late middle age with a splendid moustache and beard stood to attention as 'God Save the Queen' was played. He was duly presented with a silver trowel, far from the first in his long career, and duly cemented in stone the never-ending love–hate relationship of the French and English. He composed his features into the correct expression for the long flowery speech in his honour by the Mayor, only to find the agony extended into an equally long and flowery one by the Prefect. He then recited his own diplomatic hope that France might long enjoy the benefits of the Government of the Republic, and that cordial relations between France and Great Britain (so necessary for his own future enjoyment of the delights of Paris) 'may long continue for the good of humanity'. He meant it. To him this stone was a symbol, an *entente cordiale* . . . Now that wasn't a bad idea . . . When he was king . . .

Chapter Four

The Cannes Cricket Club had begun enthusiastically at the end of the 1880s, but had had an existence as bumpy as its pitch. The Mediterranean climate simply did not understand the demands of cricket. Nevertheless the English pressed on doggedly. Golf was all very well, ran their thinking, but cricket was England. The French remained unconvinced. Perhaps as a result of their lack of enthusiasm, the pitch's site had one or two disadvantages, the main one being the ostrich farm next door whose occupants took all too much interest in their neighbour's movements. In the tradition of good sportsmen, the English put up with it.

The same tradition led them to erect a pavilion as reminiscent of Lord's as they could manage handicapped by French workmen. It was somewhat more squat, and the balconies became one covered verandah, but the results satisfied them that they had done their duty by England, and the British flag flew proudly from the roof.

The symbol of the flag was mainly responsible for the club receiving the ultimate accolade this year – the presence (albeit unwilling) of the Prince of Wales. No lover of cricketing politics, he had successfully evaded the club in his previous private annual visits to Cannes. This year, with yesterday's ceremony, the club had taken the mean advantage of assuming he was here officially, and requested him to bat for the honour of England, appointing him honorary captain. Trapped, he had reluctantly agreed on condition that he bat No. 11, and on no account would he be called upon to field, let alone to bowl. This compromise (since the Prince's girth made his presence on the field more of a liability than an asset) suited everyone.

However, a harassed Auguste was far from appreciating the enormous advantage the presence of the Prince bestowed upon the proceedings.

'Monsieur Boris, you cannot put the *ballotine* on the hot kitchener,' shouted Auguste, agonised beyond endurance as he rushed round the small kitchen in the Pavilion, normally designed to provide only gateaux, ices and sandwiches.

'Yis. Yis, Diddiums.'

Auguste flinched at this Ukrainian crassness.

'Here, I put it on the table.' Boris was unusually anxious to please. Auguste had not yet noticed the non-appearance of his *sanglier*. Boris rushed from the kitchen into the luncheon tent erected by the side of the Pavilion, hotly pursued by Auguste, determined that no Russian should mar the perfection of a table which he had himself approved.

Left to himself, he would have served a Provençal feast of tapenades and fresh crusty bread, small succulent sardines and anchovies, oysters and langoustines, thick slices of country ham, *petites cailles*, a *salade de mesclun*, and the red sweet tomatoes of Provence. But such simple fare he knew full well would be disdained. For all the Prince of Wales's love of plain food, it had to be English. So now they had a mixture of Russian dishes, including meatballs, mixed with over-sauced, rich fare. This meal would be a disaster, and he, *maître* chef Auguste Didier, was associated with it. Only the *sanglier* would save his reputation. The *sanglier*! A sudden fear gripped him.

'Monsieur Boris,' in awe-filled tones, 'where is the *sanglier*?'

Boris looked innocently puzzled. 'The *sanglier*. Ah, Monsieur Didier—' broad hand smote brow. 'It is left behind. What catastrophe,' he said, beaming.

Auguste regarded him. 'Left behind?' he repeated, unable to believe it. Suspicion began to grow on him. 'We will send for it,' he said firmly.

'It is gone,' admitted Boris unhappily, edging back towards the kitchen.

'Gone?' repeated Auguste, neatly positioning himself between Boris and the door. 'Gone? Eaten?'

'Melted.'

'No aspic of mine *melts*,' Auguste pointed out. '*Where* is it?'

'It is dropped.' Then seeing Auguste's face, Boris added encouragingly: 'You not worry, Diddiums. I, Boris, guard the honour of Mother Russia. Do not fear. They will remember today *always*.'

Here, he was entirely correct. Auguste, however, was in no mood to consider the future when the present seemed to hold only disaster.

'They grind the faces of the poor and leave us only this,' Boris continued morosely in a cunning bid for sympathy, picking up the vodka bottle.

'*Non*,' Auguste shouted. The affair of the *sanglier* must wait. A worse catastrophe stared at him in the shape of a bottle. 'Not until after the meal, *monsieur*. I plead with you.' He wondered anew what possible standard dinners could reach at the Villa Russe, when they were not able to import the services of an Auguste Didier.

Reluctantly, the bottle was replaced on the cupboard, Boris's hand lingering lovingly on it. 'Come,' said Auguste, overcoming his desire to pummel this wretched idiot with as little respect as he had treated his masterpiece of a *sanglier*, 'we will check the coffee arrangements, yes?'

Taking a reluctant Boris by the arm, he led him through the door into the salon where the participants and guests would shortly be gathering for the match. Refreshments would be served in the salon, while the combatants donned their battle gear for the fray in the changing room.

Four footmen from the Villa Russe were busily and efficiently at work in the salon to Auguste's surprise, but nevertheless he steered Boris bemusedly round the tables, checking the Harlequin decorations and the napkins folded cornucopia style.

The salon was decorated with Phil May cricketing cartoons from *Punch*, photographs of past XIs, banqueting menus and old bats, all of which Inspector Fouchard, standing in one corner of the room, looking as out of place as W.G. Grace at a game of *boules*, regarded suspiciously as though just to spite him Nihilists or burglars might lurk behind this peaceful scene.

The object he guarded lay on a velvet cushion on a silver salver – a sheathed dagger, hilt and sheath jewel-encrusted with diamonds, emeralds and rubies.

'What,' inquired Auguste, amazed at the incongruity, 'is *that*?' He expected Fouchard to reply. Instead, Boris suddenly became animated.

'This,' he said proudly, 'is the jewelled dagger of the Romanovs. The Grand Duke, he will present it to the loser of the match. Next year, he give it to the new loser, and the same, and the same, and the same. In Russia, you killed yourself if you were handed this dagger. It is honour, you understand. Nowadays they do not insist. But it is disgrace to be presented with the dagger.' He made a graphic gesture across his throat, gurgling with bull-like noises.

Auguste was puzzled. 'Disgrace? Like the Ashes in England?'

'Ashes? What are Ashes?'

Auguste ignored him, as he had never understood what the Ashes were himself. He frowned. Jewels? And shortly the Petrov Diamond would arrive somewhere on the person of the Grand Duchess – a double prize indeed for Egbert's cat burglar. The ghost would have to wait. For the moment his services were needed here. If Egbert was right, and the thief moved in society, then he might undoubtedly be here today. Inspector Fouchard was no doubt most capable, but he looked to Auguste as if he lacked the finesse necessary to catch this particular gentleman. Whereas he, Auguste – modesty forbade him to continue the thought. Instead he suggested to Boris that he should return to the kitchen, leaving the final details to him.

Boris beamed. 'Yes,' he said. 'I milk the cow.'

'*Hein?*'

'I milk the cow,' repeated Boris patiently. 'This,' he swept a hand scathingly at the full milk jugs, 'no good for Grand Duke. He drink only his own milk and bring his cow with him. You no worry, I do it.'

He departed, leaving Auguste fervently thankful that even the more eccentric members of Plum's hadn't thought of that one.

Under the wary eye of Inspector Fouchard, he turned his attention to the dagger. Here in a corner of the room, and guarded by the inspector or his men, the dagger would seem to be in no danger. But he was a clever man, this burglar, and two prizes presented themselves for him today. This dagger perhaps was an easier target than the Grand Duchess Anna. But when would he strike? During the match itself, when the gentlemen on the batting side would be on the verandah watching the game and the guests busily occupied in social converse? Or during luncheon when everyone was in the tent by the side of the Pavilion, and the guard could be tricked away? How would this burglar make himself invisible? Just like a ghost – he laughed to himself. He had ghosts on the brain.

Auguste's thoughts were arrested by the sound of high-pitched feminine laughter outside. The guests were beginning to arrive. He scurried back to the kitchen to galvanise the staff into action. Too late he recalled he had no authority here, but it was second nature to him, and in any case necessary.

The gentlemen were flocking into the changing room,

where talk was muted, sobered, by the realisation that the honour of their countries lay with them. In the salon, where Auguste was busily serving trays of *croutons à l'Alberta* and other delicacies, the women were more concerned with how the other ladies had solved the vexed question of dress. As it was mid-morning, carriage or morning dress should have prevailed; on the other hand, this event would continue until the evening. Normally a retiring room would be provided for ladies to change their dress several times accordingly as the day made its sartorial progression. Unfortunately the Pavilion lacked this facility, as the architect, a bachelor, had seen no need, even in Cannes, to yield one inch of this exclusively male bastion to female frivolities. Great thought therefore had to be devoted to the problem. Surreptitious glances on arrival revealed to the relief of all that there had been a consensus. Afternoon dress had prevailed. Silks, even muslins, light mousselines-de-soie and chiffon veiling floated everywhere, accompanied wisely by a pile of warm shawls.

As the company regathered, Auguste began to pick out one or two faces from London. Strange to see them here – the tempestuous Rachel Gray (who had once thrown one of his *timbales* at an unforthcoming actor manager in the Galaxy Restaurant); the poet Alfred Hathaway, a new member of Plum's; Henry Washington, a constant visitor at Gwynne's, favourite of Emma Pryde (Auguste's lips pursed grimly); Lady Westbourne, frequent visitor at Stockbery Towers some years ago – and a lively one too, he remembered. The fiery young man, he was told, was the Comte de Bonifacio, the eager-faced young girl on his arm an American heiress. A mere Corsican upstart, the footman sniffed. The tall stiff-backed man was Count Trepolov – ah, what ails him? He has a face like a fallen soufflé, Auguste thought.

The hubbub of voices crescendoed, loosened by the coffee and plates of Auguste's delicacies. In one corner, the

Grand Duchess held court; in another, her husband, as befitted the challenger. What a good idea! Always before the Romanovs had been excluded from this cricket game; English only. But it had been his idea to challenge them! And they would win! He had been surreptitiously practising, and had made sure his team did also – all but one or two had valiantly complied. The rules were difficult, the English said, but that was nonsense. The ball comes, you hit it, you run, someone tells you if you are out; if they say nothing you stay in. Simple. And when you are all out, you all come in. Then you all play on the field and run about catching the other team. Igor was confident of victory.

His voice grew louder, and every so often the low tones of the Grand Duchess could be heard too. As the crowd moved, Auguste saw from time to time the flash of the famous Petrov Diamond. He wanted to see it closer, so determinedly made his way towards her with a tray of croûtons with caviar, trying not to gaze too interestedly at her bosom where the diamond rested. But their eyes met over the plate; and a faint puzzlement flared into the Grand Duchess's. Servants were not allowed to have eyes that were alive, that spoke of a person and not an automaton.

Noticing this and realising the cause, Auguste hastily ducked his head deferentially and whisked away to the Grand Duke's corner, where Rachel Gray momentarily had the advantage in noise level, a devoted Alfred Hathaway at her side. Cyril Tucker helped himself to a fillet of beef *à la Provençale* but nevertheless Auguste noticed he kept an eye on his wife's doings. He was just about to enter the corridor on what was then the quicker route to the kitchen, when he overhead a sob and a plaintive, 'My husband suspects, Nicolai. He is a brute, but I do think it better we part—'

Nicolai? The tall Russian no doubt. He remained in the doorway an instant longer, time to hear an anguished, 'Dora *carissima*. You cannot mean this. I live only for you.' (And his bees, but strict truth was not necessary at such a time.)

Alas, Dora did mean it, as was obvious when Auguste emerged into the corridor as she extricated herself gracefully from her companion and entered the salon once more, leaving a stricken Trepolov staring into the coffee cup Auguste pressed upon him as though it held the answers to woman's fickleness.

There was a limit to Dora's interest in bees. She had been prepared to tolerate them for the sake of Nicolai's handsome uniformed appearance and dark romantic gaze. But the delights of the latter had begun to pall. When the uniform was off, the results were by no means as exciting as she could have wished. Not a patch on Igor – so far as she could recall. But whatever did Nicolai mean by hissing 'Death before dishonour' at her? How strange, she thought vaguely. These Russians were very odd.

So Lady Westbourne had not changed, thought Auguste, smiling, since he had seen her at Stockbery Towers over six years ago now. Then her husband was always abroad, now he appeared to be with her, but it had not dampened her style, obviously.

He picked up a tray of almond *gauffres* and returned to the fray.

Bastide stood scornfully watching these English. Ah, if only they knew what awaited them. Vengeance should be his. Today, the battle for the glory of France must begin. He would tell Lord Westbourne that the French would never withdraw from Boussa. Furthermore the British flag at Borea should be hauled down. To the devil with international treaties. He began to pulse inside with excitement and dreams of future glory. He was only recalled to reality by Emmeline pulling at his arm.

'Basty, do have one of these Krauts.'

'Croûtons, dearest,' cried Bastide, irritated, recalled from his dreams.

Burglars? Auguste flashed around busily, trying to reconcile these people with Rose's cat burglar. Bastide? Never.

70

Trepolov was possible, the poet perhaps. Harry Washington. Now there *was* a possibility. Cyril Tucker – but it was all supposition. Even Rose had no *proof* that the cat burglar was in Cannes. Where had this rumour started? He frowned. It made sense, but there was something strange—

'*Garçon.*'

Lady Westbourne lifted an imperious finger, and after a quick glance round it was clear to Auguste that it was he who was summoned. Seething at this insult, he nevertheless obligingly presented himself.

'The Prince of Wales is arriving with my husband. Make sure you have refreshments ready.'

He bowed. But someone arrived before the Prince of Wales, pressing Auguste's hand, to the intense disapproval of Lady Westbourne.

Natalia Kallinkova cared not two kopeks for her reputation, and it said much for her charm that she remained welcome almost everywhere.

'A prima ballerina can do anything, go anywhere, no matter what she does,' she once told Auguste, laughing. 'When she is no longer prima, then she begs for her living. Today, why, I can do no wrong. Courted by princes and smiled on by hostesses.'

'Now tell me, Monsieur Sherlock,' when she had drawn Auguste away, 'where is your bad man?'

'How can I tell?' he said in despair. 'But there,' he nodded towards the Grand Duchess, and towards the dagger, 'there are his trophies, and I think he is here.'

'I think you are right, *mon chou*,' she said seriously, 'and so I shall detect too. *Voilà*,' her slim figure turned towards the crowd, skirts billowing, 'I shall begin with the oh so handsome Monsieur Washington.'

Harry Washington, Auguste considered again. He was active, and popular in society all over London. But at the moment he looked seriously discomposed, despite Natalia's presence. He was indeed. He was still recovering from the shock of Dora Westbourne's arching her body sensuously towards him, with fluttering fan and eyelashes, and announcing: 'At last, Harry, when my husband leaves for Paris, then I will be yours.'

She had departed, full of womanly happiness at the precious gift she was about to bestow. Washington, on the other hand, was as white as though he, too, had seen the Ghost of the Man in the Iron Mask. His flirtation with Dora had been a purely social ritual, based on the knowledge that that stuffed shirt Trepolov was her lover. What had happened? What the hell was he going to do? He couldn't spurn Lady Westbourne, for fear of her making trouble with Lord Westbourne. One word from him and doors that Washington depended on being open would be well and truly slammed. He'd got to stride out on to the field as though he hadn't a care in the world.

There was a sudden flurry as the footmen, in blue livery with the Romanov crest emblazoned on it, snapped to attention at a sign from the Grand Duke, and two portly middle-aged, bearded gentlemen appeared: one was Lord Westbourne, the other the heir to the throne of the British Empire. A path between swishing skirts opened like the Red Sea, as the cream of Cannes society curtsied or bowed. Albert Edward was going to do his duty by England.

Twenty minutes later, Lord Westbourne, in his self-appointed role of escort to reluctant royalty, stood opposite the Grand Duke Igor, flanked by two of Fouchard's men, looking very out of place and sandwiching the Prince of Wales, already bemoaning his lot – What the devil did they have to drag him on to the field now for? Foundation stones he understood, cricket he was far less happy about. Why couldn't these pesky English over here settle their accounts over a good round of golf?

The coin spun in the air. The Grand Duke Igor, Lord Westbourne and even the Prince of Wales watched its fateful path expectantly.

'The Three Graces.' Auguste heard an irreverent onlooker remark of the three identical stalwart backsides bent forward over the coin. A Gentleman turned belligerently. 'Do not speak slightingly of the great W. G., sir. Or his esteemed brothers. You're a disgrace to England.'

'Me,' shouted the Grand Duke, in an un-English display of triumph, as the die was cast. 'We bat, yes?'

Deploring this lack of finesse, which confirmed their view of all foreigners, the Gentlemen took the field. 'I show you who are Gentlemen,' muttered the Grand Duke gleefully.

He elected to put Count Nicolai Trepolov and Bastide in first, saving himself for a grand appearance later. He had at last grasped the fact that to bat No. 11, as he had originally intended, was not the best position to play and indeed could be said to have some opprobium attached to it, but nevertheless decided that he might be able to make a dramatic appearance to save the day. He slapped Bastide on the back. 'You first, *mon brave*. On you rests the glory of Rus – um – Europe.'

Bastide was by no means overcome with this honour. Batting was not his forte, and the Vandervilles were watching. On the other hand, Lord Westbourne was bowling. A steely resolve entered his soul. Did the English not boast that Waterloo was won on the playing fields of Eton? Very well, here at Cannes would Africa be resolved. The beginning of the overthrow of the British Empire from which the French Empire would rise triumphant.

And the match began.

The spectators, or rather those who could spare the time from the rather more important matters of discussing hats, hairstyles and Home Rule, according to sex, seated themselves on the raised verandah. Outside the luncheon tent Auguste watched the match for a few moments, trying to refrain from rushing into the tent to supervise. The disaster that would surely follow for luncheon was nothing to do with him, he tried to remind himself. He could watch the cricket. His part was done. Seeing him standing there, Natalia left her seat and came up to him. '*Voilà*, Auguste. So you are a cricket man.'

'I am not,' retorted Auguste decidedly. 'The sounds go well with a summer's day, and the smell of new-mown grass. Even the sight has sometimes elegance. And the passions it arouses. But one should think beautiful thoughts, not watch it.' He shrugged. 'Nor do I understand the game. Why every five balls do they all walk round the pitch?'

'It is a rule,' she laughed. 'And a very important one. A bitter battle is fought as to whether it should be six or five or four. More blood is split over such decisions than over the Niger River, *mon ami*.'

'But why walk around at all?' asked Auguste doggedly. 'The French are a logical nation, and know that rules must have some purpose. But look at that!'

There were cries of un-English triumph emanating from the pitch as a lithe wild-eyed Napoleon proceeded to hit his Duke of Wellington's stately best all over the battlefield. The Russian score was mounting as fast as Lord Westbourne's concern. Trepolov had some sense of decency and didn't go attacking the ball like some damned dervish. But this dreadful Corsican costermonger type was another matter, and after another over he took himself off and put on Harry Washington, and the English team regained their momentarily shaken complacency.

Alas, Harry Washington was not in his usual form, still trembling at the fate that had befallen him.

'Where is Inspector Rose?' hissed Kallinkova absently, her eye on a ball making resolutely for the boundary. 'Why is he not here looking for his burglar?'

'He has gone to see La Belle Mimosa,' replied Auguste. 'Then he will come. He had to ensure the safety of the Seventh Egg.' He stopped. What was that thought that had

74

flashed so quickly into his mind and gone? Something about the thief and the Petrov Diamond.

'Of course,' said Natalia, watching Nicolai Trepolov running between the wickets, almost as enthusiastic as if he had a bee net in his hand.

'Yo heave ho,' carolled Boris happily, coming up beside them, safeguarding the honour of Russia by alternately taking mouthfuls from the vodka bottle and testing *katushki*.

'Monsieur Boris, the *blinis*. Have you prepared them?' yelped Auguste.

Boris looked blank. An enormous hand smote a forehead. Grimly, Auguste marched back through the tent into the kitchen, with a contrite Boris trailing behind. The *blinis* organised, Auguste whirled on a plate of salted herrings that should by now be in the luncheon tent. Could any civilised palate eat such abominations?

'Do not worry. *Blinis* will be done. Do not worry, please, Diddiums,' Boris assured him anxiously. 'You have some vodka, yes?'

'*La soupe*,' moaned Auguste in despair, noticing the vast canister standing unheated on the floor. 'The soup, Monsieur Boris.'

Even in the midst of his despair, however, suddenly he stopped still. That errant niggle had returned. Egbert Rose was not here, for Westbourne was not going to see him until *after* the match. But why? he asked himself. If Westbourne knew who this burglar was, and the burglar was thought to be here, and the Petrov Diamond was here, not to mention the dagger, why did he not tell Rose immediately, so that the danger could be averted?

He tried to arrange his thoughts methodically, as though this were a galantine to be prepared. This was hard with Boris crashing around, with two Villa Russe kitchenmaids in his wake. Either, he reasoned, the burglar was not going to be here and Lord Westbourne knew it, or the burglar was not interested in daggers or diamonds. Only eggs. And the only unstolen egg (so far as they knew) was in the possession of La Bella Mimosa, who was hardly likely to be present at a cricket match. Auguste frowned. The logic was good, the ingredients were laid out correctly – from them he should be able to recognise the receipt. And yet he could not. Something was still lacking.

Egbert Rose was sorely lacking something too – the stamina provided by Mrs Rose's usual morning offering of burnt toast and kedgeree or kipper. Say what you like, but this stale bread they served here was no substitute. He knocked on the door of the ornate villa rented by La Belle Mimosa, and appropriately named the Villa des Camélias.

He was shown into an elegant morning room and was inspecting a garish painting of one of those can-can dancer ladies in Paris and wondering what the fellow was like who had painted it, when a vision hurled itself through the door bearing no resemblance whatever to her villa's gentle namesake. Already at a disadvantage being caught examining such a compromising picture, he was rendered speechless by the tigerish tawny eyes in their flaming yellow setting. La Belle Mimosa believed in setting a style and keeping to it. Rose was well used to 'unfortunate women' in the Haymarket but unfortunate didn't seem quite the word to apply to La Belle Mimosa.

'Yes,' she stormed, 'what do you want?'

'Inspector Rose, ma'am, Scotland Yard?'

'You wish to become my lover?' she inquired sharply.

Rose turned brick-red, a vision of Mrs Rose in her Sunday best flitting before him.

'No, thank you, ma'am,' he replied as impassively as he could. Then thinking this rather bald for a French lady, added unwisely, 'Though I'm sure that would be very nice.'

She looked him up and down pityingly.

'You have possibilities,' she remarked dismissively and devastatingly.

He gulped, almost swayed into inquiring what those possibilities might be, but struggled determinedly back to the matter in hand.

'I've come about the Fabergé egg I understand you possess.'

At once she was all practicality, saying briskly, 'Ah, *merci*. You come to warn me it is to be stolen, yes?'

'Possibly, ma'am. It is, I gather, the only one given by the Grand Duke Igor that remains, and we have reason to believe the burglar is still in Cannes.' What reason, he wondered, come to think of it? He was only acting on information received. Suppose it were wrong? The Grand Duke had firmly maintained only six existed, and only the most persistent questioning had brought forth reluctant admission of the possibility of a seventh.

'When do you catch him, this burglar?' she inquired. 'At the cricket match today?'

'Lord Westbourne,' he began unguardedly, only to see the kitten once more turn into the raging tigress.

'That *salaud*. Ah, all men – they take what they want, but they do not wish to pay. They gave me not true things but fakes!' She picked up a porcelain shepherdess and threw it across the room for emphasis. Rose ducked just in time. She did not notice. 'But he *will* pay, that one. No one scorns La Belle Mimosa. He is at the cricket match today? *Bon*. I will come. I will tell everyone what he is like,' she shouted, raising a clenched fist in a manner of which Bastide would have approved.

Rose wondered if Auguste would notice if he didn't turn up. Suddenly London's familiar den of villains seemed a quiet, desirable place to be.

The Grand Duke, having marched in, according to plan, to save the honour of Russia, stood poised to crown his side's triumphant innings. Unfortunately he now faced Cyril Tucker. Who would have thought this placid man could be so deceptive? It wasn't fair. He bowled straightforwardly, deceptively simply. It was only by luck the Grand Duke managed to have his bat in the way of the ball, and the bat pushed it quietly to leg. Igor eyed the next ball with misgivings, and began to be exceedingly grateful that the Prince of Wales had declined to field, and thus would not be a witness should anything of an unfortunate nature occur.

Their interest in cricket long since exhausted, three ladies were chatting on the Pavilion verandah, a discussion which led by devious means to a cautious discussion of stolen rubies, a fiction in which two of them had almost come to believe.

'Did you hear about my Fabergé egg?' asked Natalia provocatively, still mindful of her detective mission. Attention thus riveted on her, it did not take long before full confession of the true nature of the ruby thefts was made.

'You mean,' gurgled Natalia innocently, 'that we *all* had Fabergé eggs? What a generous Grand Duke. *And* there were three more – er – ruby thefts recently,' she added with relish. 'I wonder if by any chance . . .'

There was a brief silence.

'What a *busy* Grand Duke,' commented Dora thoughtfully.

Even Rachel Gray joined in the laughter that followed. It was after all well in the past, and he *had* been a Grand Duke after all.

'The inspector believes the burglar is here in Cannes,' chattered Natalia. 'In fact, here today. Either a cricketer or a guest.'

'Here?' *Now?*' They regarded her in horror as each woman quickly ran through her mind the possible unpleasant consequences of any further investigations into the identity of the burglar.

'But why? For what?' Rachel inquired plaintively. They all turned to gaze at the Grand Duchess's chest.

'For the jewelled dagger perhaps.' Natalia paused.

Or the Seventh Egg—' she added offhandedly.

'The *Seventh* Egg?' her two listeners chorused.

'Oh yes, didn't you know? I'm not sure who it belongs to,' Natalia lied happily. She liked to set cats among pigeons. 'Oh, do look at what's happening there.' She waved a hand towards the field. Enough of Seventh Eggs.

The Duke had become increasingly nervous with each over, finally being so unnerved that he advanced to meet one ball, to end the agony, and hit it fair and square almost by mistake. As it sailed high into the air, fourteen pairs of fascinated eyes on the field watched its progress. Now on the verandah chatting ceased in amazement as all the fielders raced towards the boundary in pursuit of an ostrich, which with a definite gleam in its eye had run off with the ball.

'Why not fetch another ball?' asked Auguste practically of the Pavilion steward, as he noticed the commotion from the luncheon tent.

'It is the rules, *Monsieur*,' was the shocked reply. The steward, being a fixture, was English.

The ostrich rather reluctantly ceded its prey but the Grand Duke was lbw next ball. The announcement of luncheon coincided with the end of the Players' innings for 79 runs. The Gentlemen were aghast. Dammit, cricket was their game – *something had to be done*.

Swelling visibly with pride, the Russians swept into lunch like a troop of Cossacks, Bastide sandwiched triumphantly between them. As if bolstered by their at least creditable showing, they proceeded to do equal justice to luncheon, *katushki* included. Even the Prince of Wales, depressed at the thought of the ordeal to come, cheered up at the sight of the food. These Russians didn't do themselves badly, did they? That salted herring salad looked good.

'How goes the ghost hunt?' whispered Natalia as she passed by Auguste who was anxiously superintending the tables. 'I heard he has appeared several times in the old town and the Cannois say it is not a good sign. It is said,' she lowered her voice dramatically, 'that he only appears to his own countrymen, so alas I cannot see him. And that death or misfortune comes in his wake.'

'But what countrymen? It depends,' said Auguste gulping, determined not to be thrown off track as a detective, 'on who you believe he is. If Louis the fourteenth's brother, or Molière, French, if Colonel Barclay or the Duke of Monmouth, English, or if Matthioli, Italian. And if this new contender Eustache Dauger—' He broke off. 'Ah, you laugh at me,' he said indignantly.

'Just a little,' she admitted. 'I like to see your eyes flash. So deep, so dark.' She patted his hand and moved on.

Auguste blushed involuntarily. There was something about Russian women, particularly those that sweetened life in Europe. Natalia – and Tatiana. For a moment melancholy overtook him, then he dispelled it. He was on holiday. Egbert was here, and everything was splendid. Except for the *sanglier*.

The sound of raised voices made him realise that in fact things were far from splendid so far as this party was concerned. He was a connoisseur of the atmosphere of parties and this was not right. Was it the food? There had been no complaints *yet*, but surely they must come? Or was it the rivalry of cricket? There was certainly a simmering tension somewhere . . . He decided to take round a tray of savouries – that abomination so beloved of the English – to try to discover what the trouble was. He did not have long to wait.

The *soi-disant* descendant of the Man in the Iron Mask, Bastide, was locked in conversation – if that was the word – with Lord Westbourne. 'I tell you the French flag will hang above Borea,' he shouted. '*Au diable* with your Royal Niger Company. Our flag will hang in Guinea; it will hang in *Australia*. All your empire will crumble.' He paused to take a mouthful of *caviar d'aubergines* from Auguste's proffered tray. It really was delicious. 'As I said . . .'

Lord Westbourne was listening stolidly as he had listened to similar speeches in Paris for the last six months. This latest crisis was nothing. Pretty soon some kind of compromise would be reached, the flags would be hung out to celebrate and they could all go home and watch some decent cricket. Watch, not play. He'd better make sure these Frenchies toed the line before W. G.'s Jubilee on his fiftieth birthday in July. Good God, what a thought. Better make it a June settlement – provided it didn't conflict with the Derby or Ascot. Get the work over before then, sign it later. He'd have a word with Tucker. He was at the Whitehall end. Excusing himself, he moved across to join Cyril Tucker. He was in the Colonial Office and could pull a string or two.

Bastide fumed at Westbourne's lack of reaction. These English were so superior. He must do something for his ancestors. Napoleon would strike. And so would he, Bastide!

Westbourne's wife meanwhile had once more tracked down her less than enthusiastic potential lover. 'Harry darling, I don't think we'd better be seen too much together,' Dora hissed in the corridor as they passed. That suited Harry Washington. 'But tomorrow he returns to Paris. Call for me at eleven.' It was an order.

Harry sighed to himself. Dora Westbourne was a catch in one way, but in the cricket season a decided liability. He only permitted himself to fall in love from September to May. Look what she'd done to his form this morning. If only something drastic would happen.

He walked sullenly away, watched with interest by Auguste who had not missed Dora Westbourne's pursuit.

Alfred Hathaway too looked under tension. He was. It was hard work struggling to appear pale and interesting. He had not relayed to anyone the information that he was a bowler, so he'd avoided that problem. And he proposed to

81

bat very feebly indeed this afternoon. Perhaps he could retire injured so that Rachel would rush to his rescue.

He lovingly carried his goddess a plateful of food.

'*Katushki*!' The tragic note in Rachel's voice suggested Lady Audley's secret had just been revealed. 'Oh no, *French* please. I feel French today. Not Russian.'

Cyril, overhearing this, sighed. French days usually meant a performance of which he would scarcely feel capable after a day's cricket.

'Alfred, do not strain yourself. You must take care.' The remarks were a ritual now, as Rachel ran a doubtful eye over her beloved. There was altogether a more robust approach about him recently; indeed he was increasingly persistent in his desire to join her on the chaise longue. And now he had issued an ultimatum. How annoying. After all, she had carefully explained their relationship at the very outset. 'I see you as a troubadour of old, Alfred. I see you writing poems to me. I am your lady, and you shall wear my favours.'

The only favour she had actually given him, Alfred had thought, unusually mutinous, was cuff-links decorated with tiny cameos of herself, hardly the sort of thing he could wear to the Café Royal. Instantly he was repentant.

Now, if there were not so many people about, he wanted to kneel at her feet, kiss the hem of her gown. However, her husband was nearby and might misunderstand this noble gesture. So he contented himself by saying to her in a low voice and passionately: 'I am your slave, Rachel. You know that I will do anything for you, *anything*.' The effect was somewhat ruined when he looked up to find himself staring at a tray of canapés blandly held by Auguste.

'Some sardines, sir?' Auguste offered.

Count Trepolov also was keeping an eagle eye alternately on Lord Westbourne and his lady, not on savouries. It had not escaped his notice that Harry Washington seemed to be

82

on the way in to Dora's favour just as he, Trepolov, was on the way out. Truly, women were like bees, creatures of the wild and untameable. No matter how strong the hive, they would go their own way. Yet they provided the honey of life. Tears of dark self-pity welled up. He wondered if this were an insult to his honour and decided it was. Moreover it was an insult to Russia, and therefore to Romanov honour, which he held very dear.

His lady in Paris was a distant Romanov, a fact much in her favour so far as he was concerned, increasing his passion tenfold. He had just won her gracious consent to attend the Grand Duke Igor's masked ball in two weeks' time. It might therefore be convenient not to be hampered with a mistress at that moment, but nevertheless it was still an insult – and especially from an Englishwoman. He brooded. There must be some way of avenging his honour.

'A *pyraniki*, sir?' It went much against the grain for Auguste to offer these abominations as dessert, but Boris had pre-empted his objections by removing most of Auguste's alternatives from the trays.

Trepolov absentmindedly bit viciously into the peppermint honey cake. He was immediately charmed. Was this not Narbonne honey? In his opinion Cannes honey was preferable but nevertheless the cook showed true worth. Perhaps he could be suborned.

'You do these?' he asked an indignant Auguste.

'*Non, monsieur*, I am not the cook. *There* is the cook.' He pointed to a semi-comatose Boris and marched off indignantly to put down this tray as soon as possible. Never had he been so insulted.

Like Trepolov, his honour needed to be avenged.

Cyril Tucker was a quiet, amused observer of the scene. Always there. Never noticed. This was his job at the Colonial Office and he found it excellent practice in everyday life also. And particularly wise just at the moment with things so tricky in Paris. Indeed it was almost essential with a wife like Rachel, who afforded him much quiet amusement as well as other pleasures (except after cricket matches). He kept his own counsel – usually. He'd had to tell her this latest problem since their affairs were so bound up with it, but she was so wrapped up in her own life, he thought it had hardly registered. He wondered whom she would select after Hathaway. He cast his eye round the room, but could see no likely contenders here. Ah, that young Corsican perhaps. Wouldn't last long – he looked as if he might be rather too forthcoming on the physical side for Rachel, but nevertheless he had potential, and only one disadvantage: that pretty little girl who hung on to his every word.

As it happened, the nice little thing was not hanging on to Bastide's words at all, but was in full flood about the glories of Boston, bicycling and tennis. Bastide listened with only half an ear. America had nothing to do with him. Europe must be conquered first. After this stupid conference, he would leave for Africa. For it was there that Empire must begin, and glory awaited him. *A bas les Anglais*, and Lord Westbourne in particular.

The luncheon was ending, as the hour of two-thirty approached and the match was due to begin again. The men, once more purposeful and no longer merely social adjuncts, strode forth, the English to bat, the Russians to field, and still the Grand Duchess's bosom remained unmolested, as did the dagger under a gendarme's eye.

Left behind were the staff and the washing up. This Auguste firmly refused to do. He would superintend the clearing of the food, however. It gave him professional interest to see what had been eaten, and what still remained. To his disgust, he found a number of plates of *katushki* had vanished. 'Ah, the *ballotine* – not a trace remains. It has gone.' Some slight satisfaction. Even more at the plates of *pyraniki* still remaining. He also felt a small sense of pleasure that Soyer's gold jelly remained untouched. Requested by the Grand Duchess, it was in his view a dish simply of expense, not of subtlety or taste. Typical of Alexis Soyer. All showmanship, no true art.

'Auguste?'

'Egbert. At last. I thought you had taken up residence with La Belle Mimosa.'

Rose glared at him. 'Very funny. Is she here yet?' He looked nervously around.

'Here?' Auguste asked with interest. '*Non*. I think I would have noticed.'

'That's all right, then,' said Rose, relieved. 'I thought she meant it. How's it going here?'

'No burglaries yet, *mon ami*. Not of the diamond. Nor of the dagger.'

'The what?'

'The Jewelled Dagger of the Romanovs,' Auguste intoned impressively.

Rose groaned. 'This case gets more and more like an issue of the *Strand Magazine* every day. If there *is* a case,' he added. 'You don't think,' he paused awkwardly, 'we're being taken for a ride, do you?'

'A ride?'

'Tricked. There's something odd here.'

'I feel that too,' said Auguste quietly. 'These men, they take the game of cricket so passionately that it is like Agincourt out there. And yet I feel that there is another game going on altogether.'

'So our man must be here, then.'

Auguste shrugged. 'There is a lot of passion everywhere. Much tension. Lady Westbourne, Rachel Gray, the young Comte de Bonifacio. How everyone shouts. Yet still there is no attempt on the diamond. Somehow I don't think that burglary is to be the main purpose of today.'

'Perhaps he's here for the cricket,' said Rose idly.

'Perhaps,' said Auguste, spying the disappearance of a

85

large plate of sweetmeats into the kitchen. He pursued it, Rose following him. But there was more than sweetmeats awaiting Rose in the kitchen. At the sink, vigorously washing dishes in water supplied by Boris from saucepans on the kitchener was a familiar figure.

'If it ain't my old friend James Higgins,' Rose said gleefully. 'What could you be doing here?' He was visibly cheered by this sign that his instincts were not entirely adrift.

' 'Aving a bit of an 'oliday like I said, Inspector. A working one, you might say. This pal of mine, 'e says they could do with a bit of an 'and at the Villa Russe. So off I goes. Chauffeur to 'is Imperial Grand Dukeness. Washer-upper in between.'

'You wouldn't have your eye on a particularly attractive ducal piece?'

'The Grand Duchess?' inquired Higgins, outraged.

'The diamond.'

'Certainly not, Inspector.' Higgins vigorously polished a glass. 'What do you take me for? Why, you'll be saying I'm after Fabergé eggs next.'

'Ah, Inspector, how lovely to see you.' Natalia gave Rose her hand, as he walked out to the verandah. 'It is a good match, yes?'

Rose paused, as Bastide leapt up to the wicket to bowl with a high-pitched unearthly Corsican yell, which had the umpires searching through the rule book, and the ball flew from his hand like a Napoleonic eagle after its prey. The Gentlemen had not begun well. Expectations of easy victory were replaced by alarming thoughts of a Russian win – unthinkable to have to keep that dagger in disgrace for a whole year. Encouraged by Bastide's example, the Grand Duke sharpened up his own delivery by galloping up to the bowling crease so far as girth would allow and pulling up short, delivering a feeble underarm lob that totally

86

mystified the Gentlemen of England who faced him.

By such dubious methods the English were all out for a mere 40 runs, the Prince of Wales being clean bowled first ball by a tactless Bastide as a finale. The portly figure stumped off, determined to return to the Cercle Nautique immediately for a calming game of baccarat, and was only dissuaded by Dora's womanly charms, speedily exercised in the writing room at the rear of the Pavilion.

The Gentlemen were appalled. This was a reverse greater than the summer of '78, the never to be forgotten occasion of the first Australian team to visit England, not counting those Aborigines of course. Was this Bastide, Comte de Bonifacio, another F. R. Spofforth who dismissed the mighty M.C.C. for 33 and then 19? Had he like Spofforth come down like a wolf on their fold? Could English pride take yet another knock of this magnitude? Even the great W. G. had been clean-bowled for a duck in his second innings on that tragic occasion. How were the mighty fallen. Here in their own town of Cannes as well.

Tactics were busily discussed amongst the Players' team. Or that's what they thought they were doing. In fact they weren't quite sure if they had any, but as this was what the English did, they felt obliged to follow suit. In the kitchen, a jubilant Boris was thrilled at this expression of the superiority of Mother Russia. Duty done, the vodka was playing a prominent part in his triumph.

Auguste, being half English and half French, supported neither side. He was more concerned with tea. Not a large feast should be provided, but certainly something. Had Boris organised sufficient? Surely a Russian cook could manage tea of all things, and Auguste was cheered by the sight of the huge samovars imported into the Pavilion. Why he should concern himself, he did not know, but incompetence disturbed him, over food in particular, and a mystifying unease still gripped him so that to be busy, even in such mundane ways, was a relief. He felt committed to ensure that no one lacked nourishment, and was torn between this noble objective and helping Rose to keep an eye on the Grand Duchess's bosom.

Never better than with their backs to the wall, or in this case fronts to the ball, the Gentlemen strode to their positions in the field as if in defence of Rorke's Drift. Cyril Tucker began well, dismissing the Hungarian count lbw fourth ball of the first over. Hopes were raised. They were dashed on the fifth ball when Bastide, hitting out wildly, caught the unfortunate Tucker on the hand with a straight drive and sent him back to the Pavilion for medical treatment and the commiserations that Hathaway felt Rachel should have bestowed on him. Washington walked up to take the ball for the new over. But someone else got there first, now it was clear that crisis threatened.

'Good God, look at that,' Rose said to Auguste, transfixed.

Alfred Hathaway, embarked on some inner poem of his own, was tearing up to the wicket like a Bacchante after Orpheus, long hair streaming in his slipstream. Nicolai Trepolov, mesmerised with fear, was clean-bowled and walked dazedly back to the Pavilion.

Encouraged, and not noticing in his excitement the look of horror on his Rachel's face, Alfred let rip. The next member of the team took his place at the stumps only to see both bails go flying. Hathaway had tasted blood and blood. Washington, once the bogey for the Players, suddenly became the easy option. However, fired by professional jealousy of Hathaway, his form improved dramatically and between them another five wickets fell in rapid succession. The next victim essayed a run in an attempt to save the day, but fell on his aristocratic nose before reaching the crease.

The Grand Duke walked impressively in to save the day. Twenty seconds later he was walking rather more quickly back to the Pavilion. He had gone out in grand style;

whirling round to see where the ball had gone after it whizzed past him without his even lifting the bat, he fell over the stumps, and collapsed in an undignified heap. Thanks mainly to Alfred Hathaway, dying poet, the Players were dismissed for 10 runs.

Which face displayed the more horror, Rachel's or the Grand Duke's, was hard to determine. To see the latter's, he would have run for the dagger there and then and used it in the traditional way. Luckily he was a realist. 'A game, gentlemen,' he roared to no one in particular. 'I am a good sport, yes?'

In the kitchen, Boris collapsed sobbing on the empty vodka bottle.

The Gentlemen, perking up considerably, now opened their second innings for England with Harry Washington and Lord Westbourne.

By now, it had percolated through that something interesting was happening on the field, and the spectators temporarily forgot their own tensions involved in the climactic scenes being enacted before them. The women watched avidly, as hitherto languid pats with the willow became purposeful and masterful, their menfolk growing again into white-clad heroes. The staff gathered at the entrance to the luncheon tent where their presence was not too obtrusive; the rest of the Gentlemen watched from the balcony, each dreading their turn at the wicket, none more than the Prince of Wales. Luncheon had been good, but he'd earned it.

Washington had had time now to adjust his thoughts and plan his actions, and settled down to play something more like his normal game, scoring 18 in cracking form. At Auguste's side, Boris, clutching on to the tent flap with one hand, vodka bottle with the other, gave a low moan at each run scored. He had given up all pretence at tea-making, leaving Auguste to keep an anxious backward glance to ensure that some activity was proceeding within. A battle

promptly ensued between Auguste and the Russian footmen, Auguste unfortunately being unaware of the Russian
custom whereby men drank tea from glasses, the women
from cups, and by the time the fracas had been resolved,
the match seemed virtually won in Washington's competent
hands.

'Keep your end up, Westbourne,' shouted Washington.
'Leave the scoring to me.'

Westbourne had no liking at all for Washington, but
gritting his teeth, he followed his advice, leaving Washington to strike out in the manner which had made him a
Boys' Own hero, and to thwart all Bastide's attempts to
force his enemy, Westbourne, to face the bowling.

By the time battle was adjourned for tea, the Gentlemen
needed only 11 runs for a victory, and 8 wickets were still to
fall. The meal was held virtually in tense silence.

Auguste flew hither and thither, dispensing tea and cakes
through the brittle atmosphere and forced conversation as
each side contemplated its fate. Rushing out of the kitchen
he collided with Lord Westbourne entering the study, and
both men's eyes were riveted on Dora, in Washington's
arms, secure in the happy belief that her husband was entertaining the Prince of Wales.

'Dora,' Westbourne thundered. 'By Gad, sir,' turning to
Washington.

Washington, unaccustomed to being caught red-handed,
managed a weak: 'Congratulations on a fine performance,
sir.'

'Be damned if yours was a fine performance, sir,' said
Westbourne, sidetracked. 'Play for England? I wonder they
let you play for the Harrow Juniors.'

At this unmerited insult (Westbourne was an Eton man)
Washington turned white, and ignobly fled from the scene,
banging the door behind him to Auguste's disappointment.

Belatedly, Westbourne turned on Dora. 'And you, I've
had about enough of you and your lovers. I've been doing

some thinking about these burglaries. We're going to have a talk about this when we get back to that blasted villa tonight. A *long* talk.'

With this dark utterance, he stamped out, content with venting his spleen so satisfactorily. Dora stared after him quite still with shock, then began to follow him out automatically. What a nuisance husbands were. Always in the way of one's plans.

In the tea tent, the Gentlemen had now gravitated to one side, the Players to the other, the latter debating even now some final measure that might win the day for them. The ladies were in the middle doing their social best to preserve decorum.

As Lord Westbourne stomped back in, in a thoroughly bad temper, one more shock awaited him.

Rose made a speedy approach to him. No point in waiting till seven o'clock. It was now he needed to know. Westbourne, shaken, was in no mood to think of burglars. He needed to think about these ramifications.

'After the match,' shouted Westbourne angrily, 'I'll tell you who your blasted burglar is then.' There was a sudden hush as Westbourne found himself the centre of attention. He turned hastily to the Gentlemen nearest to him and began to talk politics, always a sure way of diverting polite attention elsewhere.

'What's the latest news from the Sudan?'

'Planning on making a stand at Atbara,' said Tucker, helping himself to a cake from Auguste.

'Good man, Kitchener,' Washington pontificated patronisingly. 'Could do with him on the Niger.'

'You fellows will never understand there's a difference between the Frenchies and those dervishes,' said Westbourne, irritated. 'It's not like you all seem to think' – he turned testily to Tucker—' in Whitehall. You have to compromise, or the French are leaping about shouting "*J' accuse*" all over the place.'

There was a nervous laugh at this topical sally provided by the Zola trial.

'Compromise?' said Tucker slowly.

'Too many vested interests to compromise,' said Washington knowingly. 'Isn't that so, Lord Westbourne?'

'You're right, young man. Whitehall will see the end of the Empire if we're not careful.' He glared, and Auguste saw the Comte de Bonifacio, loitering studiedly behind Cyril Tucker, tremble. There were passions abroad today, Auguste felt once more uneasily. And yet more were about to be stirred with all the vigour of a *sauce de caramel*. Especially for his lordship.

A commotion outside, a turning of all eyes towards the door as a golden-clad figure erupted in, quivering with rage, under an enormous concoction of golden osprey feathers on her head.

La Belle Mimosa had arrived.

All eyes were riveted on her in horror, the ladies speedily taking in three salient facts. Firstly, she had stolen a march on them by wearing full decolletée evening dress at five o'clock, thus displaying her chief glories to full advantage; secondly, that in the cleft of the famous bosom resided what could only be a Fabergé egg; and, thirdly, that her breasts were large enough to support it.

The Grand Duke Igor paused mid-*pyraniki*. Natalia laughed. The Grand Duchess's lips tightened, and Lord Westbourne sought a speedy exit through the other door which unfortunately for him was blocked by his wife.

'Hah,' shouted La Belle Mimosa stridently. 'You pay me what you owe me, Charlee.'

Westbourne estimated the chances of escape through the kitchen. Dora's mouth fell unbecomingly open as she gazed at her husband's guilty-looking face, and several other men gave thanks that they had dutifully paid La Belle Mimosa's bills of account. The Grand Duke tiptoed quietly away.

'You,' said the damsel, her gaze falling on Dora. 'You his wife? I pity you.'

Dora, Lady Westbourne, might not be enamoured of her husband, but she was not going to be pitied. She drew herself up, and quickly decided a course of action. Ladies did not talk to women of that sort. To walk away was to cede the contest. To retaliate would acknowledge the woman existed. So she fainted.

Washington hurried dutifully to her side as befitted his lover's status, then remembered his invidious position and sidled away again. Westbourne, however, had eagerly seized the opportunity to slip through the kitchen, colliding with a kitchenmaid en route, muttering about reports to finish in the writing room. Thus Lady Westbourne remained untended on the ground, forced to recover by herself, until solicitously helped to her feet by Auguste, offering camomile tea and smelling salts.

Rose, still with an uneasy feeling that he was taking part in a play, determined on one last assault on Lord Westbourne. Once again his efforts were doomed to failure. Inspector Fouchard, appointing himself to the more interesting task of guarding the bosom of La Bella Mimosa, and his constable guarding the Grand Duchess, thrust his charge into Rose's hands for safe keeping. Rose had drawn the short straw, and was thus forced to seek Lord Westbourne clasping the Romanov dagger.

As he entered the study to which Lord Westbourne had retired, Westbourne simply waved an impatient hand, hardly bothering to turn round from the desk at the sound of Rose's voice. Perhaps he was busy. Perhaps still simply in shock. 'The Empire is more important than a burglar,' he replied testily, rustling papers vigorously to prove his point.

'Burglars?' roared a voice behind Rose. It was the Grand Duke in hot pursuit of his dagger which he had perceived had disappeared in Rose's hand. 'Stuff and nonsense.

You're a Nihilist, aren't you? I've caught you red-handed.'

'No, Your Imperial Highness,' answered Rose, politely cursing his presence. He could hardly insist on Westbourne's cooperation with the Grand Duke present. He would still have to wait.

'That's my dagger,' the Grand Duke pointed out. 'What do you want it for?'

'I'm guarding it, sir.'

'Damned odd way to guard it. Give it to me.'

It was an order from a Grand Duke in a country where Rose had no authority. With mixed feelings the inspector handed it over.

Play began again. Only 11 runs to win. But the Gentlemen had not reckoned with a Bastide newly heartened by glorying in Westbourne's ignominy. He was a Napoleon returned from Elba. Wickets fell, watched in mounting horror from the terrace by the Prince of Wales. Slowly talk stopped and tension grew, even the staff abandoning their duties to watch. Even Auguste was fascinated at the reversal of fate, as one by one Gentlemen took the long walk back without a single run being added. For Albert Edward the inevitable happened. Slowly and stately and cursing the day he was born a prince, he marched up to the wicket. The match depended on him. He knew it. Mama would have some complaint to make. If England's future king failed to save the day, he would have let down England. If the Gentlemen won *now*, he would have humiliated the Russians and the French. Just when he had every hope of actually achieving a little concorde between the nations.

Bastide faced this arch-enemy of his people. Letting out a whoop of joy, he raced up to the bowling crease. The Prince saw the ball coming, hesitated and hit it. Should he run? No, too much tea. He only just made it back to the crease. Audible sighs of relief. Too audible. That settled it. He'd stay put next time. And stay put he did, praying that Tucker

94

might face the rest of the bowling and save him from indignity. All eyes were now fixed on the gripping scene at the wicket.

By five minutes to the close of play at seven o'clock the scores were level. Tucker had scored a further 10, the Prince of Wales none, and the Gentlemen were still one run from victory. The Prince mopped his brow, his hands sweaty inside his gloves, as he faced the bowling for the new over. Why ever had he agreed to this torture? Croquet was a much better game. For one thing, the ladies played it. If he failed now . . .

At one minute to seven, with no runs yet scored and by now almost crying at the thought of Mama's face, Albert Edward, Prince of Wales, faced the battling Bastide for the last ball of the over. The ball was coming. In stark terror at the approaching Armageddon he forgot caution, advanced to meet the ball, and gave it a mighty drive in the manner of the great W. G. himself. It soared high into the air, over the heads of the fielders towards the boundary, with all able-bodied members of the Players' team following it. Fascinated, the Prince of Wales watched its progress as it sailed on towards the boundary and began to fall. A boundary? A catch? The future of the world might depend on this one ball.

Fortunately for the world, and in particular for the Prince of Wales, fate took a hand. The ostrich, anxious to join in the fun again, craned his long neck well forward over the boundary fence. The ball, falling to earth, crashed squarely on its skull, pole-axing the unfortunate bird, which collapsed, stunned, draped over the fence. There, like Lady Westbourne before it, it remained untended, for the ball, bouncing off the bird, was caught by Trepolov before it could reach the ground. The Players, the match in their opinion saved, were already celebrating the avoidance of disaster with enthusiastic roars of self-congratulation, when Washington, more aware of the niceties of the situation, hurtled on to the field, closely followed by the rest of the Gentlemen watching from the verandah. Summoning the umpires he demanded justice. The ball had reached the boundary fence – the ostrich's head merely being an extension of it. The match had been won by the Gentlemen.

The Grand Duke's expression slowly changed to one of melancholy. But Bastide was made of sterner stuff. Moreover, he had been reading the rules. A Napoleon disclaiming any need for a parliament, he scoffed that it was clear that the catch was a good one, since the ostrich had thrust his head into the field of play so that the ball had never reached the boundary.

The umpires' faces went white. They conferred. Clearly one of them was destined for an outstanding career in international diplomacy for regardless of the rules, which were beyond them and which in any case said nothing about ostriches, the senior of the two raised a finger – albeit nervously – to signify dismissal. The Prince was out. The match had ended in a tie.

Hubbub broke out as some of the English team, forgetting all about the need for sportsmanship, loudly protested against this Judgement of Solomon. Alfred Hathaway and Bastide came to fisticuffs. The Prince, overwhelmed with relief that his honour had been upheld, that Anglo-Russian relations were unimpaired and that he wouldn't be barred from the Folies Bergère, hastily accepted the decision and shook hands with the Grand Duke. It was confirmed that the result was a tie. The dagger would remain at the Villa Russe till the next contest.

The dagger? Where was it? The Grand Duke glanced round at the salver in which, with blind optimism, he had replaced it ready for presentation to the English. It had disappeared.

Followed by the Grand Duke's roar, 'There is a burglar here,' Fouchard hurled himself into action, overcome with horror, and instituted a search. This was what came of guarding bosoms.

The dagger did not take long to find. Opening the door of the waiting room, Egbert Rose saw it immediately. It was stuck up to the hilt in the back of Lord Westbourne, sprawled over the desk.

Chapter Five

Slowly Rose straightened up from his brief investigation and looked at Auguste, who had followed him into the study.

'Get Fouchard here,' was all he said.

Auguste swallowed, unable to take in that this was real. Cannes was a paradise of home to be dreamed of, so this could not be murder. Not the result of raw, brutal emotions that he had encountered in London. Blindly he went in search of Inspector Fouchard, who was still diligently searching lockers for the dagger while his gendarmes did their best to keep the cream of Cannes society contained in the salon. In his agitation Auguste was almost unable to speak, but his face did it for him, and with a sense of dire calamity hanging over him Fouchard followed him to the study. The scene he saw there confirmed his worst nightmares. Rose's grunt of 'Lord Westbourne' escaped him in the horror of the moment, and seeing the broad blazered back slumped over the desk he assumed the corpse to be that of the Prince of Wales, or at the very least the Grand Duke Igor. Terror overcame him and he took refuge in oblivion.

'Strewth, look at that,' said Rose disgustedly, as with a thud Fouchard slumped to the floor. Auguste rushed to the kitchen across the corridor, returning with a bottle of water, hotly pursued by Boris, and threw it all over Fouchard. Auguste was not to know that the flask of colourless liquid contained in fact Boris's emergency supplies of vodka.

'Get him out of here, Auguste,' Rose commanded irritably, waving a hand towards the cook, who was staring fascinated at the corpse, 'and get the Grand Duke in here. And get someone to go for a doctor.'

Boris, transfixed with shock, swaying slightly, allowed himself to be escorted out. 'The Grand Duke? You get the Grand Duke, Diddiums? I come too. Russia, oh Russia.'

'Get in there, Boris, and stay there. And keep the other staff there too,' shouted Auguste, goaded beyond endurance by the clinging Ukrainian, and detailing James Higgins to seek out a doctor.

Meanwhile Fouchard, licking the remains of the unexpected windfall of alcohol from his face, as befitted any decent Frenchman, scrambled shamefacedly to his feet. 'Who is it?' he inquired nervously. 'The Grand Duke?'

'Lord Westbourne,' grunted Rose, to Fouchard's visible relief, until the possible ramifications of this news dawned upon him.

'So, an English matter,' said Fouchard quickly, breathing a sigh of relief that the Sûreté could not blame him.

'Crime on French soil,' Rose pointed out firmly, meeting his gaze. He could see trouble coming.

So could Fouchard. 'Whoever has done this deed – and you cannot believe he did it himself, *cher Inspecteur* – was *English*, for his lordship has only just arrived in Cannes. So *Monsieur le Préfet* will undoubtedly take the view that the crime has its roots in England, and so will the Sûreté in Nice, and you must stay to help, *hein*?' If the Nice Sûreté were to handle the affair he, Fouchard, could hardly fail to be a scapegoat. 'This crime is linked with your burglaries without doubt,' Fouchard announced happily.

This was precisely what Rose had feared. He could hardly deny that he had an appointment with Westbourne for seven o'clock, as Fouchard knew only too well. Now Westbourne was dead before he could give Rose his information. Fouchard was well content with the effect of his pronouncement.

'Not without doubt at all,' Rose countered. 'His lordship was none too popular with a French lady here, as you must have heard yourself—'

'*Non*,' said Fouchard sharply. 'I heard nothing. The murderer is an Englishman.'

'He was sitting on a committee in Paris to settle the West African problem.' Rose had thought swiftly.

'Paris?' Hope sprang into Fouchard's eyes.

'Paris,' Rose confirmed.

With one breath, honourable compromise was met. 'The Sûreté in Paris can handle it,' said Fouchard. 'They are good at finding murderers,' he added with satisfaction.

'Murder?' bellowed the Grand Duke, shepherded by Auguste through the door, staring bewilderedly at the body of Lord Westbourne. This was not a custom at English cricket matches from what he'd been told. 'The devil must have thought it was *me*. Nihilist, of course. That's my dagger, too.'

'When did you last see it, sir?' inquired Rose, only too well aware that the Grand Duke himself was the last person in charge of the dagger. Just his luck the handle of this dagger was so knobbly with jewels; no fingerprinting would show up anything useful, even if the system were officially in use yet.

'Where I put it,' the Grand Duke answered, in the confident manner of expecting everyone to know his every movement.

'And where was that?'

'Back in the salon on the salver, of course.'

'Did anyone see you do it, *Votre Altesse Imperiale*?' put in Fouchard, thinking he should take his share.

The Grand Duke looked black. 'Room was packed. I've no idea. More important things to do. There was a match to win. Who did it?'

101

'What, sir?'

'This murder.'

Rose gave up. 'We' – it had come naturally – 'Inspector Fouchard will find him, sir.'

'Or her?' The Grand Duke looked pleased at his unexpected talent for detection.

'Now, sir, I don't know' – Rose murmured cunningly – 'if you could arrange with your chef to provide a spot of tea for everyone, we'll have to tell them soon; they'll think it strange to be kept here just for a burglary.'

'Burglary? You think it was the cat burglar did this – *thing*?' Kallinkova had swept past the gendarmes, determined to find out what was happening.

'As you're here, miss,' said Rose a trifle grimly, 'I wonder if you would like to go with Inspector Fouchard while he breaks the news to Lady Westbourne.'

Fouchard's eyes opened in alarm.

'It is your case, Inspector,' Rose said, firmly returning to the fray.

'Yours, Inspector,' Fouchard purred. 'Until the Sûreté arrive.'

'*Monsieur l'Inspecteur*,' interposed Auguste agitatedly. Fouchard took no notice. Nor did Rose.

'Scotland Yard would not wish to—'

'The Sûreté would insist. In matters where political considerations might apply, the country concerned—'

'But it had all the signs of one of your *crimes passionels*,' countered Rose. 'He was publicly threatened – by a Frenchwoman.'

'Inspector Rose,' Auguste tried again.

'*Non*. It is undoubtedly a crime beginning in London—'

'On French soil,' said Rose, coming back to checkmate.

'Egbert!' yelled Auguste. They stopped abruptly and looked at him in amazement. '*Messieurs*,' he continued despairingly, 'he is not in the salon so where *is* the Prince of Wales?'

*   *   *

The heir to the throne of the British Empire had performed a vanishing act only comparable to the miracles accomplished by Messrs Maskelyne and Cooke in Piccadilly's Egyptian Hall of Mysteries. He mopped his face in relief as his carriage proceeded speedily on its way to the sanity of the Cercle Nautique on the Boulevard de la Croisette. There he could get a good whisky and soda and reflect on his unfortunate position. He must try to remember whether Mama was at Cimiez yet or whether distance was on his side and he could concoct a sufficiently plausible telegram as to how he had managed to be present at the scene of the murder of an English lord. Not just any lord but old Charles Westbourne, one of her favourites. Now he came to think of it, hadn't she commanded him to be on the station platform at Cannes some day soon, when her railway train passed through? That meant she might already have left. And be greeted with the news in her morning newspaper, if his luck continued on its present course.

That was the end of cricket for him. He might have known something disastrous would happen. Another disagreeable thought came to him. Suppose – after all, Westbourne was roughly the same height and build, though Westbourne was much fatter of course – suppose it was someone trying to assassinate *him* again. After all, only last week someone had nearly got King George of Greece. No, he'd keep away from cricket from now on.

A frantic search by Inspector Fouchard, recollecting his original duty, revealed that the Prince of Wales was not lying dead anywhere in the vicinity, and brief interrogation revealed that he had departed of his own free will and not under restraint by some Balkan Moriarty. He had merely summoned his carriage, shot a murderous look at the Delahaye horseless carriage awaiting the Grand Duke, and gone. For this Fouchard was immensely grateful; he had no wish whatsoever to be involved in an investigation in which the Prince of Wales figured among the suspects, a sentiment with which Rose wholeheartedly agreed. He then departed with the unhappy task of breaking the news to Lady Westbourne.

Left alone in the waiting room, Rose and Auguste contemplated the corpse sprawled over the desk, noting that it faced the window with its back to the door.

'Looks like he meant it when he said he was writing a report,' said Rose. 'It's still there, all right.' There was half a page covered with confident copperplate.

'So he was killed soon after tea,' said Auguste. 'It does not take long to write two paragraphs.'

'Depends on how long he thought about it, and he was thinking hard enough about it not to turn round when someone came through the door,' Rose pointed out, 'and there are no signs of anyone coming through the window.'

'Or it meant he knew his killer well enough to turn his back on him during a discussion. Someone he knew very well.'

'Like his wife,' was the unspoken thought in both their minds.

'It must have been a murder on the spur of the moment, for the dagger was guarded all day. Only at the end of the tea break did it reappear again without a guard. Provided the Grand Duke speaks the truth when he says he left it there,' Auguste added.

Rose groaned. Fouchard would never get involved if the Grand Duke were a suspect and even he, Rose, quailed at the thought. 'There'll be witnesses,' Rose said hopefully. 'Even if the guests didn't notice, the servants would be clearing the tea after all. They'd have seen it there. Even Higgins—' The awful truth jolted him. Jewels and Higgins went together like safe and cracksman. And Auguste had blithely dispatched him to hunt down a doctor. But he couldn't see Higgins going as far as murder. Or could he?

'If this were one of those Sherlock Holmes mysteries, the villain would have left clues a mile high,' said Rose disgustedly. 'I never seem to have his luck,' eyeing the desk and floor completely free of such things as telltale hairpins and cuff-links.

' 'Ere's the bloke you wanted,' cried Higgins cheerily, ushering in Dr Earl from the Villa Beatrice, who bustled in eagerly. This was a change from the griping pains of new arrivals. Moreover, although titles were two a penny in Cannes, Lord Westbourne was different. His death would undoubtedly be fully reported in the English newspapers, perhaps even Her Majesty might take an interest. With luck Archibald Earl might well make the columns of *The Times*.

'Going out in style, eh?' he remarked jovially, observing the jewelled hilt, as though he attended murders in Cannes every day. '*Cherchez la femme*, eh?' He began his examination as Rose paled at the thought of La Belle Mimosa. It wasn't a pleasant one.

'I'd say he's been dead two and a half hours at the most, perhaps less. Is his wife here? Need attention, does she?'

'She's being told now. Two and a half hours – that brings it to just after tea, as we thought,' Rose said to Auguste. 'The dagger must have been taken almost immediately.'

'But surely some people would still be in the salon, and then there'd be servants around?' objected Auguste.

'Any later and we could eliminate the Russian side, because they were on the field.'

'Could have run in for a trip to the toilet,' said Rose doggedly, if unrealistically. No way was he going to eliminate the foreigners at this stage, and leave the burden on the English side.

There was a commotion outside as Fouchard returned, followed apparently by half the Cannes police force and Lady Westbourne pushing her way through, Natalia trying in vain to prevent her.

'I demand to see him. He's my husband.'

'Madam.' Rose fielded her expertly before she could enter.

'Don't you dare stop me, you common little man!' she shrieked.

But the shriek was cut off as he reluctantly stood aside and she viewed her husband's body and the dagger. 'How odd,' she remarked conversationally, 'he never liked rubies.' Then her eyes glazed. 'How could he do it?' she moaned, and collapsed gracefully on the floor.

With an 'I told you so' look Dr Earl cleared his throat and advanced in professional manner, but Natalia forestalled him, shooting him an indignant look as though he were responsible.

'Camomile tea,' cried Auguste. 'I will obtain some camomile tea. There is some in the store . . .' He rushed into the kitchen, expecting to find preparations for refreshments in full flood. But the kitchen was empty save for Boris, and there were no signs of any sustenance at all. And Boris was sprawled insensible over the small working table.

'What are you doing, you foolish man?' howled Auguste, shaking him violently. 'Food, we need *food*, and tea. Monsieur Boris, rouse yourself.'

Boris opened a bleary eye. Tears began to pour out of it unheeded into the remains of Auguste's galantine. Unsympathetically Auguste shook him again.

'Get up, get up,' he cried, pulling at his arms. 'We need tea, and food. There is much to organise.'

'The Englishman,' cried Boris. 'The poor Englishman. He is dead.'

'Yes, yes, but it's not your job to worry about that. You must look after the living.'

'But we lose the match,' said Boris anxiously. 'The honour of Mother Russia is lost. Why the Grand Duke no win match? Why he fall over? He is wonderful man. The Tsar is wonderful man. But the people—'

'Yes, yes, food,' yelled Auguste, cutting across this diatribe.

'*Piroshki?*' murmured Boris lovingly, beginning to motivate himself.

'*Au diable*, your *piroshki*,' muttered Auguste, rushing out with a tray of camomile tea for Lady Westbourne.

He handed the tea to Natalia, who proceeded to coax Dora back to life, while the men stood awkwardly by. Inspector Fouchard took advantage of the pause, having now ascertained from Rose that Auguste's qualification for his presence ran deeper than camomile tea.

'May I say what a privilege it is to meet Monsieur Escoffier's favourite apprentice? Ah, how I recall the *civet de lièvre* you prepared at the Faisan Doré. Why, it must be over fifteen years ago?'

'*Alors*,' said Auguste with pride. 'That was my first named dish. The year was 1881 and the *Maître* Escoffier permitted me the honour of putting my name to the dish, *civet de lièvre à la façon Didier*. It was a small thing, but all the difference to the taste when I added the – ah, *non*, I keep my secrets. But tell me, *Monsieur l'Inspecteur*, did you also taste my *loup de roche aux herbes*?'

'No,' Fouchard said with interest. 'Tell me your method.'

Egbert Rose coughed, and guiltily Auguste returned his thoughts to murder, as Natalia, averting her eyes from the corpse, rose to her feet, raising Lady Westbourne who clung to her, a dead weight.

'Shall I take Lady Westbourne to her home, Inspector?' She looked from Rose to Fouchard. 'I fear she will answer no questions today.'

'We will call upon *madame* tomorrow,' said the inspector, determined where he could safely be so.

'*Merci, monsieur*,' said Natalia meekly, winking at Auguste, who pretended not to notice, conscious of his status as specially co-opted detective. 'And, if she inquires, the body?'

'Remains with the police, *madame*, for the moment.'

'And now,' said Fouchard firmly after they had gone, 'we will go to tell everyone what has happened. And you,' pointing amicably at Rose, 'will do the telling.'

'But—' Rose began.

'First, they must have apéritifs,' broke in Auguste anxiously. 'I hear them now. Give me five minutes, I beg.'

He slipped out as a small army of servants carried by all sorts of carts and carriages scurried up to the Pavilion with emergency rations organised by *Maman*, with *Papa's* enthusiastic support. Thank goodness *Maman* was in one of her English moods. Today she could have organised the British Empire, had she been called upon to do so. Tea for a hundred or so people presented no true challenge. *Papa* was agog with curiosity. If the Grand Duke had been assassinated there would be no surprise, for Grand Dukes tended to come and go. But an English milord was something else. Every charcuterie in town had been ransacked in order to provide something palatable. More tea appeared, champagne hardly seemed fitting, however desirable. Boris was now completely *hors de combat*, eyes glazed, lurching hopelessly around, oblivious of Auguste's rushing hither and thither. Auguste was endeavouring to be both detective and *maître d'hôtel* for the matter of tea, torn as usual by twin loves. In despair he wondered what on earth he was doing. He was supposed to be having a holiday. And now here he was not only serving and cooking food, but involved in a murder once again. What the secretary of Plum's was going to say to him, he shuddered to think. He hoped *The Times* never heard of this affair. On the other hand, there was nothing like detective work for clearing the brain, a loving assembling of ingredients, and the fitting of the pieces together to make a whole *plat*.

Chivvying the staff of the Villa Russe into the tea room with refreshments, Auguste brought up the rear. He attracted no attention. Fifty pairs of eyes saw him and turned away; he was only the chef. But to his alert eyes, it was clear that the company had divided itself into groups. The Gentlemen had banded together with their womenfolk, the Players were together with their ladies, and the others, outsiders to their coterie, remained apart, including La Belle Mimosa, who accepted and drank from her teacup, declining stronger beverage, as though nothing more potent than this delicate liquid had ever passed her lips. As Auguste returned to the study he saw the gendarmes at the door struggling to keep out yet another element; the news was clearly all round Cannes, and the newspapers, including one strident English voice announcing himself as the *Cannes Gazette*, were determined to make full use of this unexpected variety for their pages, resigned usually to who was in town and who was not. Now they had an event of a most exciting nature.

'They grow impatient, Inspector.' Auguste was careful to preserve the proprieties in public, despite his friendship with Egbert Rose.

Rose turned to Fouchard who nodded fervently. 'Let's go,' he said in the manner of one setting out to St Giles' rookery.

'And *you* speak to them,' Fouchard reiterated nervously. 'Then we think,' he added somewhat ingenuously. He was not accustomed to violent crime, and felt obscurely indignant that fate had once again singled him out. Only last year the Grand Duke of Mecklenburg-Schwerin had thrown himself from the balcony of the Villa Wenden; this, however, was infinitely worse. Murder! And one of the English community. How pleasant it would be if they should have their own police force . . . a permanent detective from Scotland Yard for such unfortunate eventualities among the *hiverneurs*. He eyed Rose speculatively.

As the three men entered the room there were several heated discussions in progress. The most spirited came from the raised voices of the Gentlemen. Once again they were thrashing over the vital question that had held all right-thinking Englishmen's attention for the last three years: was the bottle of champagne brought on to the pitch to celebrate the great W. G.'s achievement of scoring his hundredth hundred at Bristol in May '95 a magnum or a jeroboam. The Russian concern was of less magnitude. They were merely arguing about the ostrich (not having understood the English challenge), and whether neck before boundary meant something like leg before wicket to the Gentlemen. The women were discussing the question of whether the forthcoming Russian royal wedding was really worth the penalty of remaining in Cannes unfashionably late in the season.

Into this maelstrom plunged Inspector Fouchard: '*Vos Altesses Imperiales, mon ami* Inspector Rose of Scotland Yard wishes to speak with you.' He sat down, congratulating himself that he had handled the situation rather neatly.

Rose, with the confidence of not being on his home territory, decided on the bold approach: 'I'm sorry to say, ladies and gentlemen, we've had an unfortunate occurrence. Lord Westbourne's been murdered, and' – waiting for the murmurs of satisfaction at this confirmation of their guesses to die down – 'it's for certain that someone here knows something about it.'

It took a moment for this to sink in, then they realised the impertinence of the suggestion, and the gasps were even louder.

'Surely, Inspector,' said Washington, 'some tramp must have entered through the window, bent on burglary, stabbed him and left the same way.'

' 'Fraid not, sir. Why leave the dagger behind?'

'He was surprised by someone,' said Washington nonchalantly.

'Window not disturbed, sir,' said Rose, scotching this firmly on the head.

'Then it was a servant,' said Washington, impatiently

now. 'You don't seriously imagine a *cricketer* – one of us – would stab a man *in the back*?'

There was a general murmur of approval at this conclusive evidence.

'I don't imagine, sir. I look for facts,' Rose countered stolidly.

Count Trepolov stood up, drawing his full six foot two inches erect. 'At least the Players can have nothing to do with this unfortunate business. I trust we may retire. We were all on the field—'

'Do you know when he was killed, sir?' inquired Rose mildly.

The Count flushed and thought quickly. 'The lord retired to the writing room at the end of the tea interval and the Players were all on the field after that. No one on our side would wish to kill Lord Westbourne. The idea is ridiculous.'

'I disagree. He stood for English imperialism,' shouted Bastide, eyes flashing. 'Africa is French.' He stood up, carried away with a chance for fervour. 'To us the glory.' Remembering an old print of Napoleon in his youth, he pushed his sharp-featured profile forward, his fist upraised, and held the pose.

'Oh, Basty, you are wonderful,' breathed Emmeline, her cheeks flushed pink, then she uneasily thought perhaps it was not so wonderful of him in view of the fact that they were looking for motives for murder.

'Maybe, sir. Someone didn't like his politics. Now, if you'll sit down.'

Somewhat deflated, since his announcement had caused no great stir, Bastide did so, but was rewarded by a comforting squeeze of Emmeline's hand.

'But it's more likely,' Rose continued, 'that this burglar I'm after killed him and that he's here today. As you all heard, Lord Westbourne thought he knew who it was. It seems to us that his lordship had to be got out of the way

111

before my lad could get to his victim.' Two bosoms swelled, and there was a strident female laugh.

'*C'est ridicule, ça.* If it is this burglar, and he is here, why do I have thees still?' La Belle Mimosa pointed dramatically to the egg. 'Unless it is 'im – he gave it to me.' The finger now pointed straight and devastatingly at the Grand Duke.

At this outrage to all rules of society, consternation broke out. The Duke cowered, the Grand Duchess's eyes glittered, though whether at La Belle Mimosa or her husband was not clear. Or wasn't until she rose composedly to her feet, not to address the gathering, but to depart.

'If,' announced the Grand Duchess Anna in dulcet tones to Inspector Rose, 'you wish to find this murderer, *it* is here. You heard *it* threaten to kill Lord Westbourne and now Lord Westbourne is dead.'

La Belle Mimosa was on her feet with the dexterity that World Champion Jem Mace would envy in the ring and confronted the Grand Duchess bosom to bosom, hands on her hips.

'It is your husband's, thees,' she jeered, thrusting out her breasts and patting the egg.

The Grand Duchess hardly hesitated. '*Vraiment? Bien!*' An apparently languid white hand darted out like a snake's tongue, wresting the egg away from its moorings, and the Grand Duchess passed on leaving La Belle Mimosa shrieking impotently with rage, only held back from physically attacking the Grand Duchess by her guards. She took refuge in words. 'But he sleeps with me,' she jeered.

The shapely head did not turn or pause, but a cool voice was heard to remark: '*Pauvre homme.* And to have to pay too.' Only then did she look carefully at the egg and with a slight sneer on her face turned and deposited it with a gesture of disgust in a nearby aspidistra pot.

There was a silent round of applause for the departing Grand Duchess, broken by a rich, full, female voice: 'Cyril, am I suspected?' Rachel Gray had ceded the limelight long enough.

'No, Rachel,' said Cyril Tucker. 'Not you in particular. Everyone.' He was going to have a difficult time this evening, he could see that. He took temporary refuge in his own nirvana. He knew every cricket score since the Lion of Kent scored his first century. He mentally selected Gloucestershire versus Surrey in 1880 and replayed the finish, in the hope that such excitement would shore him up to face the journey home with his wife.

The Grand Duke also suffered from forebodings about the evening ahead and seemed anxious not to follow his wife. Being a possible suspect for murder seemed a reasonable alternative at the moment.

'Even me?' he inquired. 'You suspect me?'

Rose had learned much from his case at Stockbery Towers. 'Only a formality, sir,' he said smoothly.

The grand-ducal brow remained furrowed.

The Grand Duchess's carriage, fluttering its white ribbons and with the coachman's hat turned sideways to denote its grand-ducal occupant, drew off, and the company, dismissed by the police, gradually made their way to their belated dinner engagements. La Belle Mimosa was carrying the egg, somewhat less ostentatiously than previously. The Grand Duke inconveniently remained, despite being obviously in the way of the police who were now removing the body. He gazed at the departing ex-Lord Westbourne uneasily. 'Are you sure,' he inquired of Rose anxiously, 'that it isn't the Nihilists?'

'Why should the Nihilists wish to kill Lord Westbourne, sir?' replied Rose patiently.

'Thought it was me,' offered the Grand Duke apologetically. 'All in white. Both of us in blazers.'

'But, *Votre Altesse Imperiale*,' put in Auguste deferentially, 'you were on the cricket field for all to see. No one could have mistaken Lord Westbourne for you.'

113

'That's true.' The Grand Duke cheered up. He peered at Auguste. 'You're the relief cook, aren't you? Boris told me about you. Not bad, not bad at all, that luncheon. You've got a future ahead of you. Any time you want a job come and see me. Time old Boris was retired.'

'*Merci, Votre Altesse Imperiale,*' murmured Auguste straightfaced.

'All the same,' the Grand Duke reverted to his favourite theme, 'I want a guard at our ball. And I want *you*—' He stabbed a finger at Rose.

'It is the local police's task, sir—'

'Couldn't tell a burglar from a bortsch. No, it's you I want. I've an idea that's where your fellow will strike next.'

'Your – er – vehicle awaits you, sir,' announced a footman. The Grand Duke's face fell. Home was suddenly less inviting than the cricket club. He'd have to do a lot of thinking on the way home.

'Come and have a look.' He waved a hand at Rose and Auguste and they obediently followed him out to the roadway at the rear of the Pavilion. There, awaiting him, was the Delahaye, Higgins, and the cow which was attached to the motor car by a rope.

'There,' said the Duke proudly, admiring the motor car and ignoring the cow. 'Just a fad. Won't last. Anna won't ride in it.'

But Rose's attention was on the chauffeur. 'I'll be along to see you, Higgins,' he said meditatively.

'Muriel and I will look forward to that, Inspector,' announced Higgins, as he leapt down to usher the Grand Duke up.

Inspector Fouchard departed to make urgent contact with the Nice Sûreté, fervently wringing Rose's hand, kissing him on both cheeks, to Auguste's amusement, and announcing amid protestations of eternal gratitude that he was his saviour.

Rose emerged physically and emotionally ruffled with

the distinct feeling that he was being outmanoeuvred and also that he was going to have a lot of explaining to do at the Yard. He mentally began composing his telegram.

'I think for you, dear Egbert, a cup of tea,' announced Auguste thoughtfully, as the Delahaye moved off at a snail's – or rather a cow's – pace.

'To hell with tea,' said Rose forcefully. 'This is France, I'm officially on no duty whatsoever, and I need more than tea.'

Auguste searched the small kitchen, eyed wistfully by the gendarme left on duty, and produced *un marc de Provence*, which Rose, coughing slightly, pronounced satisfactory.

'That's lubricated me nicely. Now, Auguste, your ghost is going to have to wait. There's more important work for you.'

'So are your Fabergé eggs, *mon ami*.'

'Not necessarily. If it's our burglar. And if it *is* our burglar, then we can look at those who were in England at the time of the robberies and are here now.'

'But suppose it's someone from Paris – La Belle Mimosa may have known him there. Then there is *le jeune Comte* who believes that glory lies in war and death. Suppose he killed him for the glory of France, in the hope that the conference would collapse?'

'Or Lady Westbourne herself. Had a row with her husband and stabbed him—'

'She would have to have brought the dagger with her,' Auguste pointed out.

'True. Still, why not? The lady wasn't feeling very friendly towards him when he left for the study.'

'And there is something you forget, Egbert. Dora Westbourne was robbed of an egg, and we know she is not always a faithful wife. *Cherchez la femme* as the good doctor said. I heard today a conversation which suggested she had parted from one lover, and then was with Lord Westbourne when he observed that she had undoubtedly taken another.'

'*Voilà*, I am here.'

115

They jumped as Natalia returned from her duties with Lady Westbourne. She had clearly overheard some of their conversation. 'If it is this burglar who stabs Lord Westbourne and you find him, I get my egg back, *n'est ce pas*?' She smiled at them. 'So I help you, because I do want my egg back. Very much.'

'I don't know—' Rose began dubiously.

'Ah, but I move where even you cannot, Inspector. I hear what you cannot. Gossip. Some nights I dance, but when I am in Cannes then I can detect. Come, let us go to dine. I have my carriage here.'

'My hotel—' Rose began.

'Ah, Inspector, hotels can wait. Tonight you need something special.'

Hobbling past her carriage was a familiar figure, at least to Auguste. It was the ancient Cannois he had met at the port.

'*Monsieur*,' he asked, puzzled, 'what are you doing here?'

'*Le meutre*,' the Cannois replied, spitting scornfully.

'What, *mon ami*, do you know about this murder?'

'It is only an Englishman. No need for excitement.'

'But what—'

'Did I not say nothing good would come of it? Once the *Masque de Fer* is seen, trouble comes.'

'You would like to be taken back to the town, *monsieur*?' inquired Natalia, leaning down from the carriage.

He looked at her. '*Cherchez la femme*,' he said cryptically, and hobbled off chuckling to himself.

'Come, Auguste, Inspector. You at least will ride with me, will you not?' and they climbed up beside her with alacrity. Happiness filled Auguste's heart and swept aside thoughts of murder. For this moment he tried to think only of Natalia. After all, he was on holiday.

Chapter Six

The police headquarters at the rear of the town not far from Rose's hotel was as ahum with activity as Trepolov's bees on a brood comb. Rose was impressed by what Fouchard's men had so far achieved in a brief morning's work, perhaps pleased by their unusual temporary assignment in tracking down a murderer. The Sûreté in Nice had, as Fouchard predicted, promptly handed the case to Paris. If he were a villain with the choice of being hunted down by British crushers or French gendarmes, he decided he'd choose the British. His admiration for Fouchard shot up. He was presented with names and addresses of all those present (even La Belle Mimosa's, he was amused to notice); vigorous inquiries were rapidly noting those known under the useful Registration of Foreigners Act to have travelled from England recently, and the Sûreté Générale in Paris, he was told, was working on Lord Westbourne's movements there. The greater number of persons who could be established to have been in England while the robberies took place, the greater role Inspector Rose and the Sûreté would have to play in the proceedings, was Fouchard's reasoning. Moreover, he might with good fortune share in the credit when this monster was discovered, but escape blame should he elude justice.

'*Mon brave*,' Fouchard began excitedly, if informally, as he ushered Rose into his office. 'Inspector Chesnais of the Sûreté is on his way here. I think you may know him? He managed to take the evening *rapide* and will be here this evening. This tells me,' he added with gusto, 'that there may be political implications. My friend, this is a grave affair,' he finished revelling in the thought.

'Yes, I had the pleasure of meeting the inspector,' Rose replied. The word pleasure was diplomatic. 'There's one thing you should consider, however,' he added thoughtfully and evilly. 'If the murder was not political but was connected with the robberies, the robberies are going to continue. Our friend will still want that seventh egg, and the Petrov Diamond into the bargain. It seems to me that you and your men had better be on the alert.'

Fouchard thought this over. He comprehended exactly what Rose had in mind.

'The Grand Duke's masked ball,' he said resignedly. 'Two weeks from today.'

Rose nodded. 'I think you'll need all your forces there if we haven't nabbed the blighter first.'

Fouchard was not acquainted with the words nab or blighter, but the meaning was starkly clear. 'Then,' he said simply, 'we must make sure we do.'

Thus motivated, they took a cab up the hillside to where the Villa Russe gleamed white in the late morning sunshine, and were shown into the huge morning reception room intended to impress visitors, and succeeding. Decorated in white Carrara marble and gilded bronze, it was based on the Great Throne Room of the Winter Palace, with Rastrelli busts of Romanov ancestors and busts by Rodin of the Grand Duke and Duchess. The Grand Duchess's was superb. The Grand Duke's was not, having resulted in something like a cross between the sculptor's Balzac and a ballet dancer. It was displayed in a somewhat dark corner.

The doors were thrown open and the grand-ducal pair made their entrance. A united front, thought Rose, amused. Whatever had passed between them after their return to the villa the previous evening, no sign of it remained this morning, at least to the outsider. The Grand Duke muted his usual boisterousness as soon as mention of the murder was made.

'You find this burglar,' he commanded, 'before our ball. It is for my birthday,' he informed them, pleased, before adding gloomily, 'I do not wish to find myself a victim of my own dagger.'

'It is difficult,' explained the Grand Duchess. 'We cannot change the ball, because of Igor's birthday. The day of St Benoit, the 14th March in our Russian calendar, the 26th here. Always we have this problem. When do we celebrate? This year both the 14th and the 26th in the French calendar are in Lent. But I do not think many people will stay away from our ball for this reason.' The glance she gave her husband suggested he might arrange his birthday more conveniently next time.

Having politely put such questions as they could, and discovered that neither the Grand Duke nor Duchess had observed anything of use to them, Fouchard requested formal permission to interview the servants on duty at the Pavilion the previous day.

'Servants?' The Grand Duchess's brow puckered, in slight surprise, as if forgetting for the moment where they were kept.

'The Pavilion kitchen door to the corridor faces the study door,' Rose pointed out. 'It's possible one of them might have seen something. Or that they might have noticed whether or not the dagger was lying on its salver while they cleared the tea from the salon.'

They had, however, been forestalled. Auguste was already deep in conversation with the kitchenmaids. Madame Didier, imported once more from retirement, in order that some kind of luncheon might be served, since Boris still seemed glazed by the events of the day before, was bustling round the kitchen, intent on producing a little light luncheon of *rouget à la Niçoise, moules au safran* and *aubergines à la façon Escoffier*.

119

The latter dish had been taught to her by her son, whose culinary powers, she sometimes conceded, were *pas mal*. All the same, he had much to learn, and she maintained a sharp eye on his creation of the *farci* for the aubergines. Indeed, since most of Auguste's thoughts were for once more upon detection than upon culinary creation, the food lacked the attention it normally commanded.

'A few questions only,' he murmured innocently in answer to the unspoken question writ large upon Rose's face. It was perfectly obvious he had already been active in discussing the matter on everybody's mind.

Interrogation in two and a half languages (lapses into Russian between the staff being common) was a complicated process.

'After Lord Westbourne entered the study, did any of you see anybody go in there after him?' Fouchard demanded authoritatively.

'Yes,' said Boris eagerly. 'I see *him*.'

'Besides me,' Rose said patiently.

Boris's face fell in disappointment that he had not been of use. 'The Grand Duke,' he offered sullenly.

'I saw the Grand Duke come out, *monsieur*,' offered the newest kitchenmaid, eyes big as the Sèvres saucers she served at teatime. 'He came through the kitchen, and bumped into me.' This was an event that would be talked of for the rest of her life.

'Did not,' rumbled Boris.

'You weren't there, Mr Boris. You'd gone to milk the cow.'

'It is the cow's fault,' he commented and relapsed into silence. What responsibility the cow bore for the murder remained unclear.

'I saw a lady,' offered a footman, but could put no name to her.

'What was she wearing?' Fouchard asked sharply.

A consultation in Russian took place between the footmen.

'White,' came the eventual reply.

As the dagger appeared entirely to have escaped notice while the staff cleared the tea, this remained the only positive information to emerge.

'So now we hunt the Woman in White,' said Auguste.

'Not only Sherlock Holmes, but Wilkie Collins too, eh?' grunted Rose.

Lady Westbourne, whom Fouchard had generously granted Rose permission to see alone, was at home. She had spent the morning furiously thinking and dressing for the occasion. It was so convenient that it was Lent, and that accordingly she had brought suitably sombre dresses with her; the grey silk with lace would suffice for the moment to give the requisite air of fragility, until her Paris dressmaker was able to dispatch the mandatory black clothes. True, there was a ladies' tailor in the Boulevard de la Croisette or the English store of Folkett-Browne, or even Madame Verrine in the Rue d'Antibes, but after some thought she decided that their products could not produce the correct effect of helpless widowhood for which she was striving. She needed to be set apart, not accoutred in garments whose origins would be all too familiar to Cannes society.

It was only now therefore that she had had time to consider her feelings over Charles's demise. In the short term, it was undoubtedly a relief; in the longer term it was highly inconvenient. Widows, however charming, were not so sought after as widowers; and Washington, to whom she was pledged at the moment, lacked the qualifications necessary for a husband, whatever his as yet untested advantages might be as a lover. Morever, should she in her widowed state even consider a lover? Society would not tolerate it. Perhaps she could consider dear Harry as escort only? Or would that too do damage to future matrimonial prospects? It was all very difficult.

Genuine tears came into her eyes. Charles had always been there, she realised, and now he would be there no longer, solid, reliable and providing. There was a funeral to arrange, solicitors to contact, police to see— Uneasiness crept over her once again as she remembered the unfortunate scenes that had taken place publicly yesterday. *Charles* of all people – going to a woman of the streets. Well, not the streets, from what she had been told, but certainly an 'unfortunate woman'. She didn't look in the least unfortunate, Dora was thinking bitterly, as she swept into the morning room where Rose awaited her, derby in hand.

She accepted his expressions of sympathy and gratitude for seeing him, with sweet womanly grace. A lace handkerchief fluttered in trembling fingers as she seated herself.

'May I ask you, ma'am, whether your husband gave you any clues about the identity of this burglar? He was going to give me, as you know, positive identification, but he never got the chance.'

'Not a word, Inspector.' She hesitated. 'It was awkward, you see,' she continued winningly. 'He did not know I had a Fabergé egg. I had only told him about the ruby, for fear of upsetting him. I was so very, very fond of him and Igor was so very long ago and so – *unimportant*,' she lowered her voice, 'when I think of dear Charles.'

'Quite, ma'am. Nevertheless, it seems the eggs might have been important enough to the burglar for him to kill your husband.'

A hand flew to her mouth. 'Oh no. So you could say in a way I *killed* Charles.'

'No, ma'am,' Rose stoutly contended, before advancing into a minefield. 'Nothing to do with you. Even if there hadn't been your egg, there were six others.'

'Oh yes, so there were.' Tremulous smile.

'I saw it came as a shock to you,' Rose added carefully, 'that your husband was a friend of Miss Mimosa.'

At once she was cool, the eyes glittered. 'No, Inspector, not *friend*. It was some business transaction he was advising her on. My husband never consorted with other women.' At once she perceived she was on dangerous ground, since a connection could easily be proved, but she had no option other than to continue. 'Our marriage was happy; we were like two lovebirds.'

'Indeed, ma'am. Now, as you fainted, quite natural-like in the study, you threw out some interesting words. "How could he do it?" you said. Who would you be thinking of, ma'am?'

Her face drained of colour, apart from the cosmetics supplied by Messrs Nicholls and Passeron of Nice. 'Did I?' Her voice rose. 'How foolish of me. I meant I thought he had committed suicide, thinking I would be angry at La Belle Mimosa's statements. How foolish. As if I could be angry with Charles.' The lace handkerchief was uncurled from its tight little ball and put to proper use.

'Suicide with a dagger in his back, ma'am?' Rose had not forgotten her insults of the previous day.

Her face turned ugly. 'It could have been done,' she cried sharply. 'It's your job to find out who did it if not, Inspector. Not mine. I have far too much to do. The funeral . . .'

'Good coffee, this,' said Rose appreciatively as he sipped the strong brew at the small café on the Rue St Antoine. 'Not that I don't prefer a nice cup of tea,' he added hastily. No need to let Auguste think he was flinging his derby over the windmill about France.

'We have tea here also,' replied Auguste slightly indignantly.

'Don't taste the same,' pronounced the authority, and proceeded to bring Auguste up to date on his interview with Lady Westbourne and the police inquiries.

'She was furious enough to stab him – did you see her face after La Belle Mimosa dropped her two pennyworth into the conversation? But women like her aren't given to running around with daggers. They employ other methods of revenge,' Rose concluded.

'But on the spur of the moment, *mon ami*, who knows? And there still remains the Woman in White.'

'That means finding out what they were all wearing. Not my field. And they'd lie. I can hardly line 'em up on an identity parade like we were in the Mile End Road. The only woman it could not have been was La Belle Mimosa. Unless she went in later of course.'

'Natalia would remember what the ladies were wearing,' said Auguste confidently. 'So how do you progress with your burglar inquiries?'

'Harry Washington was in London at the right time. So was Cyril Tucker, naturally, and Alfred Hathaway. The Comte de Bonifacio was in Corsica, but Count Trepolov began his winter holidays in London.'

'The Tsar does not work his guards too hard.'

'In Trepolov's case it's more honour than duty, I gather. Chiefly ceremonial post. Would you want someone like Trepolov if you were in the Tsar's shoes?'

Auguste shivered. 'For me, I would not like *at all* to be in the Tsar's shoes. The people grow restless, so I hear. The Grand Duke is fortunate to live in London.'

A less fortunate fact for Rose, however. 'I don't see Cyril Tucker as a burglar; after all, he's in the Colonial Office. So that leaves Washington, Trepolov and Hathaway for this list. Do you see young Alfred shinning up drainpipes?'

'*Non*. Nor Trepolov.'

'Mark you,' Rose ruminated, 'don't you forget that snoozer at the Savoy – he was a Frenchman.'

Auguste laughed. 'And I recall the elegant Captain Jones who so successfully relieved French ladies of their fortunes in Paris.'

'*Touché*. Talking of gallant escorts, there's always Lady Westbourne's. He could be said to have a motive.'

'Trepolov again?' inquired Auguste. 'But he ceased to be her lover, so I believe, yesterday. And Lady Westbourne clearly has in mind a new lover.'

'Revenge?' queried Rose hopefully.

'Perhaps,' said Auguste. 'I think we should visit the gentleman.'

The Prince of Wales too was enjoying a post-prandial cup of coffee in his club, the prestigious Cercle Nautique. Here he felt safe. If he stayed in a private house, he was at the mercy of its owners, who exhibited him like a prize duck; if he stayed at a hotel, every Tom, Dick and Harry under the sun was booking in; if he rented a villa, he had to surround it with half the French police force, which made it highly embarrassing for guests on arrival, especially the more personal ones. The *Cannes Gazette* had its eye on him every minute and lady friends would find their movements followed with such avidity in the social columns that it was abundantly clear to the cognoscenti whom they numbered amongst their very particular friends – a fact which might or might not be welcomed.

He was uneasily aware that sooner or later the police would be making inquiries about old Westbourne. He had had no time for him, but who on earth would want to murder the old codger? Now he came to think of it, Westbourne was probably his own age, but somehow he seemed years older – because he connected him with Mama, he supposed. He had little doubt where Westbourne's allegiances lay.

And what was Her Majesty going to say about all this? He trembled at the thought of the eagle eye, which would transfix him from the Royal Train as he dutifully lined up with other dignitaries on the Cannes railway station platform as her train passed through. And he trembled even more at the summons to Cimiez that would follow.

She'd already pinioned his movements by arranging a state visit by the President of the French Republic in April. 'So that you may see how these things are done, Bertie,' she

125

had informed him. Nonsense, she wanted to ensure that, once *again*, he didn't enjoy a decent holiday.

Washington believed in the opposite approach, as in his batting tactics. When under threat, you hit out. Unfortunately Rose's ball developed a spin that Washington hadn't bargained for.

He glanced nervously around the public rooms of the Hôtel Gonnet. Since the hotel was full of nothing but talk of Westbourne's death, it did him more good than otherwise to be seen talking to Rose and Auguste in the salon. Unfortunately he was lbw straight away, through misunderstanding exactly where the inspector's questions were leading.

'I would hardly wish to murder Lord Westbourne on the strength of one day, Inspector,' he tried to say easily. 'Nor have I actually' – he wondered how to phrase this—' in the circumstances made it *de facto*.'

'Burglary, sir?'

'Burglary?' His face grew blank. 'I thought you were referring to—' He broke off.

'I'm interested in a jewel thief who pinched six Fabergé eggs in London. What did you think I meant?'

Washington could hardly reply. He turned red, realising that he had been on the point of an unusual indiscretion.

'I am a cricketer, sir. What do I know of burglary?' The charming smile managed to reassert itself, seeming to ask how could anyone suspect such a gentleman.

'Just routine, sir,' Rose smoothed.

It transpired that Washington had been in England throughout the period of the robberies, and moreover had attended precisely those social functions that had been followed by the disappearance of the rubies.

When they had gone, Washington stared blankly into his future. He was at a crossroads. Where and what should he do? When they began making deeper inquiries . . .

* * *

As one artiste to another, Natalia Kallinkova was sympathising with Rachel Gray over *marrons crème* and *éclairs de chocolat* at Rumpelmayers where ladies gathered for afternoon tea. Rachel Gray was eyeing Natalia jealously, wondering just how she managed to consume these cream cakes and was still able to dance. She herself was inclined to the statuesque and her Platinum Anti-Corset took much of the credit for her elegant figure on stage.

'This evening I cannot dine with you, alas. I dance,' explained Natalia in between bites of chestnut cream.

'I sympathise. I fortunately am resting,' proclaimed Rachel in gravelly tones. In fact she had no choice.

'How wise,' Natalia cooed, knowing the situation perfectly well. Rachel Gray might be an outstandingly good actress but many actor-managers preferred to have a lesser actress and less temperament.

Natalia patted Mephistopheles, who wondered what had so revolutionised his life with so many outings. He slobbered over her foot in appreciation. The ladies had met apparently by chance. In fact it was a chance carefully engineered by Natalia. She was pondering how to introduce the subject of dress and the burning question of yesterday's murder without descending to the obvious when Rachel Gray saved her the trouble.

'I did so admire your dress yesterday, Kallinkova. Such a striking colour.'

'Thank you, dear Miss Gray, and I yours. White was the colour, was it not?' Natalia held her breath, Rachel was last on her list. Her knowledge of the vagaries of fashion had increased a hundredfold during her investigations.

'Simplicity is best,' Rachel nodded, gratified, 'as Miss Bernhardt and Mrs Siddons found. Also my namesake, the Divine Rachel, was seen to best advantage in white. Purity of expression,' she added.

'And how bold and imaginative to wear to a cricket match,' Natalia enthused. There was a pause as Rachel wondered whether by any chance she had detected a slight note of sarcasm, but decided not, as Natalia's face was so obviously exuding warmth and friendship.

'Tell me,' said Natalia, continuing confidentially woman to woman. 'Do you think Lord Westbourne's death is really connected with our eggs? That the robber is so unscrupulous that he would *murder* for them? And how, this is what terrifies me, how did this evil man know about our eggs?'

Rachel leaned forward eagerly. 'That's what puzzles me also. It is quite terrible. If Cyril ever found out about the Grand Duke . . . Of course, Igor merely gave it to me as a tribute to my genius,' she added hastily.

'Of course,' murmured Natalia sympathetically.

'But Cyril might misunderstand.' Rachel paused. 'I have my *admirers*, but Cyril knows they mean nothing to me. I would not like to think Cyril might come to know of Igor. He is so very quiet I never know what he is thinking . . .'

'A treasure,' put in Natalia infelicitously, for Rachel looked at her doubtfully.

'He would do anything for me,' she affirmed. 'I have that knack of commanding devotion in people.'

Natalia looked suitably impressed. 'Ah yes, that young Alfred.'

'So sweet,' murmured Rachel, uneasily thinking of his fervent declaration: 'I'd do anything for you Rachel. *Anything.*'

Count Trepolov was bending lovingly over a hive when Rose and Auguste arrived, fingers hovering, trying not to yield to the temptation to open the hive yet again. It had been a mistake the other day, a false alarm, and incalculable harm might be done if it were again too cold. He rapped on the wood, and a pleasant hum inside told him all was well within. Lucky little bees.

Would that he had some such hive to creep to, some such

queen to worship, some such ordered existence to live. Soon he would have to return to St Petersburg to take up his duties yet again. By that time he would perhaps have won the hand of his lady; and by that time the pangs of love for Dora, Lady Westbourne, would surely have died. Meanwhile life was hollow. Even mead could not totally redeem it. His own mead, liquor of the gods, created from his own honey flavoured with the flowers of the Cannes hillsides.

'Sir—' His manservant was ushering out that English policeman and someone else. One of the kitchen servants, he recalled, and apparently now interpreter.

'You are a policeman,' he accused Rose.

'Yes, sir, and investigating the theft of rubies and the death of Lord Westbourne.'

'And why you come to see *me*?'

'Just a formality, sir.' He was getting tired of this phrase. 'As you were in England at the time of the robberies, and present yesterday, we just have to ask for an account of where you were, in case the two things are connected.'

'Me? A *burglar*.' A rare smile crept over Trepolov's lips, but it did not reach his eyes, Auguste noticed. 'This is very funny. You think I am a burglar and I kill Lord Westbourne for *that*?' He went off into a peal of laughter till an angry buzzing from within the hive recalled him to his senses. 'Bees do not like upsets,' he said to Rose reproachfully.

Not only bees, thought Rose warily, edging away from the buzzing. A Londoner, bees were no different from wasps in his view. 'What were you doing in London, sir?'

Trepolov looked startled. 'I was in London because there is no point being here in February.'

'Why's that, sir? The weather?'

'The *bees*.' The man was a fool. 'There is nothing to do in February, but in March and April in Cannes the bee year begins. So of course I must be here.'

'Did you see the dagger lying on its salver during the tea break yesterday?'

129

'I waited for the Grand Duke to come back to discuss tactics. I see it in his hand.'

'But not after that?'

'*Non*,' he said abruptly.

'You went out to the field with the Grand Duke?'

'Yes. No.' He changed his mind belatedly. 'With the Comte de Bonifacio. First I go to the *cabinet de toilette*.' He looked at them defiantly as though they would deny a man the right to such freedom.

'Did you know Lord Westbourne – and Lady Westbourne?'

Count Trepolov stood up. 'I am a man of honour, Inspector.'

His eyes strayed wistfully to the hives. Bees were so much less complicated than human beings. 'I have no interest in Lord Westbourne,' he said fiercely. 'Or Lady Westbourne,' even more fiercely. 'I like only *honey*.'

Alfred Hathaway was lying fidgeting on the chesterfield, toying with an ode and trying to feel ill after his exertions of yesterday. Instead he found to his consternation that the idea of a brisk ride to the Mauvarre pine forest didn't seem at all a bad idea.

His health, however, underwent a severe setback when Inspector Rose arrived. Apart from yesterday, he had last seen the inspector at the Café Royal during the unfortunate days of its dominance by Mr Oscar Wilde and Lord Alfred Douglas. In those days he was a young aspiring poet from a middle-class home and he hadn't had the least idea that there was anything strange about their behaviour. He had thus been forced to hide his ignorance, which ill became a bohemian poet, when the trial burst upon a horrified society. By association he blushed in Rose's presence.

Burglaries? He was a poet, he told the inspector with some dignity, though in fact flattered at the idea. 'Alas, I do not have the health,' he cried, 'to climb drainpipes, Inspector.'

Remembering his performance of yesterday, Rose was not so convinced. 'Where were you after the tea break, sir?'

Alfred smiled in happy recollection. 'I worshipped at the feet of an angel.'

'Pardon?'

'Mrs Tucker, the divine Rachel—' he breathed. 'Who would not worship such a creature? They speak of Mrs Patrick Campbell. She is nothing compared with Rachel Gray – You meaner beauties of the night/Where are you when the sun doth rise?' he intoned somewhat inaccurately.

'And you were with this angel – er – Mrs Tucker from the tea break on?'

'Who could forsake the divine Melpomene?' he inquired. 'She did, I recall, leave me for a few moments.'

'Why would that be?'

'I did not inquire the reason.' He blushed again. 'I assumed it to be a visit to – ah – the ladies' retiring room.'

'But you felt no such desires?' Blow me if I'm not falling into the way of speech, thought Rose.

'Before I joined her,' Alfred announced unhappily, whether because of awareness that this admission brought him within the ranks of possible murderers of Lord Westbourne, or because of some obscure feeling that poets should have no such earthly needs was not clear.

'*Maman*, *Papa*, Inspector Egbert Rose.' Auguste presented his guest with pride.

Madame Didier seemed uncertain whether or not to curtsy, but something in Egbert Rose's face convinced her that shaking hands, albeit diffidently, would suffice.

'My pleasure, ma'am – sir. I hope I don't intrude.' They both rushed to deny that any friend of Auguste's at any time could possibly be said to be an intruder. Their home was his.

'My son has told us of your work in London. That you are a great policeman like *Monsieur le Préfet Lépine*,' offered Monsieur Didier.

Rose smiled to himself at just what the Commissioner would say to one of his humble inspectors being rated alongside the famous Lépine of the Paris police, and settled down to enjoy his visit. Hands folded primly in laps, the Didiers regarded this strange beast from England while Auguste interpreted.

'I'm English myself, *monsieur*,' announced Madame Didier with pride, 'though it is many years since I have been there. I was born in Lewisham.'

'I know it well, ma'am. I was born in Blackheath myself.'

'Fancy that. Almost next door,' said Madame Didier, well pleased. 'Auguste has told you no doubt that I was at the Thatched House Tavern,' she added with pride.

'He did indeed, ma'am. Under the great Richard Dolby.'

'Oh Auguste. How could you? He never listens, that's his trouble, Inspector. I expect you've noticed that, *monsieur*. It was my *mother* who worked in the kitchen there at the time he created his great recipes. I always tried to teach Auguste to cook from Mr Dolby's recipes. Jumbles, Mr Rose.'

'Pardon?'

'Jumbles,' she repeated. 'How Auguste used to love them as a little boy. Auguste, I used to say, you'll have to be a cook when you grow up – no one else could keep up with your appetite!'

'I know what you mean, ma'am,' said Rose gravely, enjoying himself immensely at the sight of Auguste's embarrassed face.

'After the Thatched House I went to a castle,' she confided to Rose. 'And there I met Auguste's *papa*. He had come to work in an English garden for experience in Cannes, you see.'

Papa said something to her and her face grew turned pink.

'And he took back the fairest rose to France,' translated Auguste for Egbert's benefit.

'Auguste tells us,' *Maman* said doubtfully, 'that he is employed as a cook in London.'

'He cooks the odd dish from time to time. Not bad,' said Rose kindly.

'It is true we have trained him,' said Monsieur Didier hesitantly, 'but still he will make the *brandade sans l'ail. Incroyable*!'

'What's he say, Auguste?' asked Rose, as Auguste angrily riposted to this slur.

'No matter,' muttered Auguste.

'You can tell your father, Auguste, that I say you're a top chef and that I didn't know what eating was till I met you.'

Auguste did so, while his parents beamed, though *Papa* was slightly hesitant that he might have mistranslated.

'Of course in London we don't take food so seriously as you do here,' said Rose wistfully, gulping slightly. The Hôtel Paradis's mutton cutlets *à la provençale* – eaten too late at night – were too rich a fare not to have effects.

'But who would doubt the importance of food?' said Monsieur Didier, puzzled. 'Why, even the judge at the trial of Monsieur Zola has decreed that provision may be made for a restaurateur to provide meals for him while in prison.'

There were nods of agreement that this was only right and proper.

'Did I not tell you, Egbert, that here you would find the true food of Provence?'

The *repas*, hastily thrown together at news of Rose's arrival, was not that of the Faisan Doré, not that of the Hôtel Paradis even, it was simply – Provence. Auguste gave a heartfelt thank-you to *le Bon Seigneur* who had decided that this should be one of *Maman*'s French days. The aroma of garlic arising from the dish of mushrooms lovingly placed on the table by *Papa* set Rose back a little – until he tasted the *sanguines* and they beamed in pride at his expression, almost forgetting to eat themselves in their pleasure at his enjoyment of their meal. Stuffed sardines and a *salade de mesclun* dressed with walnut oil followed, in preparation for the *plat* – *la pintade*.

'Ah!' An involuntary sigh of happiness escaped Rose when the bird was placed on the table.

'Your wife does not cook *la pintade*?' Monsieur Didier inquired, surprised.

'No,' said Rose regretfully. 'Mind you, we eat very well,' he said hastily.

Auguste spent many evenings at the Roses' home, and knew very well that Mrs Rose's offerings would be considered a serious mistake on any table in France, and yet – and yet how he enjoyed those companionable meals with the warm fire crackling, his gentle teasing of Mrs Rose, her girlish blushes, the games of whist that followed. How different, how much the same.

Somewhat later, they set out into the dim light to walk back to the Hôtel Paradis. Neither felt like talking after the happy evening, particularly of murder.

Above them loomed the old fort and the church. 'Here,' said Auguste, laughing at the memory, now that he was comfortably full of *Maman*'s food and Châteauneuf du Pape, 'is where I saw the ghost. He walked there – and vanished. *Pouf*, like that.'

Rose looked at the high walls and the steep drop. 'Odd,' he said, 'how the dark plays tricks on you.' He shivered. 'For all your Lérina liqueur inside me, I'll be glad to get back tonight. I'm not surprised you thought you saw a ghost. There's a funny atmosphere around.'

'Here?'

'Yes, and around this case.' Rose paused. 'Went to see a play once with Mrs Rose. *A Midsummer Night's Dream*. There was a bit in it reminds me of your ghost – something about in the night how easy is a bush imagined a bear.'

'But there are no trees to imagine bears or ghosts here. Just the bare road and then nothing, though it is true what you say perhaps about the case. There is so much, is there not? We have politics, we have Fabergé eggs, we have

ghosts and lovers, and Russian Grand Dukes. It is like a play itself, is it not?'

'Just what I was thinking yesterday,' agreed Rose.

'And in your play, Puck puts the juice of a flower in people's eyes to mystify them, confound them . . . just like this case. But who is our Puck?'

The Paris train drew in late on the Saturday evening. Ranged on the platform to greet it, in the manner of the Prince of Wales awaiting his own superior authority the previous week, were Inspector Fouchard and his sergeants. A figure stepped out of the train. Inspector Chesnais of the Sûreté had arrived.

He did not stop for formalities. 'So,' he said jovially, rocking back and forth on his toes, hands clasped behind his extremely plump body, 'your English inspector, he thinks it is burglars. What are burglars, *pouf*? *Alors*, to your office, Fouchard.' Wagging a finger in the air, he marched out of the railway station, followed by Fouchard and his men. How could such a fat man have so much energy in him? thought Fouchard, so late in the evening too. He resembled a *boule* perched on a pair of small feet dancing along the road, thought Fouchard viciously. To the *office*? Tonight? His spirits sank low.

'*Eh bien*, Fouchard, courage,' Chesnais announced genially, aware of the falling temperature in the atmosphere. 'To us the glory. The English do not think of wider implications. They are blinkered at Scotland Yard. I have met this Rose, a fine man, but no *vision*. He does not see beyond his boots. And, *mon ami*, his clothes. Can one be a detective in clothes like that?' He removed his elegant ulster complacently. 'Now, you show me the evidence, I will show you the criminal.'

Three hours later he was still as bright as a button, and Fouchard was dozing quietly in the corner, pretending to read a file.

'So!' roared Chesnais.

Fouchard jumped.

'I have solved this crime, *mon ami*. My investigations, and what I see here, tell me. If your English detective does not see it, then he is a fool.' He paused impressively. 'I *know* – and tomorrow an arrest will be made. Nine o'clock, Fouchard. Nine o'clock, *prompt*.'

Chapter Seven

Auguste shivered. Nine o'clock on a March Sunday morning was no time to be standing on a quayside, even in Cannes. Egbert Rose, with only the contents of a stale croissant inside him, shared his views. A wave of longing for Highbury with the comforting sight of the Sunday roast on the kitchen table, and fatty bacon and overdone eggs before him, overcame him. But when the news reached him by way of a young gendarme sent by Fouchard, there had been no alternative. It might well be that Chesnais had incontrovertible evidence. It might also be that Chesnais needed an hour of glory quickly. With all of Paris still talking of *l'affaire Dreyfus* and the merits and demerits of Monsieur Zola's imprisonment, a blow needed to be struck for French justice – whether it hit the target or not.

They did not have long to wait for the inspector. A police van soon disgorged Chesnais, Fouchard and an eager-looking gendarme, excited at this unexpected promotion from his usual *surveillance sur îlot* at the Flower Market.

'Ah, Inspector Chesnais, may I present my sergeant, Sergeant Didier.'

Fouchard looked somewhat surprised, but for fear of endangering good relations at the Faisan Doré remained silent. After a startled look at Auguste's straw hat, willow-pattern tie and pale blue shirt, Inspector Chesnais obviously put this down to Scotland Yard eccentricity.

'You are French, Sergeant Didier?' he asked, puzzled.

'Half French, *Monsieur l'Inspecteur*,' Auguste replied hastily.

Chesnais had no time to waste on sergeants, however.

'*Bon*,' he said briskly. 'Forward. We go to arrest,' he paused impressively, 'the Comte de Bonifacio.'

'So I gather, Inspector.' Rose eyed with disfavour the choppy white waves outside the harbour. 'It seems very unlikely to me. I take it you've a strong case?'

'But of course.' Chesnais was hurt at any suggestion that his methods were other than painstaking. 'The Count was heard to make inflammatory remarks to his lordship at a meeting of the conference. He burst into the chamber and was heard to utter threats of death.'

'Against Lord Westbourne's life?'

'That's what he meant,' said Chesnais. ' "Death to the British Empire", and shouting at Lord Westbourne. And next day Lord Westbourne asked for extra security on his house because of these threats.' He was triumphant.

'May I suggest that it's more likely to have been La Belle Mimosa than the Comte de Bonifacio? We know she followed him down from Paris, and she was still shouting about killing him only yesterday.'

'*Non*, Inspector Rose, *les poules de luxe* do not kill clients, even those they do not like. It gives them a bad reputation, you realise. No, we have our man. He can give no explanation for what he was doing after the tea break, before he took up the bowling.'

'*Bonjour, messieurs*.' A bicycle hurtled to a stop beside them, its rider waving cheerfully. Bowler-hatted, frilly-bloused and check-bloomered, Kallinkova dismounted gracefully, and smiled at them happily. 'You look surprised, gentlemen. Perhaps also a little shocked. But it is good exercise. Why do you not approve of bicycles?'

'It is not the bicycle, *ma mie*,' murmured Auguste, choked with laughter at Rose's face, but the endearment earned him an odd look from Chesnais.

'Where are you going?' she inquired.

'*Madame.*' Chesnais struggled to overcome his horror of women in men's attire. He wondered if he should arrest her, but having recognising the famous Kallinkova decided this would be unwise. He merely averted his eyes to somewhere left of her bowler hat. 'To arrest the murderer of Lord Westbourne.'

'*Vraiment?* Then I shall come,' she announced, looking from Rose to Auguste, and parking her bicycle in the ticket office of the steamer service.

'*Non,*' chorused the gentlemen.

'No?' Surprise gave way to outraged femininity. 'Ah, it is my bloomers. Do not worry.' She gave them a sunny smile, whipped a rolled-up bundle out of her basket on the back of the bicycle, and disappeared into the ladies' waiting room at the departure quay for the Ile Ste Marguérite. One minute later she reappeared, decorously clad, albeit rather more bulkily than before, in a somewhat crumpled skirt. '*Voilà.*'

Thus checkmated, Chesnais found himself torn between irregularity and a desire that his triumph should be crowned by the presence of one of the world's leading ballerinas. He compromised by stomping off to the police boat, and allowing whoever so willed to follow.

The sight of policemen on the tiny Ile Ste Marguérite was an event and the few residents peered out of their windows as Chesnais and Fouchard led them officiously up the one narrow street of the island. Auguste had always loved this island, a place of secrets and magic where he could wander among the pines and eucalyptus, play at being Légionnaires in the woods with his friends, and swim in the warm waters. How sad that now this small island too was touched by the tentacles of murder instead of the usual warmth with which it had been blessed by the gods.

There was no answer at the small house rented by Bastide. It took no great detective work to work out where he was, however. It was a very tiny island and apart from this one

139

short street of houses only one building existed – the Fort itself on the Pointe Croisette, built by Richelieu, its mellow stone shining gold in the pale sun.

'I think I know, *Monsieur l'Inspecteur*, where he will be,' said Auguste regretfully, and once Fouchard had arranged permission for their entrance he led the way past the old stone buildings over to the far side where the governor's buildings were. Leading out of them were the cells for the important prisoners. Here was the very stuff of Dumas, here the window up at which Auguste had gazed so many times as a boy. The window of the cell of the Man in the Iron Mask.

Here, nobly positioned at the parapet above the steep cliff, staring out over the sea towards the hill of La Californie and the misty blue mountains of the Alpes Maritimes, and the Esterel on the other side, stood Bastide, who turned to face them as they approached.

'So you have come, *messieurs*,' he cried disastrously, 'to take me as you took my illustrious ancestor Napoleon, to take me as you dragged off his noble forebear *Masque de Fer*, to incarcerate me as you did him in the Bastille—'

'Very well, *monsieur*. It shall be as you wish,' said Chesnais briskly. He had no time to spare for dramatics.

Rose groaned at the headstrong impulsiveness of youth. 'You seem to be expecting us, sir.'

'I admit nothing save the glory of France,' cried Bastide dramatically. '*J'accuse*—' An arm was flung theatrically as he sought an object for his verb. '*J'accuse Sa Majesté, l'impératice*— Of course I expect to be arrested; it is the way of all great men. They wish to do away with me.'

Yet even as Chesnais, now transported with delight at the straightforwardness Bastide was giving his task, formally arrested him, Bastide became silent as though reality had now raised an unfortunate question-mark.

The handcuffs put on by the constable with hands trembling with excitement, an indignity not suffered by

140

Napoleon, seemed to set the seal on the onset of depression, and he sat silent in the boat as it returned to the mainland.

Natalia squeezed his fingers sympathetically as well as she could for the handcuffs. 'Why are you arresting this poor boy?' she asked indignantly. 'You think he is your burglar?'

'*Non, madame*, this has grave political considerations. Very complicated.' This to imply that a mere woman could not grasp their intricacies. 'It was an assassination intended to change the course of history.'

'No,' bleated Bastide, finding some kind of voice. 'I deny it.'

'If this is a mistake,' Auguste told him gravely, 'we will discover it.'

'Sergeant,' thundered Chesnais, earning a surprised then amused look from Natalia, 'the case so far as the Sûreté is concerned is closed. It is not for sergeants to have opinions.'

'*Entendu*,' muttered Auguste, sympathising at long last with the problems Rose had to endure at Scotland Yard.

At the sight of the police van at the quayside, Bastide roused himself to one last stand. 'Take me, I beg you,' he quavered, as he stepped on to the Quay St Pierre, 'along La Route Napoleon that I may be inspired by the spirit of my great ancestor. He too knew adversity.'

'Yes indeed,' Auguste agreed. A man who never knew the pleasures of *la cuisine*, who drank coffee in preference to wine, who ate simply to live and thus never knew what life was about; Auguste guiltily dragged his thoughts back to the unhappy boy being pushed into the van. Was he a murderer?

'If he is,' remarked Rose, as the van was driven along the narrow roadway to the Allées de la Liberté, 'I'll eat your straw hat, Auguste.'

There was one other horrified observer of the scene. Emmeline Vanderville, walking back from Holy Trinity English church to the Hôtel du Parc, was brought up short by the spectacle of her beloved Bastide bowling along in what

141

undoubtedly looked like police custody. The constitution of American eighteen-year-olds is good, especially heiresses', but this was a severe jolt. Emmeline turned pale, then turned round and began to run helplessly after the police van, picking up her trained skirt. She tripped over the cross-lacing of her kid boots, which were not accustomed to this strenuous exercise, and came crashing down, and Natalia rushed to pick her up.

Emmeline was unhurt, impatiently disregarding grazed hands, and demanded to know the meaning of what she had seen, clearly seeing Natalia as one of the devil's battalion. Natalia put her arm through hers, and they walked along the quayside as she explained. Emmeline grew pale, both from horror at Bastide's plight and her own. What would her parents say?

'Basty couldn't do it,' she said firmly, once common sense had reasserted itself. 'Why, he couldn't even shoot pigeons at the Cap Croisette when we went. The idea's ridiculous. All that stuff about France and glory – he doesn't mean it. He's a lamb really,' she said fondly.

Natalia doubted the lamb but agreed that Bastide, the wicked murderer, did seem unlikely.

'He did make a lot of threats,' Kallinkova explained gently. 'The police seem very sure—'

Emmeline's mouth grew round. 'You believe it too,' she accused.

'No, but I keep an open mind. Someone undoubtedly killed Lord Westbourne, and your Bastide was undoubtedly threatening him.'

'So was that awful woman and no one's arrested her,' pointed out Emmeline passionately. 'Can't *you* do anything?' she asked ingenuously. 'You're famous, aren't you?'

'I'll try,' said Natalia stoutly, but her pessimism (now she had met Chesnais) came through.

'You don't believe him either,' cried Emmeline

142

vehemently, glancing round for help from the heavens. The heavens did not oblige, but the beach did.

Alfred Hathaway was determined to recover his accustomed ill-health. At the beginning of March the bathing establishments had reopened for the season, but custom was slim since the wind was undoubtedly not warm, rain was all too frequent, and the sea icy cold. It was just what Alfred needed. The shock of the cold water had made him gasp for several minutes, but by the time he came out he was positively glowing with enjoyment. He was splashing happily at the edge of the water on his way back to change from his red-striped bathing costume when he beheld a beautiful sight. An elegantly dressed young lady whom he vaguely recognised was flying purposefully down the beach towards him in a purple hat, its ribbons streaming. Mindful of his undress and only thankful that it was not complete as at Brighton where he heard gentlemen bathed with nothing on at all, he stood there transfixed with shock. He was naturally very wet and much of the wet communicated itself immediately to Emmeline, as she flung herself passionately into his arms.

'Mr Hathaway,' she cried, 'you'll help me, won't you?'

The smell of her otto of roses mingling with the sea salt rushed to Alfred's head, which promptly dispatched a telegram around his body. Alfred found himself only too willing to help her in anything.

'So this is where you learned to cook,' said Rose, looking round the small, elegant restaurant in the Rue d'Antibes. 'Bit different to the Ratcliffe Highway.'

'*Pardon?*'

'Where I learned, so to speak. On the beat.'

'From *Maman* I learn to cook. Here I was trained. Monsieur Escoffier came here, only a year before I myself. It was not so great a restaurant then, perhaps more like your Ratcliffe Highway. But how he transformed it! From a poor café it has become a restaurant of high renown. Indeed, he almost created restaurants in Cannes, one could say. Before that, one ate with ladies in hotels only, but now—' Auguste waved a hand towards the illustrious inhabitants of Cannes partaking of Sunday luncheon *en famille* with great gusto.

'*Eh bien*, my friend, now what do you do? An arrest has been made, but no burglar has been caught.'

'I don't like it. I can't feel that young hot-head stuck a dagger in Lord Westbourne, can you? I'd like to carry on, but it's nearly another two weeks to the Duke's ball—' He broke off, aware that he'd lost Auguste's attention. He was absorbed in the menu, switching attention only to the waiter with whom he had whispered consultations of great seriousness, much in the manner of Sir Frederick Treves conferring with colleagues over a royal illness. Aware at last of Rose's gaze, he said grandiloquently: 'Do not concern yourself, dear friend, I will choose for you. I wish this to be an experience, far removed from the Hôtel Paradis. You will see how French cuisine can transport you to Olympus.'

'I've been there already, thanks to you, Auguste.'

'Naturally, but now you will taste Provençal cooking in its own home as every cuisine is best enjoyed. Today, truffles – the kitchen's diamond, as Brillat-Savarin so truly says. The truffles of Provence never taste so exquisite in London as here; they lose their savour, and gain in price. So,' his eyes sparkled, 'we will have the *faisan truffé*, the *specialité de la maison*, with a *sauce Périgueux*, or, as I prefer to say, *sauce aux truffes Provence*, as I would not choose truffles of Périgord here; they are black as are our own and all very well, but to my mind our own possess the more exquisite flavour. Of course—'

'Monsieur Didier,' The waiter deferentially called him back to the matter in hand.

'*Alors* – to begin, *huitres marinés* – that is, oysters marinated with a little *sauce ravigote*—'

'I rather fancy these *coquilles à la provençale*,' said Rose, making a bid for independence. Mrs Rose was doubtful about scallops.

'As you wish, *cher* Egbert,' said Auguste, looking anxious. 'I cannot help but feel, however—'

'Never have them at Highbury,' Rose said firmly.

Auguste yielded, against his better judgement. Another ten minutes ensued while the agonising choice of wines was made, and the wine waiter departed. Even then Auguste was clearly pondering whether the right choice had been made.

'I think it's a mistake.' Rose was determined to get back to the case before food arrived to distract Auguste yet again.

'You think I should have chosen the Châteauneuf?' asked Auguste anxiously.

'The Comte de Bonifacio, Auguste,' Rose reminded Auguste patiently. 'My guess is that as soon as my telegram reaches the Yard with news of his arrest, they'll be sending another one ordering me back, burglar or no burglar. I might get back again for the ball, but in the meantime it's up to you.'

Auguste heaved a sigh. 'But I am on holiday, Egbert.'

'Good, so you've plenty of time,' Rose said hard-heartedly.

'I have been advised to avoid detection, for my health.' A slight Gallic exaggeration.

'The day you do that will be the day you hang up your saucepans for good.' Rose paused over a mouthful of rich *sauce provençale*. Delicious, but . . . 'Chesnais has no proof against the Comte. He'll have to release him, and then the case will be wide open again.'

'He does not need proof, my friend. Bastide must *prove* his innocence, and he only says he accompanied Trepolov on the field. Yet he and Trepolov were the last to appear. He gave the excuse that before they went out he was seeking

145

the ball in the changing room, but no one saw him there.'

'Nor have *we* any evidence against anyone else. Far as I can see anyone could have done it. I'll show you the notes Fouchard slipped to me. I don't think he's too happy about Bastide's guilt, but he's not going to get involved.' He stopped as the silver covers were whipped triumphantly off the *faisan truffé* and eyed them with misgivings.

'Truffles and pork stuffing you say?'

'Indeed, *mon ami. La truffe*, the food so dear to the Romans, was forgotten by mankind until early this century. Some, like Kettner, say it was no great loss. But he is no true gourmet, that man,' Auguste added heatedly. 'Or else he has never tasted truffles in France. Taste now,' he waved a lordly hand, as though he had personally snuffled the tubers out from under the ground. 'Can you wonder a pig that can hunt these down is so highly prized? When they arouse thoughts of love in women and men alike, and their aroma transports them, like love itself, to paradise?'

'You don't seem to need help of that sort, Auguste.'

Auguste went faintly pink, and laughed.

'I still think,' said Rose, 'that this burglar business is linked in somehow. And *someone* must know something about it. Get in amongst them. As Miss Kallinkova's – ah – friend, they'll accept you here. Someone must know *something*.'

'I will do what I can.' The idea of escorting Natalia was an appealing way of working at detection. 'At the funeral they will all be gathered together. And now, my friend, some' – enthusiasm restored his voice as he whispered to the waiter – '*Charlotte Hélène*. Ah, no one can resist this, it is made with crystallised violets. Monsieur Nègre himself, who has originated the idea of sweetmeats of crystallised flowers – you have seen his shop in this very street – has supplied the violets.'

Some hour or so later, Rose, released from his pleasurable torment, almost staggered as they walked out into the sunshine. In the Allées de la Liberté, a band was playing and he sank down in front of the bandstand gratefully.

'It was that liqueur did for me,' Rose said forcefully. 'What the devil is in it?'

'That is known only to God, not the devil,' replied Auguste. 'The *liqueur de Lérina* is made by the Cistercian monks at the monastery of St Honorat, one of the Iles de Lérins. But it is good for you – made from local flowers and herbs.'

The band was playing loudly, and he had to shout to make himself heard.

'Maybe,' said Rose. 'But if they drink it themselves it must be a merry old monastery. Let us look at these notes Fouchard has produced.' It was an effort.

Auguste studied the lists for some while. 'Lady Westbourne claims she went to the ladies' retiring room after tea, so does Mrs Tucker, but they do not admit to seeing each other. Miss Kallinkova went straight on to the balcony, verified by several people. La Belle Mimosa has no alibi since no one would sit with her, and no one claims to have seen her. Miss Vanderville says she was in the salon with Bastide, but Bastide says he was getting the ball from the locker room where no one says he saw him. Not good, *mon ami*. Cyril Tucker went out on to the balcony, Trepolov claims, and Washington confirms it, that he was in the gentlemen's cloakroom, and then went on to the field with Bastide. Alfred Hathaway says he escorted Mrs Tucker out to the balcony, after her return from the retiring room but this contradicts what Mrs Tucker told us. There it is. Some of them are obviously lying. But who?' Auguste finished. True, he did not expect to receive a definite answer, but when there was no comment at all he glanced at his colleague. Despite the climax of the 1812 Overture being rendered with verve, Inspector Rose was fast asleep.

Auguste smiled. It was a fitting tribute to Monsieur Escoffier's former restaurant.

'Pah,' said a voice. Painfully sitting down on his other side was the old Cannois.

'*Bonjour, monsieur*,' said Auguste cheerily.

His good cheer was not returned.

'A French bandstand under the eye of that *salaud*—' The old man spat in the general direction of Lord Brougham's statue, gazing down beneficently on the town he had created. 'Have you found him yet?' he inquired abruptly of Auguste.

'They have arrested him, *mon ami*.'

The Cannois thought this over. 'This is not possible,' he pronounced.

'You have evidence to prove he is innocent?' Auguste asked eagerly, recollecting his presence at the ground.

'*Non.* But how will they keep him?' the Cannois asked in interest.

'They have charged him with murder.'

'Ah. He is in the Bastille again?'

'*Again.*' Auguste was jolted. Then, 'The Bastille, *monsieur*?' he queried doubtfully. 'Who?'

'*Masque de Fer, mon fils.* How today's youngsters are obtuse! It is very clever to arrest a ghost, *n'est ce pas*?'

Now this was more like a holiday. True, he had promised Egbert, who as Auguste predicted had been summoned back to Scotland Yard a week ago with a 'now it's up to you, Auguste', to continue the investigation; and the sight of Emmeline in the carriage in front pricked at his conscience. But he had done his best with little to show for it. The funeral had come and gone, and all his painstaking and subtle questions had led nowhere either as regards Lord Westbourne's death or the burglaries.

The funeral might have gone, but Lady Westbourne had not. Clearly determined not to waste a villa paid for in advance, she had remained and had reached the stage when she had decided it would be permissible to take an

148

outing with a suitable escort – such as Harry Washington. Today's carriage visit to Grasse provided a most suitable opportunity.

Auguste was rejoicing too, seated next to Natalia, with Emmeline opposite them as the carriage wound its way along the Grasse road. He recalled all these villages from his youth, trundling up through Mougins in an old farm cart at harvest time, tasting the grapes on the hillsides. Grasse had seemed a long way away in those days, a place of magic and wonderful smells, from the flowers grown all around for the perfume factories. The smells lingered faintly to enchant the air even at this time of year, but the mystery of childhood had vanished. Still, there was much to enjoy, particularly at Natalia's side.

He was particularly amused to see that Emmeline's neck in its high-necked frilly blouse was almost permanently turned towards the carriage in front, where Alfred Hathaway's, riding in the Tuckers' carriage, was almost permanently turned towards their own. A pleasant game of lawn tennis at the Hôtel du Parc last Monday afternoon, hastily suggested by Alfred as a palliative to the shock of her beloved's arrest, had proved such an unexpectedly exhilarating experience, especially after his bathing exercise, that it had been followed by several more meetings. Alfred was a little disconcerted to find that Emmeline was such an *active* young lady and was reluctant to lie on sofas so that he could hold her hand and commiserate. However, once he had accepted this aberration on her part, he found himself positively enjoying the croquet, walks and visits in which this energetic young lady sought solace, and rejoicing that his health permitted him to take this excursion to Grasse, he had accepted a ride in the Tuckers' carriage with unwonted enthusiasm, which Rachel had taken to be a tribute to herself.

A sensitive young man, however, Alfred had not lost sight of the fact that dear Emmeline – matters had progressed quickly by English standards – was in need of his assistance only in order to free her beloved Bastide.

As trains and coaches and carriage excursions organised by Thomas Cook were deemed to be for the *hoi polloi*, the party had decided to take their own carriages, which could usefully be left at the Hôtel Muraour et de la Poste to await their return. Doubts however were aroused when it was discovered that the coachmen awaiting their return would have recourse to the proprietress's excellent wine, home-made from her own vineyard.

Ah, this was the true France, decided Auguste, as they sipped a glass of wine in Madame's garden. Soon it would be summer and the English would be gone, fearing the effects of the vicious sun. Did they ever wonder how the French endured this torment? he pondered, laughing at yet another oddity of the British. Or was it fashion, not nationality, that demanded this need to empty the Riviera during the summer months?

Emmeline was chattering to Alfred who had somehow managed to join them, since Rachel had unwisely attached herself to Lady Westbourne, and was now sorely regretting this good nature.

Auguste leaned forward. '*Mademoiselle*, forgive me, but if we are to secure the release of the Comte de Bonifacio, I must ask you this. You say that after tea on the day of the murder you were with the Count in the salon and then went to the balcony.'

Emmeline went pink. 'Yes,' she muttered, with a sidelong look at Alfred. The latter began to make half-hearted movements to go, but recalling his new role as protector, grasped the excuse to stay.

'That's not what he says,' Auguste pointed out.

'Oh. Then he's protecting me, you see,' said Emmeline, in a rush. 'My reputation.'

'You mean you—'

'Oh *no*. I didn't stab Lord Westbourne, but Bastide and I

were – well, we were alone – just for a few minutes,' she added hastily. 'In the Pavilion office. You don't mind, do you?' For some reason she felt the need to ask Alfred.

'Ah,' said Auguste. 'But of course.'

The thought that such an angel might be willing to share her beauty somewhat more positively than Rachel filled Alfred with a happiness it was hard to justify considering she was in love with someone else. For a moment he battled with the ignoble thought that he'd rather like Bastide to remain in custody, but decided this was dishonourable.

'And did anybody see you, *mademoiselle*?' Auguste asked hopefully.

'No,' said Emmeline, downcast. 'That was the idea,' she pointed out. Then she brightened. 'There was that old man, of course.'

'An old man,' Auguste repeated resignedly. At Emmeline's age who knows what she might define as an old man. Even – no, such a thought was not to be considered.

'Yes,' she continued, 'he was peering through the windows, spitting at us.'

'Spitting?' cried Auguste, trying to imagine the Gentlemen or the Players peering through windows and spitting.

'I don't think he was English. Or Russian. He was rather – well—'

Could it be – an idea was presenting itself to Auguste, just as Rachel descended on them.

'Dearest Alfred,' she announced somewhat forcefully, 'shall we depart for the *parfumerie*?'

Auguste soon wearied of hearing how it took 45 pounds of rose leaves to make 1 gramme of Otto of Roses and 2¾ pounds troy of orange petals for 1 gramme of Néroly, but regained a certain interest to hear that Néroly Bigarrade was made from the flowers of the bitter-orange tree. He contemplated a *sauce bigarrade* used not for duck but for game. How would it taste? he wondered. For himself, the *bigarrade* was too heavy for duck. He watched violets and jasmine laid between sheet after sheet of glass for extracts for pocket handkerchiefs in the factory of Messrs Jean Giraud, heard how they were used in pomade. But how foolish. There were better uses. It was so wasteful when one could *eat* these delights. They could be crystallised in sugar, as in the *Charlotte Hélène*. And other flowers, flowers for colour, flowers for taste – how important was the eye in achieving the subtlest effects. One day perhaps he would run his own school in London – not like Mrs Marshall to teach everyday cooking, but *la vrai cuisine* so that the old arts should not die out . . . The history of cooking too. So much was known in mediaeval times that had been lost in today's practical fast-moving world. He was snapped out of his reverie by Rachel Gray, cooing mellifluously at his side. 'Dear Alfred, you may buy me some perfume. Roses, I think.'

Alfred obediently did so, but as it also struck him as a good idea to buy some for Emmeline, the gift lost its effect and Rachel turned very pale.

After the exertions of the parfumerie, Natalia managed to get permission from the owner, Monsieur Malvillan, to tour the home of Fragonard to view his paintings. All her charm was needed. Auguste was admiring the famous series of paintings intended for Madame du Barry. The Four Ages of Love. Ah, how easy love seemed then. What games. What innocent pleasure. Emmeline looked wistful and Alfred moved a little closer, merely to comfort. His action did not go unnoticed by Rachel Gray. It was the last straw.

'Alfred, do come here and admire this with me.'

'One moment, Mrs Tucker,' he said absentmindedly. 'We will come.'

We? 'You said you would do anything for me,' Rachel cried, hand to heart. 'Is it so much to ask?' Her voice rose, attracting attention.

Emmeline looked at Alfred in surprise. Why did he want to do anything at all for this woman old enough to be his mother? She looked too old to play tennis.

'And so I would,' Alfred said nervously, keeping his voice low, aware of all ears upon them, however studied the turned backs.

'Rachel, dearest,' intervened Cyril, seeing danger signs on Rachel's face, 'I feel—'

'And you, at the cricket match, Alfred. So brave, so foolishly impulsive, just to save my honour.'

'What?' Alfred was confused, staring at this virago as if hypnotised.

'I see you now, dagger in hand—' she cried, arm outflung as in her lauded rendering of Lady Macbeth.

'Oh, I say,' squeaked Alfred. Cyril's 'Rachel', Emmeline's 'Oh', Natalia's 'Stuff and nonsense', and Lady Westbourne's timely faint all combined to make this a most interesting tour for the owner. It was not often that his philanthropy in opening the house was so rewarded. Nor was it over. Natalia's clear voice rang out. 'Perhaps it was fearing yet being impelled to see what he had done that sent you into the study after him?'

'Me?' Rachel's face took on the air of one caught without her lines. 'You lie!'

'You were the only woman in white, *madame*,' pointed out Auguste. 'The footman saw a woman in white enter the study just after tea.'

The party had gathered round in a group, far too interested to pay attention to Lady Westbourne, who scrambled to her feet alone and very cross. Why hadn't Harry come? It was his job to comfort her.

Cyril could not help Rachel now. She opened her mouth and shut it. Then opened it again. 'It was an error.' She rolled her r's in a manner that the divine Sarah would envy.

'An error for what?' inquired Auguste politely.

There was a short pause.

'I was under the impression,' replied Rachel Gray with what dignity she could muster, 'that it was the lavatory.'

The Casino des Fleurs was not a thriving concern. It had little competition in Cannes, for there were many who could not afford the prices of the Cercle Nautique, but somehow despite the attractions of its *petits chevaux*, lawn tennis, reading room, theatre and restaurant, it had not captured the hearts of the Cannois, nor, more importantly, of the *hiverneurs*. This evening, however, its fortunes looked fair to change. Although its reading room did not carry the same cachet as that of Mr John Taylor, tonight its theatre, despite the fact that on Tuesdays the band played at the Cercle Nautique, was about to transform its hitherto unremarkable achievements. Even the Prince of Wales had abandoned the Cercle Nautique in order to see Natalia Kallinkova dance in *The Sleeping Beauty*.

Lord Westbourne was now interred in the new cemetery by the side of Lord Brougham, but his murderer was as yet undiscovered. Soon Rose would return for the ball and Auguste had nothing further for him except that Rachel Gray had possibly entered the study with evil intent. But for what reason? It seemed hardly likely she would go to such lengths to prevent her husband from discovering about the Grand Duke Igor. Perhaps there might be some other reason? After all, her husband was in the Colonial Office and Westbourne an emissary of the Queen. He must mention this to Egbert.

Moreover Bastide still remained in custody. This irked Auguste. He now had a witness whose evidence could free Bastide – if only he could find him again. But for once the old Cannois – for it must have been he – had disappeared as surely as the ghost of *Masque de Fer*. Agog with his information, but without the old Cannois in person, Auguste had rushed to Fouchard.

Chesnais refused to release the Comte, so Fouchard told him. It was natural in his view that sweethearts should wish to protect their lovers, even at the expense of their own reputations. Chesnais stood firm. He had his man, and Bastide continued to languish in jail. Auguste had spent much time since Rose had departed conscientiously sifting evidence; since he had been banished from Natalia's bed for a while so that she might prepare for performances in Monte Carlo and tonight's in Cannes, it had been no great hardship.

But since Emmeline had told him of the old Cannois, he had vanished as surely as the Ghost of the Iron Mask.

Auguste sat in the small balcony with his mother and father, for once not noticing the unaccustomedness of their best clothes, so excited were they. Did Auguste go to the ballet every evening in London? they inquired.

Auguste had seen Natalia dance in London several times, but here it seemed different. They were closer now; he felt every movement she made on stage, every emotion she shared with the audience. The complete mistress of technique, she abandoned herself to the sensuousness of the music, sweeping him into a land of heady romance and delight. Even her audience, fashionable though it was, with the Prince of Wales present, paid close attention. From the balcony Auguste looked down upon row after row of deeply cut décolletée evening dresses, jewels, fans and opera hats. Had this anything to do with Kallinkova's art? She would dance as happily and as well to an audience of two chimney sweeps as to this splendid gathering. Natalia . . . the supreme artiste. Did he love her? Could you love a will o' the wisp? An enchantment, a dream . . . It was a precious butterfly, something to cherish, to adore and then to see fly free with the summer air.

Later, as he lay restlessly at her side as she slept, his mind still whirled with the music, the light, entrancing figure on stage and the enchantment of the evening. Cannes itself had enchantment, nothing was quite real. He did not belong to this world of princes, nor did his parents. Yet such was the spell of the place, you could dwell in a world of enchantment like *The Sleeping Beauty*. He turned to look at Natalia, her peaceful face, her classical beauty, her dark hair spread out around her; thought of the gaiety that danced around him, enmeshing him in its toils, thought of her warmth in his arms, and began to drift into sleep. This case too was an enchantment – no, he would not think of murder. Perhaps he would awake and find it solved. Yet characters in his drama paraded relentlessly in front of him, the courtiers in Aurora's palace springing back to life around him, Florizel kissing Aurora awake and finally—

He sat up abruptly. It was crystal clear. 'I have been asleep,' he cried out loud.

'*Bon*,' murmured his Aurora sleepily. 'I too try.'

'Why did we not see the truth? Not who, but why?'

Chapter Eight

A glowing red sun was thrusting up over the horizon of the sea as Auguste walked home along the Quai St Pierre through the early pink light. He had chosen a long route home, in order to have time to think. Normally it was hard enough to leave a sleeping Natalia, to force himself into a chilly dawn, but today he did not mind so much. There was much to think about, and walking along the quayside where the fishing boats were landing their catches, gazing at that pink-grey morning light over the Croisette peninsula, seeing the red glow of the rising sun light up the sky, feeling the sharp chill of the air – this was the Cannes he loved. The Cannes that belonged to its people, not the *hiverneurs*. In another three or four hours this world would be swept aside, still there to be found in the flower market, in the shops, but serving as a background to the fashionable *hiverneurs*. In the morning it came into its own once more.

Here it was possible to see things clearly, to try to recall the flash of inspiration that had come to him so vividly last night, only to vanish with his dreams. He had been so convinced that Inspector Chesnais was wrong, that Lord Westbourne had not been murdered for political reasons. That seemed too much like – like – he sought to express the thought completely and fully – a recipe by Soyer. The ingredients were right, the method was right, the inspiration was right. And yet the final dish failed somehow to satisfy, to glue together like isinglass in a jelly. So, what must he do? He must dissect the jelly once more; melt it down, lay out the ingredients and study them, go back to that basic concept that had come to him in the night. But what was it? It had seemed so clear, yet when he slept again, Morpheus had snatched it from him. Seek it as he would, it had vanished.

Sometimes in a recipe this indicated that the idea was of no value, that the night-time inspiration to make a sauce for *gibier* from fruit was wiped from memory for very good reason. Daylight would show that were the two to be united in a *plat* catastrophe would follow. Somehow he did not think that would be the case now, but strive as he would, it would not return.

Instead, sitting down by the sea wall, he turned his thoughts to Natalia, yesterday's night of magic enchantment and the unexpected bounty that this holiday had bestowed on him – until it evened the score by sending murder also. Yet enchantment it was, he knew, by the cold light of dawn. A kiss of heaven to bless him for a few weeks, a few months, who knew? Soon she would vanish, as she had done before, as she warned him would happen again. In their story it was not Cupid but Psyche who would vanish with the light of day. How much would he mind? As much as when dear Maisie married? As much as when—

He sighed. Was he doomed for love always to treat him so? For the woman he loved always to be a dream, beyond his reach? Did he always seek out Tatianas? She was in Paris, further away than he was to her in London, but it seemed closer.

Firmly, he put such thoughts behind him. This battle he had already won in his mind. He had much to be thankful for, he had a future, and for the moment at least there was Natalia. The New Woman. He began to laugh as he thought of the checked bloomers, of Egbert's face, and irreverent thoughts of dear Edith, Egbert's wife, clad in the same unbecoming garments, passed through his mind. But the twentieth century beckoned. Who knew what lay on its horizon?

When he crept into his home quietly in order not to disturb his sleeping parents, he found his father already up, cleaning the kitchen stove, and preparing the vegetables for the day. He shot his son a reproachful look.

'You had better change those clothes, my son. It might occasion comment.'

Auguste reddened, having forgotten that he was still clad in evening dress and opera hat. How glad he was *Maman* was still asleep. He quickly ran to change his clothes for more informal wear.

Even these did not pass muster, for when he returned his mother was bustling around preparing chocolate in the *chocolatière*. She eyed his Joinville scarf and ring critically. 'It's high time you got married, my son. Why do you not?'

How could he explain?

'Because there is no one like you, *Maman*.' He planted a kiss on her cheek and she bridled.

'You dally with ladies' affections,' she accused him. 'I see it now. You are a Gilles de Rais.'

'*Maman*,' he protested, '*ce n'est pas vrai*.' If only she knew he was a victim, not a sadist.

'I want some grandchildren,' she announced. 'If only to teach them the secret of my *brandade*. It is obvious that you will never learn it correctly. But for all that, you are not bad. I am told that you did quite well at the buffet.'

'*Merci*, *Maman*,' he said meekly.

'What she wishes to ask you, my son,' his father interpreted this high praise, 'is whether you will assist Monsieur Boris in the preparations for the ball on Saturday?'

'What?' Auguste yelped, the chocolate leaping out of his bowl in his agitation. 'Ah, *non*, Saturday, and today is Wednesday. What can I do? It is impossible.'

'There. I said he could not do it,' said his mother triumphantly.

'*Naturellement*,' Auguste said quickly. 'I *could* do it. I am a *maître*.' He looked at their doubtful faces and began to doubt it himself. 'But it is my holiday,' he explained pathetically, 'and Monsieur Boris—'

He left the sentence unfinished. He did not need to complete it. They nodded sympathetically. 'Monsieur Boris is a good cook, but he has his failings,' agreed his mother. 'And just at the moment he has many failings.'

Auguste groaned. Even so, a little part of his mind was gripped by a familiar excitement. A grand ball, and what a problem for a *maître* chef. In Lent the food must be just so; not too ostentatious but good enough to celebrate a Grand Duke's birthday without making his guests wonder if they were breaking the Lenten abstentions too greatly. Light dishes would be the answer? Perhaps eggs? No. He could not trust a strange kitchen and staff with soufflés. Perhaps he would just go along to give some advice, and not stay to help. Yes, that could be achieved without difficulty. Besides, he reasoned, he might even get closer to solving the crime this way. And, if he were present at the ball, as Egbert would be, perhaps he might see something that would help. Even prevent robberies. Fish, of course. An all-fish menu. And what better place than Cannes to serve it with the sweet fruits of the Mediterranean so plentifully at hand. He would go to speak to the fishermen on his way to the Villa Russe . . . He might even see the old Cannois.

Fate, which had thrown him in Auguste's path so often before, seemed resolute in its refusal to lend a hand. He was to be found neither on the Croisette nor by the port, in none of the cafés. Auguste had hung around the flower and food markets, but there was no sign of him. He had vanished as completely as the ghost of *Masque de Fer*.

This was a kitchen in despair. Auguste stood in the doorway of the kitchen entrance at the Villa Russe, aghast. You could smell despair in the air. This was not a humming, thriving unit marching forward with a purpose, as a kitchen should be, but a shell in which sporadic bursts of activity

160

might or might not take place to produce what might or might not be edible meals. The kitchenmaids had lifeless eyes; they drifted, they did not dance in foot or mind. The assistant cooks toyed with salamanders and spits without interest. Even the roasting food on the spit seemed to be floating aimlessly as though it had no will to turn itself into succulent delicacies for the palate.

In the centre, seated at a table, a long list on a board in front of him, was Boris; but compared with the Boris Auguste had first met, this was a shrunken, defeated man. He looked up listlessly as Auguste entered, greeting him merely with a perfunctory hug, overwhelmed with the enormity of the occasion.

'You come to help, yes?' There was no doubt in his voice.

In the midst of this desolation, Auguste was clearly descending as *katushki* from above.

'What,' Auguste inquired grimly, 'is your menu for the ball supper? Let me see it.' The man must have catered for hundreds of balls before, surely? What was he worrying about?

Boris looked at him blankly.

'*Zakuski*,' he offered.

'What?' Auguste howled. '*No* meatballs, *no*, *no* meatballs.'

'No, no. *Zakuski, pas de katushki. Hors d'oeuvres*, Boris added. 'With vodka,' he explained.

Auguste cast his eyes to the heaven from which in Boris's view he had descended, and set grimly to work. He examined larders, order books, pantries, still-room, refrigerators, and then toured them again. Then he sat down with a reluctant Boris, edging the bottle away inch by inch in the hope that the Russian would not observe his movements.

'*Eh bien*, fish,' he said. 'We need fish. For three hundred and fifty people. We have twenty-four turbots with *sauce homard*, twenty-four salmon, forty plates of lobster salad, thirty-six salads of fillet of soles and salmon—'

'*Kamchatka* – crabs,' interrupted Boris, suddenly inspired.

'Crabs, certainly,' agreed Auguste cautiously, 'but how—'

'With wine, cook with wine,' explained Boris eagerly.

'Very well. Crabs.'

'And trout with *kasha*.'

'What is *kasha*?' asked Auguste suspiciously.

'It is *kasha*.' Boris waved his hands, and a kitchenmaid brought some for inspection.

'*Non*,' said Auguste firmly in disgust, looking at the buckwheat and imagining trout stuffed with this abomination. '*Non*.'

'Is my kitchen,' Boris pointed out.

'Is my holiday,' stated Auguste, rising to his feet. Principles were principles.

A large greasy hand clasped his prized Norfolk jacket. 'You stay. No *kasha*.'

Mollified, Auguste sat down again.

'*Ecrivisses à la provençale, coquilles de St Pierre au gratin*. So much undervalued this fish and yet St Peter himself has blessed it with his thumb-mark. Though some say the mark is that of St Christopher who picked it up to amuse *le bébé Jésus* as he carried Him across the sea. In England we call it the John Dory. And you know why? Because St Peter is the gate-keeper of heaven, the *janitore* in Italian. *Voilà*, John Dory. Language is interesting, my friend,' as he wrote dishes down busily on the list of calculated quantities. 'There was an English actor who travelled great distances to eat this fish and always with one sauce. The marriage of Miss Ann Chovy to Mr John Dory was made in heaven, he said. This is English humour. I myself feel anchovy—' He broke off.

Boris was asleep. He shook him none too gently with no result but a low rumble.

'And the *pièces montées*,' went on Auguste with his list through gritted teeth, 'six *grosse meringues à la chantilly*,

162

nougat, pies, and groups of truffles in between.'

'It's time for him to see the Grand Duchess, Auguste,' Madame Didier interrupted anxiously. Mother and son regarded the recumbent Boris.

'I shall have to go,' said Auguste finally. It might not be a bad thing, he was thinking. It would be sensible to be acquainted with the Villa Russe; such knowledge could come in useful on the night of the ball. Servants could go where guests might not.

The Grand Duke and his Duchess were in the ballroom, superintending the installation of the decorations. The ball would overspill in the orangery beyond, and a candlelit path led to the belvedere, for any wishing to admire the stars and the Bay of Cannes by night. Refreshments, for any not satiated by the buffets in the salon, would be placed in the belvedere. Although it was Lent, the Grand Duke was relying on the Almighty to overlook this sin and provide a warm day for the event. The Grand Duchess sat in a Louis Quinze chair and considered the effect of her décor for the ball, while workmen ran about at her beck and call. The Grand Duke appeared to be one of them, countermanding orders as fast as they were given. The decorations took a suitably Lenten tone in including many hundreds of branches of palm, but upheld the honour of the Romanovs in that they stood in emerald-encrusted pots.

Perhaps like the great restaurateur in the Siege of Paris, thought Auguste irreverently, noticing the palms, he should have provided stuffed donkey's head, and promptly offered a silent prayer of apology to *le Bon Seigneur*.

A slight frown crossed the Grand Duchess's face as Auguste bowed before her.

'Monsieur Boris is not well, *Votre Altesse Imperiale*. I am – ah – the temporary cook, Auguste Didier.'

'Yes, I recognise you. You were the chef at Stockbery Towers, were you not?'

Auguste admitted this honour.

'The Duchess spoke highly of you. Have you come to join our staff?'

'No, *madame*, I merely assist Monsieur Boris.'

'Let me see the menu.' She studied it intently. 'It is excellent, Mr Didier. But please—'

Auguste gulped. At least she had accorded him the *Monsieur*. These Russians were correct. Except Boris of course. He was not a correct cook, *pas du tout*. Perhaps he was correct for a Russian cook, but not in any civilised country.

'Not quite so much herring,' she continued. 'Despite what Boris might tell you, not all our guests wish to dine mentally in St Petersburg.'

Auguste was charmed. They understood each other. All might have been well save for the sudden irruption of the Grand Duke into their midst.

'What's this?' he asked querulously, in tones that reminded Auguste of the Duke of Stockbery querying crayfish from the River Len.

'Plum's blackberry fool,' said Auguste. 'My own recipe.'

'I don't like it,' said the Grand Duke.

'But our guests, Igor, may,' pointed out the Grand Duchess. 'We must please them.

'Why can't we just keep things simple? Either plums or blackberries, not both. Look at this. *A la soubise*. I like to see what I eat, not have it smothered in some froggie sauce – especially if it's made from their milk.'

'No milk, sir – I start my sauces from the basic concept of a well-flavoured stock. Too many sauces go wrong from the beginning because of ingredients . . .' He stopped in mid-sentence. The thought had come back, and this time he would remember it.

By the time the hansom cab drew up at Kallinkova's villa on the route de Fréjus Auguste was bursting with impatience to tell Natalia what had happened.

A little *light* luncheon, she had said. 'I am a dancer, not the fat lady at the circus.' All the same Auguste was glad to notice that it wasn't that light – the *coquilles* were cooked to perfection, and the *salade* adorned with a dressing that the Chevalier d' Albignac himself would envy.

'Your maid does all this?' he inquired incredulously. Devoted though he was to the ancient Marie, who he was quite sure was perfectly well aware of his comings and goings, he could not see her producing such fare.

'*Non*, it is mine,' said Natalia nonchalantly.

'Yours?' he breathed. This was indeed an angel descended from the heavens. 'With all your gifts, your genius of dancing, you cook *as well*?'

She laughed. 'Perhaps it should be the other way round for you, *mon cher*. I cook – and I manage to dance a little in between. So now, *chéri*, tell me this great idea of yours. You have solved the murder?'

'*Non*, but I have seen the method of cooking.' He paused impressively. 'It was the Grand Duke.'

'Igor was the murderer? *Ah non*,' she said, startled.

'No, no, naturally not. But he gave me the clue. Be simple, he said. Go back to the beginning. So I did. And then I saw. All along we have been blinded by this burglar, so sure that we centred our thoughts on Lord Westbourne. We did not listen when the Grand Duke spoke. When he told us that perhaps the murderer mistook Lord Westbourne for him. They are the same build, his back was to him, they wear the *de rigueur* blazers. But who would wish to kill the Grand Duke? I ask myself. And I come back again; the ladies who do not wish their husbands to know; a *crime passionel*. Though that does not satisfy—'

'I cannot believe that, Auguste,' said Natalia sharply. 'And there's one other possibility you must consider, if mistaken identity is the question. That it was not the Grand Duke, but someone else the assassin wished to kill.'

'But who?'

'The Prince of Wales.'

*　　*　　*

His Royal Highness the Prince of Wales was having a
wretched holiday. First a cricket match with a murder at the
end of it, then having to face Mama. He shrank at the
memory of having stood on that platform waiting for the
train to pull in, waiting for that small beady-eyed face to
peer out of the window and summon him in, haranguing
him for five minutes of hell. Then he had to attend the
funeral on Mama's behalf and, worst of all, drag himself all
the way to Cimiez (missing a damned good game of baccarat at the home of his friends the Goelets) and tell her all
about it. Goodness knows why she didn't go herself. She
liked nothing better than a nice slow walk round a cemetery
as a rule. Had he done the murder himself was the unspoken
implication of her every word. No one seemed to think he
might have been the intended victim, not the murderer, and
he wasn't going to point it out. He was just going to hide in
the Cercle Nautique with a certain planned number of
expeditions in closed carriages to certain addresses and that
was that.

He pondered over how to refuse old Igor's invitation.
Damned if he was going to another event with that lot.
Why, suppose he were the intended victim? He'd be laying
himself right open to a repeat effort.

'My dear Igor and Anna,' he began carefully. 'It is with
the greatest disappointment that I am unable after all to
attend . . .'

La Belle Mimosa was out for a parade on the Croisette at
the time when all good people and others had decreed was
the fashionable time to do so. Driving in her carriage had
some advantages – it was far less strain on her Italian kid
boots for one thing – but far more fun could be obtained by
walking along the boulevard with gentlemen on tenter-
hooks in case she might acknowledge them while out walking with their wives, and torn as to the etiquette of raising

166

their hats or not. La Belle Mimosa had made no concessions to Lent, and the ladies loathed her even more for it. Her bright yellow silk dress and parasol could be seen the length of the boulevard. Only Auguste did not notice until in unladylike fashion she placed herself directly in his path and stood still. He bowed.

She looked him up and down and twirled the yellow parasol. 'Rumpelmayers,' she suggested. 'No, too many women. Dull. Take me to the Gray d' Albion.'

Auguste gulped. He was, after all, a cook, even if a *maître* chef. Then he laughed at himself. He had been too long in England. Here a *maître* chef might dine at the Hôtel Gray d' Albion as might anyone else.

Whether La Belle Mimosa was his ideal choice of companion was another matter.

'I am,' she informed him as they crossed the roadway, 'without *un ami* at the moment.'

'Indeed,' murmured Auguste, wildly wondering whether this called for commiseration or for a firm booking. He was saved from answering by her frank, 'But then you are the *ami* of Kallinkova – for the moment. She doubtless would not like it and I like her.' The first smile he had seen on her face flitted briefly across it. 'I do not like many women, me.'

Outside the Gray d' Albion she stopped.

'*Non*,' she said. 'I change my mind. We go to my villa.'

Auguste froze. True, tea at the Gray d' Albion with La Belle Mimosa posed embarrassing problems; tea at her villa opened up even more alarming possibilities. Much was spoken of ladies' reputations, he thought bitterly, how about men's – forced between ungallantry and compromise? He wondered for a moment how Egbert had fared in the same circumstances, as he obediently found a hansom and escorted her to the Villa Mimosa. Like Rose before him, he was impressed at her taste. If the ladies adorning the salon were anything to go by, he wondered irrepressibly what those in her bedroom might be like, quickly suppressing any desire to find out.

'*Eh bien*,' she remarked cheerfully, as a severe middle-aged maid brought in tea on Sèvres china. 'I like this English tea custom. I like Englishmen too. I like that Inspector Rose. I wish him for my lover.'

Auguste choked over a mouthful of Earl Grey.

'Indeed,' he murmured weakly, wondering how Edith would treat this news.

'He has good hands,' the expert pronounced. 'Whereas you,' she looked him up and down, 'your eyes speak much, but do they fulfil their promise? Your body is handsome, but this—'

'*Madame*,' Auguste mustered his dignity, 'your tea is superb.'

She laughed. 'You think too much of love to love love itself. Happy the lady who wins you, but you will never understand us, I think. Nevertheless, I am willing to try.'

'*Madame*, I—' It came out as a strangled yelp.

'I jest,' she said soothingly. 'You could not afford me,' she added more practically, straight on to: 'You think I perhaps killed Westbourne, yes?'

'We think it likely that he was killed by the thief whose name he was to give away.'

'Ah, the burglar of the Fabergé eggs.' Her eyes went to the small side table where the egg was carelessly displayed in all its beauty. 'You are wrong. The burglaries have nothing to do with it,' she ended dismissively.

'How can you know?'

'I know.'

'How—?' he said sharply.

She laughed. 'I will not tell you.'

'But you must tell us if your egg is to be safe,' Auguste pleaded.

'It will be safe,' she replied scornfully. 'Ah, *mon ami*,

this I do know. Pah!' She spat delicately and for no apparent reason into her saucer.

'So if your egg is safe, we need not guard it if you come to the ball?' Auguste suggested cunningly.

A moment's pause. Then: 'I do come to the ball. I wear my egg.'

'But does it not worry you?' Auguste asked puzzled. 'Don't you want the egg?'

'Who would not want a Fabergé egg?' Her tawny eyes gleamed. 'Don't be foolish. If it is stolen, I will know who has it. I will ask him for it back.'

Auguste's brain reeled. 'But he may be a murderer. And if you know who it is, *tell* us.'

'He will not murder me, my friend,' she replied smugly. 'And only if it is stolen will I know the thief,' she added, though Auguste sensed this was more to keep him quiet than to express the truth. 'I do not wish to slander anyone, do I?' she added, with a smile as sharp as the diamonds that adorned her.

It was all happening again. The egg, the Petrov Diamond, Fouchard – Auguste reeled in disbelief.

'Perhaps I did do it, *hein*?' she asked innocently. 'You think I am a murderess, Didier?'

'Where were you after the tea break?' he muttered. He had a distinct feeling he was being outmanoeuvred.

'I went to the balcony with Kallinkova. She was the only one who would talk to me,' La Belle Mimosa replied. The tawny eyes glinted, and looked him up and down. 'When Natalia finish with you, you come to me, *hein*? I could teach you much, I think.'

Auguste walked back home to recover. He was very puzzled. There was something strange about La Belle Mimosa and her egg. Considering that the thief had come to Cannes to steal it, she was taking it very calmly, for all her explanations. Why did he get the feeling that he and Egbert were dancing to a tune? Marionettes in the hands of La

Belle Mimosa perhaps? Or someone else? By the time he reached the winding road to the fortress and the Rue du Barri, it was growing dark, and he seemed to be the only person on foot. From behind every closed shutter came smells of garlic, tomatoes, peppers, and his footsteps quickened, wondering what *Maman* would have for dinner tonight that would make the rest of the day seem worthwhile. All the elaborate dishes he would be helping to prepare at the Villa Russe for the next two days contained less of the true savour of the south than the comforting *marmite* of *Maman*'s. He turned the corner under the watchtower, where the people of Cannes had watched for the Barbarians coming, so his father used to tell him. He imagined them huddled there, day after day, silently watching the sea for the sight of sails. There had been other visitations too along this coast, St Paul himself some said, and St Patrick of Ireland, the Romans, the Moors, the Piedmontese, all had come and gone, and the independent kingdom of Provence had risen and fallen. Now Provence was part of France. Yet always it would maintain its special quality, that underlying hint of its savage past. Words left over from its Provençal language that had nothing to do with the elegant written French of today. *Lou mes di foui*, they called March in Provençal, the month of madness, for this was the month that the moon had her greatest influence. It was shining not brightly, but enough to give a ghostly luminosity to the buildings that crowded both sides of the narrow street.

Suddenly there it was, right in front of him, fleeing in the dark, a faint glowing figure seeming to float over the ground, hatted and cloaked. Gulping, and resisting the temptation to dive straight into the Rue du Barri, he forced himself to run. Surely that figure was too substantial for a ghost? he argued. Surely you should see through ghosts? No, he recalled other sightings, so real you could have sworn they were alive . . . until they vanished. His echoing footsteps seemed laboured as in a dream, no noise from the scurrying figure in front. Its footsteps were soundless. In the dim gas light it vanished out of the pool of light into the gloom and was swallowed up. Panting, Auguste raced to the corner convinced he would see it on the next stretch. As he turned there was a figure in front of him and he cannoned into it. It was the old Cannois.

'Did you see it? Him, *monsieur*?' he panted, all thoughts of Bastide flying from his mind.

'It? Him? Who?' grunted the old man, very peeved.

'*Masque de Fer, mon brave. Où est il?* The ghost.'

'No one came here,' said the Cannois. 'I heard you running. Who's that running? I asked. Must be old Iron Mask. But it was you.'

'He has vanished,' said Auguste, slowly staring round. Where had he gone? On one side of the road a steep drop too far for a human to jump, on the other a sheer wall rising to the high gardens above.

'There is one possibility' – Auguste was still grasping the old Cannois, as if scared that he too might vanish – 'these steps . . . No, they were lit. He could not have reached the bottom before I got there.'

'But he is a ghost, *mon fils*,' pointed out the Cannois in surprise. 'He has no need to escape. He is a *ghost*.'

Auguste gulped, reason fighting senses. '*Eh bien*,' he said at last with dry mouth. '*Monsieur*, I am glad to see you.'

'Pah,' retorted the old man.

Inspector Fouchard was not delighted to see the old Cannois, nor did he react well to the realisation that he would now have to approach the Sûreté again with confirmation that their prized capture was probably guiltless. He put Emmeline and the old Cannois through strict interrogation, eventually pointing out in triumph that only Emmeline's word testified that Bastide accompanied her from the office straight out on to the balcony again and not via the study. 'Or suppose, *mademoiselle*,' he said hopefully, 'you did it together.'

171

His voice tailed off as eighteen-year-old American innocence stared back at him outraged, with murmurs of Papa. Inspector Fouchard hastily rethought his position and reluctantly agreed to wire the information to Paris. When Auguste had relayed to him the information that La Belle Mimosa's egg would once again be on display at the masked ball, Inspector Fouchard's cup was full.

Count Nicolai Trepolov waited, derby in hand, at the railway station on Friday. The Nice Express *rapide* was pulling in and happiness was his. He would taste of the mead of the gods. He would be able to show her his bees.

With a triumphant belch, the train came to a stop and soon from a first-class carriage the beloved figure emerged. His heart swelled with pride. To think: a distant cousin of the Romanovs, and *his* love. And soon she might be his for ever. The thrill of it temporarily ousted the bees from his heart. She was walking towards him. Soon she would be at his side. Oh, the honour. The Princess Tatiana Maniovskaya, soon to be his wife, thus to unite him with the Romanovs for ever.

Another passenger descended from the train, not from the first-class cars however. Inspector Rose had returned to the Riviera, though hardly in such comfort as the Princess. The train was very crowded, and he had not slept at all. He was not alone. With him were Bastide Comte de Bonifacio, and Inspector Chesnais. Bastide had been released grudgingly by the Sûreté with Chesnais insisting that a close watch be kept on him.

Scotland Yard had returned Rose to the battlefield, and his small room at the Paradis seemed almost like home again. Back at Highbury, faced once more by Mrs Rose's cooking, he had almost forgotten the dining room here, and the smells of its food had faded. Now they rose up in his nostrils, enticingly, and it was some time before he could move himself from the table to seek out Auguste. Not that he needed to devote much time to the search.

Auguste was a dervish in the centre of a whirlpool. After tomorrow, nothing. I shall not touch a cooking pan till I return to Plum's. I shall not eat – no, that was too much. Meanwhile forty *entremets* needed to be approved, the bread ordered from the Vienna Bakery, Monsieur Nègre's supplies of confectionery checked. (How grateful he had been for this large order in Lent.) Here at least others did the cooking, but the strain fell on the master brain – himself. Boris sat despairing mightily but doing nothing.

Rose smiled to himself. He had seen it all before. Would Auguste ever stop? He doubted it.

'Ah Egbert.' Auguste ran to him eagerly. 'You have returned just in time, my friend.'

'The Factory became worried now that Lord West-bourne's murder's wide open again and telegraphed to me in Paris, once they heard the news from the Sûreté. I'm officially on the murder now. Robberies take second place.'

'Come, my friend. I have much to tell you. While you have been away, as well as concerning myself with the release of *le pauvre* Bastide,' Auguste said with some pride, 'I have been thinking. Let us take some refreshment in the belvedere.'

'The what?'

Auguste pointed towards the golden edifice at the far end of the gardens.

'That's what it is, is it? I'd been wondering.'

Followed by a footman bearing suitable apéritifs for the hour of sunset, they walked down the long gardens to the belvedere.

The sun would soon make its final dive behind the horizon in the bay, the sky glowing reds and pinks in the west, and velvet soft above their heads in the still, warm air.

Rose sat down, taking the pink kir offered to him by Auguste somewhat dubiously.

'Ah, do not fear. It is a drink invented by a bishop and thus acceptable to *le Bon Seigneur*,' laughed Auguste.

Rose took a sip, then another, and began to relax as Auguste related what had happened in his absence, and offered his conclusions that Lord Westbourne's death might have been a case of mistaken identity.

'The Prince of Wales?' Rose paled, setting his kir down in a hurry.

'Possibly, but more likely the Grand Duke.'

'Why would anyone want to kill the Grand Duke?' He paused. 'Oh no. If you're thinking what I'm thinking, Auguste, it's ridiculous.'

'It is possible, my friend.'

'The Nihilists,' said Rose resignedly. 'That's all we need. Wait till Chesnais hears this one.'

'I forgot to mention,' Auguste added carelessly. 'La Belle Mimosa is more deeply involved than we thought. She knows something, *mon ami*.'

'Oh?' said Rose uneasily.

'But she will not tell us, until she is certain. You seem to have made a friend in that one,' added Auguste, rewarded by the red flush that filled Rose's thin cheeks.

'If this were England, I'd know how to deal with the lady,' he retorted darkly. 'But here' – he paused, looking at the golden edifice encircling them, with its onion-shaped cupola – 'I feel as if I'm in a birdcage. Two nightingales in the Emperor's birdcage, eh? And with just as little to sing about, the way this case is going.'

Chapter Nine

Inspector Fouchard and his men marched, as purposefully as the Grand Old Duke of York on his outward journey, up the hillside of La Californie to the Villa Russe. Chesnais, impatient for action, had preceded them, and he and Egbert Rose were escorted into the Grand Presence. *Le Bon Seigneur* had been merciful to the Grand Duke and accorded him a fine day. Even now an army of servants was installing the huge gilt-painted plaster candelabras in the grounds, each one bearing three four-foot candles in the Russian national colours. They were arranged over a wide area in avenues forming a four and an eight in honour of the Grand Duke's years. At the apex of the four was the golden belvedere, also lit by candles, these arranged roughly in the shape of the Romanov double-headed eagle.

His birthday it might be, but the Grand Duke seemed ill at ease as he received them in the morning room. Behind him on a finely carved desk was a gleaming working model of the St Petersburg–Cannes Express constructed in pearls and amethysts. He had clearly been playing with his new toy as they entered. An animated picture projector and a box marked *Fatima's Danse du Ventre* and *The Diamond Jubilee of Her Majesty Queen Victoria* also bore witness to the event. But the Grand Duke still did not look like a happy man.

'You have guards on all the gates?' he inquired anxiously.

'Two on the main entrance, two on the tradesmen's and

one on the side gate. And two on every entrance into the house itself, including the cellar and the chimney. Everybody entering will have to display an invitation card and all the servants are being given identity cards.' Chesnais waited for praise of his efficiency. The honour of the French Police Force had been impugned by Rose, but would quickly be redeemed. If possible, by the re-arrest of the Comte de Bonifacio.

'And no one can enter unobserved?' Igor asked anxiously. 'Over a wall perhaps?'

'To escape our men, they'd have to get one of these flying machines working,' Chesnais said confidently.

'And what if he is here already?' demanded Igor. 'One of my guests here, or a servant?'

'I'll be at your side, sir, throughout. And Inspector Fouchard will have guards on all the rooms.'

'At *my* side?' The Grand Duke looked startled.

'Inspector Rose believes that you may well have been right, that Lord Westbourne was killed in mistake for you,' announced Chesnais cheerfully. Tact was not his strong point. 'That being so, today offers a wonderful opportunity – *pardon*,' hastily recalling his audience, 'a tragic opportunity for another attempt. But nothing will happen, rest assured.'

The Grand Duke's face was panic-stricken. He had shouted wolf so often that he had come to disbelieve in his own assertions. The fact that the police were taking them seriously was a most alarming innovation.

'The Nihilists,' he breathed. He thought over the implications. Then: 'No, you are wrong,' he announced more cheerfully. 'There would be no Nihilists at a cricket match. The English would not tolerate it. It is thieves you must expect tonight,' he continued fiercely. 'They want the Petrov Diamond. They shall not have it.'

Rose coughed apologetically. 'There may be other people who have reason to dislike you, sir, besides the Nihilists.'

'Nonsense,' cried Igor, hurt. 'I am kind to everyone. Why should anyone wish to hurt me?'

Rose plunged in. 'There's the matter of the ladies who received the eggs, sir.'

'The eggs?' The Duke's eyes grew glassy. 'You think—' He broke off. 'Ah,' he said, delighted, 'I see. You think because they are no longer my mistresses, they wish to kill me. No, they *lof* me,' he explained loftily.

'La Belle Mimosa doesn't seem to love you, sir. She hasn't love Lord Westbourne either.'

The Grand Duke lost a little of his confidence. 'You keep her out of here,' he said firmly.

'She has an invitation, sir. It would be difficult—'

The Grand Duke's eyes bulged. 'Not from me, she hasn't. Or from the Grand Duchess,' he muttered as an afterthought. 'It was a mistake,' he added rather plaintively and somewhat obscurely to Rose. 'Used to be able to tell: if a woman wore jewels in the daytime, she was a demi-mondaine – nowadays everything's going down the drain. Why, I even saw—'

'And we have to assume,' Rose cut across a possibly interesting reminiscence firmly, 'that she will be wearing her egg to the ball tonight.'

The Grand Duke's eyes blinked nervously. 'Will she?' he muttered.

'We'll be guarding her, but our priority must be the Petrov Diamond. Will the Grand Duchess be wearing it?'

'No. It's with the other jewels. Under your guard,' the Grand Duke pointed out.

Rose frowned. He'd just come round to the Grand Duchess's way of thinking that a bosom was as good a place as anywhere to keep it safe.

'Sir, I don't like it.' Rose hesitated. 'There's your new chauffeur.'

'Higgins. Good fellow. What about him?'

'He's a publican, sir, from the East End of London.'

'I know that, he's on holiday here.'

'He's also the biggest receiver of stolen jewels in London.'

The Grand Duke frowned. 'Nonsense, he's a good chap.'

'He may be a good chap, sir, he's also a good fence.'

'Then that just serves to prove my point, doesn't it?' said the Grand Duke with irrefutable logic. 'His presence means that damned burglar is going to be here tonight. Now look, I can't waste time here discussing the servants. The jewels are in the Petite Bibliothèque and as many of your fellows as you like can guard them there. It's more sensible than following Anna round the whole evening. I'll show you.'

He led the way up the marble and gilt staircase now smothered with lilies and roses, their purity given material elegance by the diamond-studded holders which secured them to the balustrades. The small library, on the second floor, was combined with a study for the convenience of guests.

'There.' The Grand Duke pointed to the desk which bore an ancient and somewhat scruffy wooden chest about eighteen inches by twelve. 'Look at this,' he said proudly, opening the box with his key. In the bottom, on a bed of opals, Siam rubies, Persian turquoises, garnets, chrysoberyls and topaz lay the Petrov Diamond.

'The Orlov Diamond's bigger, of course,' ruminated the Grand Duke, 'not to mention the Great Mogul. Women are never satisfied,' he brooded. 'Got her eye on the Tiffany yellow now. She thinks I'm made of money.'

'You've no safe, sir?'

'What do I need a safe for? There's enough safebreakers in the world without me putting in a safe to attract them. If they want it, they'll get it anyway.'

Again, such was his overpowering personality that Rose could not think offhand of a rebuttal to this argument.

'The chest is supposed to have belonged to my ancestor, Tsar Peter. Used it when he went to London. Before he was Tsar of course. Some kind of tradesman, wasn't he? Anna was going to throw it out. But I said no. Might come in handy. And it did. Who'd expect the Romanov jewels to be in there?' he asked proudly.

'Who indeed? thought Rose. Only all the world and his wife, if I know Igor. He looked out of the windows down to the garden beneath. 'I don't see anyone in evening clothes shinning up this pipe unnoticed,' he said. 'But we'll post someone at the bottom in case. And a couple of guards up here. You've told no one?' he said routinely.

'No one,' said the Duke vigorously. 'Anna of course knows.' He smiled brightly.

By a natural progression of thought Rose next tracked down James Higgins. He found him in the stables polishing the lamp holders on the horseless carriage and vigorously whistling 'All Things Bright and Beautiful'. He was taking no notice of the obvious hatred emanating from the French coachman lovingly polishing his spurned carriage wheels.

'Certainly I'll be 'ere tonight, Inspector. It's my duty. The old Hayebox might be needed.' He patted it virtuously. 'We got to know each other, this old 'orse and me. Days it took to bring 'er down, and I wouldn't leave 'er now if you offered me the Crown Jewels and no questions asked.'

'Forget about jewels, Higgins. We don't want the Stepney swell mob in here, do we? Remember I'll be watching. You *and* Muriel.'

'I'm sure Muriel will appreciate that, Inspector. A soft spot for you, she 'as.'

He lightly ran his chamois over the gleaming radiator.

'And remember, Higgins, there'll be someone at your side, all day.'

'That will be very pleasant, Inspector. I always enjoy 'aving someone to chat to.'

A toothy grin and he resumed his whistling. He had switched to 'Onward Christian Soldiers'.

* * *

179

Boris had at last galvanised himself into some kind of action, impressed by the imminence of the event. He rushed around after Auguste reiterating then countermanding his orders, and tasting his own concoctions, since Auguste showed no inclination to do so. Madame Didier, glancing at her son, detailed herself to restrain Boris's peregrinations, so that Auguste could continue his eleventh-hour rescue without hindrance.

So much remained to do, and he had so little time in which to do it. The ices were to be stirred in the refrigerators, the galantines to be garnished, the *salades* to be supervised. And the fish! It was all very well this fish menu, but it posed difficulties as most dishes had to be prepared today. At six in the morning the tradesmen's entrance had been chock-a-block with fishermen, and the kitchen resembled Billingsgate. Lobsters, crabs, crawfish, scallops, oysters and turbots lay in baskets, and the smell of the salt combining with the heat of the stoves made the kitchen almost unendurable, even for Auguste. Now the turbots reposed in their fish kettles, salmon fastened unseeing eyes upon their chef, boiled *écrevisses* waited pink and fat, ready to be peeled by the kitchenmaids, the crawfish were ready for Auguste's preparation of the dish of dishes, *crawfish à la provençale*, the recipe with which the *Maître* Escoffier had made his name in 1869 at the Favre in Nice.

Thank heavens, thought Auguste in despair, that he had had the sense to moderate the fish menu with some *entremets* of egg and cheese dishes, some *soufflés d'épinards aux anchois*, and naturally, also, *aux truffes*. He recalled making the latter dish at Stockbery Towers in Kent with Kentish truffles, and the difficulty with which he had persuaded the Duke that Kentish truffles, although naturally not like those of Provence, had a distinguishing flavour of their own. Unconvinced, the Duke had sampled the dish, and had afterwards waxed so lyrical about Kentish truffles that he promptly purchased his own trained dog to hunt them out.

Auguste was in the middle of a discussion with himself on the perennially interesting subject of whether *crawfish à la provençale* was or was not superior to *homard à l'américaine*, when he was jerked back to the present as a pageboy shot in, piping:

'Monsieur Didier and menu to the Grand Duchess.'

She treated him as if he were their cook, he fumed. Did she think he was their *servant*? Then, recalling the standards that had to be maintained at this ball, and the stories of the balls at the Winter Palace, he could not find it in his heart to blame her for wanting the best – himself.

The Grand Duchess had replaced Igor in the morning room and was in the process of taking morning chocolate with a guest, as Auguste ran feverishly upstairs watched suspiciously by one of Fouchard's men. This Sergeant Didier was an impostor in his view. Some policeman, he was. The *soi-disant* sergeant's head was still spinning with dishes and plans and receipts, as he entered the room.

'The menu, *Votre Altesse Imperiale*.'

A head turned slightly at the movement, and Auguste's life changed for ever.

The morning room became at once a paradise and a hell; his heart held him captive as the world kaleidoscoped around him. For one moment he looked into her eyes, then calmly she set down her cup upon the silver trolley, and with a murmur to the Grand Duchess rose to her feet. The Princess Tatiana did not look back as she walked towards the far door, but had Auguste not been so swept away on glory and misery he would have seen a certain tenseness about her shoulders, a slight hesitation on the threshold. Then she was gone, the flunkeys closing the door behind her.

'Monsieur Didier.' There was a note of impatience. The Grand Duchess was not used to her servants gazing spellbound at other people while she was addressing them, and she was forced to repeat his name somewhat sharply before he came to his senses.

'My apologies, *madame*.' Auguste stumbled over the words, head still reeling. *Tatiana here?* 'May I suggest we serve the turbot with a lobster sauce rather than with mayonnaise—' *She is related to the Romanovs, why should I not have considered that she might be here?* 'The langoustines will make a blaze of colour, so they should not be next to the sturgeon, whose glaze is mixed with lobster coral—' *She has not changed. Was it a dream?* 'The cod and the caviar, *madame*—' *She looked at me and walked on. She cares no more.* 'The cod will have a sauce of grief—'

'*Une sauce de grive?* Thrushes, Monsieur Didier?' Her tones were cold, since Auguste's abstraction was obvious. She then recalled that her ball was tonight, and even though this cook seemed as mad as Boris, he had to stay. Auguste was therefore reprieved from instant dismissal from a post he had no idea he was occupying.

Auguste walked trembling back to the kitchen, all interest in food leaving him. Tatiana in Paris was bearable. But Tatiana in this very house – ah, that was different. Suppose she was married? The torment. How could he endure the next twelve hours? He might see her again; he could not bear the exquisite torture of that thought. He must throw himself into his work, forget her. Forget that his dream of life was centred on the floor above.

He took a deep breath full of resolve, and erupted into the kitchen. '*Petite Marie*, what do you do with that salamander? You think it is a warming pan? Jean-Paul, you call that a garnish? *Alors*, Monsieur Boris—'

Equally elaborate preparations were going on in villas and hotels all over Cannes. A masked fancy dress ball in Cannes, especially at the Villa Russe, was an event. Madame Verrier had been swamped with work. Balls were as hard work in the dressing room as in the kitchens. Ideas had been ruthlessly stolen from the Nice masked ball at Mardi Gras. Thus there were several *Mesdames de la Lune*, dressed in ivory satin and diamonds, and at least three lady devils, tastefully arrayed with golden horns and black dresses heavily encrusted with rubies.

Rachel Tucker at the Villa Sardou discovered that her Phèdre dress, a copy of that worn by the great Rachel herself, required an entirely different corset, and mourned that she had not bought the one with the Pompadour embroidery and suspenders that had looked so versatile.

Emmeline Vanderville impatiently tugged at her new pink spider-web tulle dress and twisted and turned to look at the effect of the lace butterfly decorated with diamonds that her maid had just placed in her hair. But she was not concentrating on them. She was looking at the posy of Neapolitan violets that had just arrived from Alfred. What a sweet romantic gesture. She'd pin it on her dress so that he would see them. They didn't last as long as amethysts, but they were so pretty and she could always press them between the pages of her very private diary. The orchids supplied by Bastide remained in their box.

Dora, Lady Westbourne, was in a quandary. As a widow she should not attend a ball, yet she could not miss it. She would ensure that if she could not dance, Harry would not either. Such a pity she had to wear black. She had briefly considered going as a lady devil. Such interesting costumes at the Nice ball. But she had decided in favour of Mary Queen of Scots . . . She too had lost a husband by murder, *and* she, too, had a lover. Yes, she should look as regally fragile as Mary.

Natalia Kallinkova had arrived early at the Villa Russe and was taking tea with her acquaintance Princess Tatiana. Not hampered by having to consider a change of corset, she had simply brought her costume with her, and its satin folds were even now being lovingly hung out by Marie in an upstairs bedroom.

'I shall go as the Queen of Hearts,' she confided to Tatiana. 'It is an old English rhyme. She stole some tarts.

So I shall wear some real tarts which *mon cher ami* Monsieur Didier will supply from the kitchens. Ah, he is a knave indeed, that one. It is not tarts but hearts he steals, all on a summer's day,' she laughed.

Tatiana continued to sip her tea, her face impassive.

The newest scullerymaid had barely finished washing the marble steps for the fifth time that day before the first carriage arrived. Showing invitations at the gates was a novelty, and speculation was intense. The Grand Duke, standing at the entrance to the ballroom to greet his guests with the Grand Duchess, was not yet masked, and was arrayed as an opulent Turkish Sultan, his splendid red turban encrusted with emerald bands; his Grand Duchess, who had not wished to be taken for a common lady of the harem, had chosen Scheherazade. Both roles displayed their jewels in quantity. Six seamstresses had worked for a week to sew them on to the costumes. Peter the Great's box, however, still contained the largest items of the collection, including of course the Petrov Diamond, the Grand Duke assured Rose.

Rose fidgeted by his side. No fancy dress for him; he even felt uncomfortable in his faithful old tailcoat and old-fashioned collared waistcoat. The Duke, once accustomed to the idea that he might indeed be a target, now refused to let Rose out of his sight, and he had been enjoined to share the grand-ducal luncheon. He looked forward to telling Edith all about it. From Highbury to Grand Dukes! From bangers to *bisques*.

Cannes society, or rather its top echelons, was now flocking into the ballroom, and Rose's unease grw. How on earth to feel master of this situation, when in theory anybody might be carrying a dagger in his costume. Indeed, one was. The Grand Duke. As Rose's eyes took in the Grand Duke's costume, he became painfully aware of a familiar sight sticking out of one of the Turkish Sultan's boots. A jewelled dagger. It gave him a nasty jolt, for a moment thinking it the very same dagger used to kill Lord Westbourne.

The Grand Duke had followed his eye. 'Ah,' he said, pleased. 'I take notice of what you say. I protect myself. This is the Dagger of Prince Tanarov. He displeased one of my ancestors.' He did not go on to elaborate, and Rose did not press the point. He was too busy thinking of the possible ramifications of a jumpy Grand Duke imagining every bush a Nihilist bear.

The ballroom was huge by Cannes standards, even if not by those of the Winter Palace, and as if to provide a reminder of this fact, the main decorations consisted of a huge representation of the Winter Palace, twenty feet high and thirty feet long, constructed from lilies and decorated with greenery, with small diamond clusters composing the windows. The Grand Duke believed in having birthdays in style. By its side and tastefully hidden behind a tall screen of palms was the orchestra.

'Are they checked?' frowned Rose, glancing at Fouchard.

'*Oui*. Local men,' said Fouchard loftily. 'No danger. Do not worry so, Inspector Rose. No stranger can enter the grounds of the Villa Russe tonight.'

He spoke too soon. One of his men came rushing through the crush of people. 'We have him, sir!' he cried excitedly.

'Who?' asked Fouchard sharply.

'A Nihilist, sir.' They had been well indoctrinated in the art of Villa Russe protection. 'He doesn't deny it.'

Fouchard rushed off, filled with horror, and Rose's unease grew. Where there was one . . . But his fears were misplaced on this occasion. He recognised him at once as Fouchard returned, trophy firmly in his grasp. It was the old Cannois.

Auguste had other things on his mind than the capture of Nihilists. Food. Only food. He must concentrate and not think of Tatiana. Now was the important time when the

185

kitchens disgorged their masterpieces and the *plats* were laid in the supper room and garnishes were added; when the *maître* must stand back to criticise his handiwork, to bring it one step nearer perfection. There stood his creations, pristine, untouched, gifts from heaven. The hot *plats* were in their chafing dishes, the salads arranged to delight the eye. Liveried servants stood proudly by their charges. Ah, this was the supreme moment for a chef. Afterwards there was a different kind of satisfaction for a *maître*, when dirty, messy plates bore a testimony of their own.

Auguste went to superintend the tables in the supper room while Boris floundered around below. The food was to be served from golden and silver dishes, on to Sèvres china plates. Even the Villa Russe could not run to 400 golden plates, but to make up for it, each table groaned not only with food but with huge living green plants, carried on silver pergolas up to the ceiling, with fresh orchids and roses peeping between the leaves. Auguste regarded these almost disparagingly, lest their splendour detract from the glory of his food. The eye was so important. Not *all* important, but certainly a part of it. He would not go so far as to insist on the theatrical displays of Monsieur Grimod de La Reynière, who heralded the arrival of each dish with flutes and trumpets; there was a need, it was true, to create a sense of anticipation, but not to overwhelm the food itself. *His* food, at least, did not require this.

He was still lost in anxious admiration of his achievements when Natalia came in, recognisable only by her Queen of Hearts costume, in white satin with red satin hearts. Few jewels for Kallinkova. She mischievously placed a kiss on his cheek, seeing he was in the midst of his professional checking. She felt only a slight reaction.

'So,' she said softly. 'The lover thinks of other things. Of detection perhaps?'

'I feel we are pawns on a chessboard,' he said apologetically, gratefully leaping to this excuse. Because he had seen Tatiana, that was no reason to slight Natalia.

'Then think like a knight, *mon ami.*' She laid her hand gently on his cheek. '*Eh bien*, where are my tarts?'

Think like a knight, forward and along. Round sharp corners – like the Ghost of the Man in the Iron Mask. It had disappeared. But if one accepted there were no such things as ghosts then it had to go somewhere. Absentmindedly he changed the order of two *plats*, refixed a white Piedmontese truffle on the glaze of a sturgeon. Always before, the method and routine of cooking had helped his detection; perhaps this time also it might. Suppose each *plat* here represented a person present at the cricket match: this sturgeon was the Grand Duke, the centrepiece, and perhaps the intended victim. This turbot, Lord Westbourne. These pink salmon, the ladies. His eye went round the tables. All round the edges were the lesser *plats*, the *entremets*, the vegetables, there to supplement, to serve . . . the kitchenmaid . . . A wild idea came into his head, so extraordinary he sat down, head in hands. His dream returned to him. Ah yes, now he remembered. The idea grew. He thought it over. But how? Why?

'Natalia,' he said slowly. 'I have been blind. It is maybe so simple, just at right angles to the line we followed. Like chess, as you say. They told us themselves, and we did not listen. We have been so busy thinking of everyone's motives, first to kill Lord Westbourne, then to kill the Grand Duke. But I of all people have been guilty of thinking the *vegetables* were there to supplement. They *are* the *plat*. We took no notice of the servants. We thought of them as witnesses, but not players in the game. Why not? *Why not?*' He waved a decorative crab claw around in growing triumph. 'Why am I here myself?' he demanded.

'To cook.'

'And *why*?'

'Because Boris is not capable.'

'And *why* is that? What is different after the cricket match than before?'

'Lord Westbourne is dead.' She considered, following his thoughts. 'But why should Boris wish to kill Lord Westbourne?'

'He didn't – he intended to kill the Grand Duke.'

She stared, then laughed. 'What? Ah, *non*, *mon ami*, that is *pas possible*. Everyone knows that Boris is devoted to the Grand Duke. He has served him for twenty years.'

'Yes, and perhaps that is why he was not killed sooner.'

'Oh, Auguste, you're being ridiculous. Simple? You're making things complicated.'

'Am I? Suppose he is a Nihilist. He was in Paris when that group was discovered some years ago. His task is to kill the Grand Duke. He waits his time. You Russians are patient people, and it is the Nihilists' way to lie low. Some day he will do it, he reasons, but only when the honour of Russia, safeguarded by the Romanovs, is at stake. And at the cricket match, what happens?'

Natalia opened her mouth, but Auguste swept on.

'The Grand Duke made an idiot of himself. He threw away the chance of victory for the Players and fell over the stumps on the first ball instead of scoring magnificently as he had boasted earlier. He laughed, but Boris did not. I heard him, Natalia. The honour of Russia, he kept saying. And then see his horror when he discovered Lord Westbourne was the victim. He was drunk, he is short-sighted, he saw the Grand Duke enter the study but not come out. Don't you remember I told you he blamed the cow? He went out to milk the cow and did not see the Grand Duke leave. So he enters and there is a broad blazered back. He took his chance to avenge Russian honour. But he killed the wrong man, and in his distress, his answers to me came out oddly. I thought he was drunk, but he was following his own reasoning.'

'The honour of the Romanovs is the honour of Russia,' she repeated thoughtfully.

'And he loves Mother Russia.'

'If you are right,' said Natalia doubtfully, 'you should tell the inspector.' Then as Auguste promptly began to rush out, she remembered something.

'*Eh, Monsieur le chef*, you forget my tarts.'

Auguste rushed back. Natalia could have anything, *everything* she desired.

Seeing Rose was easier said than done. When he eventually succeeded in reaching the inspector, it was impossible to talk to him alone, and the Grand Duke insisted on listening in.

'Boris?' He roared with laughter. 'Anna,' he shouted, 'this cook thinks Boris tried to kill me.'

'Poor man, he is mad,' said the Grand Duchess kindly. 'Just send him back to the kitchen.'

It took some time to convince the Grand Duke of Auguste's right to be heard on the matter, and his annoyance began to grow. For all his fear of Nihilists, he knew Boris all right. The idea was ridiculous. Nihilists weren't to be found in kitchens, but gathered together in dark corners, plotting. If Boris were a Nihilist, he'd have poisoned him years ago.

Auguste himself began to lose confidence in it as a theory. Theory was all right, but was it *practicable*? He had to admit it seemed unlikely. He wasn't seeing things clearly. It was Tatiana preying on his mind. She might be here now, masked, and he not recognise her. He must return to the kitchens, where he belonged. No detective, no lover.

'You've done it this time, Auguste,' said Rose gleefully. 'I don't say you're wrong, mind. In any case, I'll stick to Igor like glue. Afterwards I'll speak to Chesnais and get him to make inquiries. He was in on all that bombing business in Paris. The important thing is to make sure nothing happens this evening. It's the jewels we must watch. No one's likely to try a murder on with me standing here.'

*　　*　　*

189

Bastide, Comte de Bonifacio, was almost crying. He might as well have stayed in prison for all the attention he was receiving. Emmeline was behaving most strangely. She had arrived with her parents some time ago but seemed to be dancing with a matador. She must be under the impression it was him. Moreover, there was a Musketeer here, trying to share in his glory. *He* was the descendant of the true Man in the Iron Mask. These tales of Dumas were mere fiction. To have a Musketeer present detracted from the true Bonifacio heritage. He sulked, grateful only that he had not insisted on the iron mask, but had chosen the velvet one. The historical facts on this point might be disputed but it was so much easier to eat this way. Moreover, it looked somewhat more romantic. But now someone else was similarly clad. He was used to there being two or three Napoleons at every ball he went to, but competition here hurt him sorely.

That reminded him. Surely Emmeline would have discovered by now that he was not the matador? It was time to disillusion her. As the dance ended, he walked up to her.

'Dearest,' he began in the accent that would announce his identity immediately to her. 'Your dance card,' he requested. 'I am here now,' waiting for her tones of thrilled surprise.

'Oh, hello, Basty,' she said in tones of no surprise at all.

He stiffened. Did this mean she was aware that it was not he dancing with her but another?

'*Who*,' he demanded of the matador, much as the Caterpillar of Alice, 'are you?'

Alfred Hathaway had absolutely no desire to slink away from an inherently unpleasant situation, as two weeks earlier he might have done. Now a new boldness came over him. 'Alfred Hathaway, sir, at your service.'

'An Englishman,' Bastide sneered. 'My dove, come.'

His dove showed no desire to come, and clung to her matador, but she thrust her dance card at Bastide. 'You can have the polka,' she said generously. She did not want to hurt him.

'But the supper dance?' he asked in horror. 'Surely I

may escort you to supper?' This was persecution.

'No, Alfred's taking me in to supper, Basty,' she announced brightly.

Bastide was unwise enough to show Alfred an unromantic fist, and was promptly rewarded by Alfred rapping out unthinkingly: 'Sir, name your seconds.'

The Comte, with scarcely a moment of hesitation, grandly named two gentlemen in the manner of Napoleon designating Marshals Masséna and Soult for the honour.

'Pistols?' It sounded good.

'Fists,' glared Bastide. He was going to get this over.

Alfred beamed, remembering the lessons he'd taken as a boy at his local Tunbridge Wells boxing school.

'Fists?' shrieked Rachel Gray, coming into the fray with finely judged technique. 'He is a poet. He is not well. He is dying.'

'Don't be foolish, Rachel,' said Alfred impatiently, throwing off her restraining hand. 'I'm not dying.'

'We shall meet again, sir,' said Bastide grandly, turning on his heel to stalk away, an effect somewhat marred by his tripping over the Iron Mask's cloak.

'You foolish child.' Rachel turned vehemently on Emmeline. 'You will be responsible for the death of England's greatest poet.'

'He might win,' pointed out Emmeline practically. 'Anyway, you don't die of fists.'

'Rachel.' Cyril, dressed as a rather slimmer W. G. Grace, complete with false beard, hurried up and put a firm hand on her arm. 'Recollect, I pray you.'

They looked at each other. 'Very well, Cyril,' she said slowly.

Nicolai Trepolov was suffering from the pangs of disprized love. At the last moment his jewel had been snatched away. His beloved had refused him. He could not believe she could mean it. It was too cruel. Moreover, it was a slight to his honour. Not only had the Princess Tatiana refused him, but for her to have told him she could never marry for she was in love with the cook! A Romanov, albeit a distant one, to be in love with a cook! The disgrace. To what levels had the standards of the world fallen! These upstarts, with their talk of revolution. There must be something that would change her mind. Perhaps if he invited her to his villa, suitably chaperoned of course, and offered her his honey-sweet mead, an elixir guaranteed to induce love . . . Were not sacrifices of mead made in olden days to the god Priapus? He hastily put aside this improper thought. They would both drink deep of the divine potion and then she would return his love. He would show her the hives, he would tell her he would be as faithful as a bee, and life should be of the sweetest honey. He might even give her his recipe.

Lady Westbourne was taking advantage of her mask to escape some of the censure that she might incur. But even she dared not dance, an inconvenience since Harry was plainly bored with this inactivity. How handsome he looked in his d'Artagnan costume. So brave, so dashing when he swirled that long cloak around him.

Harry was indeed bored. He wanted to dance, but could see no opportunity of so doing. Then Phèdre's eye fell upon him. Balked of Alfred, she would find Harry Washington a more than acceptable alternative. How fortunate that, as everyone was in theory in disguise, convention demanded that Dora could in no way blame her for what she was about to do. Taking advantage of Cyril's temporary absence, she laid her hand on Harry's arm.

'Dear d'Artagnan,' she cooed, 'it was your name on my dance card, was it not? Or was it Danton?' she inquired innocently.

She had hardly escaped to the floor with her prey, however, than a ripple ran through the room. Upon the steps,

192

pushing by a stupefied Grand Duke and Duchess, stood a radiant figure. La Belle Mimosa had no need to kowtow to Lent. Dressed in her usual colour, she looked ready for Easter, and in her bosom resided once again the Seventh Egg.

Inspector Rose was beginning to relax, though it was hard work following the Grand Duke as he talked to his guests. He had enough to tell Edith to keep him busy till Christmas. He could hardly dance round with him too, so he had allowed the Duke one stately dance and then reclaimed him. However there were no reports of trouble on the gate, apart from the old Cannois, who, it transpired, had merely been endeavouring to see his granddaughter, the newest scullerymaid. There had been no attempts on the jewels, which remained unmolested in their wooden chest. Auguste reported that Boris was still charging around in the kitchen and showed no desire to show his head above stairs. Hard to believe Boris was a murderer. A Nihilist required a developed political intelligence and that did not fit Boris. Was he a dupe? Was there anyone here who could have put him up to it? Now, that was a thought. Trepolov? No, an Englishman? His brow furrowed. The supper dance was in progress now. In the supper room Auguste would be running around like a scalded cat, metaphorically if not literally. Rose grinned. He'd seen it a dozen times now, and it never failed to amuse him.

In the supper room Auguste lined up his troops for the fray. The guests would drift in in ones and twos, then groups, then suddenly all 400 would be demanding to be served at once. Then just as suddenly – or so it would seem to him – it would all be over.

Here they came now. Was that not Lady Westbourne looking very cross? It was. She demanded caviar and champagne. The first plate was prepared.

The candles in the gardens illuminated their paths,

showing the huge '48', and at its apex the eagles of light from the belvedere. Now that the supper interval had arrived, the belvedere presented the perfect place for little uninterrupted intellectual discussions.

'Alfie,' breathed Emmeline, transported on a wave of romance in the arms of her poet.

'Emmeline,' breathed Alfie, swept away by her closeness, by the touch of her lips, so eager, so warm. This then was love. For once he felt no need of words, no poems rushed into his head as he devoted himself to the sensuous joys of physical encounter.

'You have betrayed me, Delilah.' A white-faced Bastide stood at the entrance to the pergola.

Alfred advanced eagerly to defend his lady's honour. 'Sir,' he said. 'Withdraw.'

Bastide had no intention of withdrawing. Advance was more in his mind. Advance with a swift right hook.

Unfortunately for him, Alfred had been well trained and Bastide staggered back, clutching a bloody nose. But he was made of no mean stuff and came at Alfred again, catching him in the midst of squeezing Emmeline's hand in triumph and meanly taking advantage of it. As Alfred received the full force of Bastide's fist on his chin, a solid figure in white rushed between them, arms flung wide. About to let fly, Alfred pulled back unsteadily and collapsed on the floor.

'He is dead,' moaned Rachel.

Close behind Rachel was Washington. This at least was more interesting than standing at Dora's side . . .

The crawfish were popular, Auguste noted with approval. And the sturgeon. Alas, the turbot was less well regarded. Perhaps the lobster sauce had been a misjudgement, Auguste thought anxiously, determined to keep his thoughts on the table less he be tempted to wander the room in search of his beloved.

Dora, waiting in vain for Harry, realised that he must

194

have followed Rachel Gray in that ridiculous white costume. She promptly set down her plate of lobster salad and set off in hot pursuit. She had seen Rachel going into the candlelit avenue of the straight side of the '4', and no doubt that ridiculous boy had followed. They might be alone in the belvedere even now . . . She set off, but when she reached the belvedere they were not alone. There was animated discussion going on between them, Cyril Tucker, that young American girl and two young men. She decided to join in, with force.

'Harry,' she began, meaningfully.

Moodily circling round the loops of the '8' was another figure crossed in love. He had wished to show the stars to Tatiana. She had declined. He must think about his course of action. The matter would not rest here. He arrived, attracted by the noise of argument, at the belvedere. Dora's eye fell on him. Any port in a storm. 'Darling Nicolai,' she shrieked, 'please come here.'

'I have the *zakuski*,' said Boris, looming up unexpectedly at Auguste's shoulder. 'Where you want them?'

'You're too late,' said Auguste through gritted teeth. 'They are having their dessert. They do not want hors d'oeuvres *now*.'

'What? You mean they will not eat my *zakuski*?' Boris looked threatening, and Auguste uneasily recalled that this was his suspected murderer, and Boris was carrying a kitchen knife for cutting his beloved *zakuski*. Balked of serving his *zakuski*, who knew what Boris might do? He looked round. There was no way he could allow Boris to wander round unguarded with plates of *zakuski*. Or with a knife. Nor could he abandon his post for the moment to ensure that Boris returned below.

'Take them down to the belvedere,' he said, checking that the Grand Duke was safely present in the supper room. 'There are people there who have not eaten. They may wish to eat *zakuski*.' Poor things.

'Yes, yes,' said Boris eagerly and disappeared obediently.

Auguste looked round desperately for Rose, and caught sight of him halfway through a meringue. He managed to speak to him without attracting the Grand Duke's attention.

'We're safe enough so far, then,' said Rose. 'But I don't like it. It's going too smoothly, and Madame Mimosa has a smile as thick as a lump of melon on her face.'

La Belle Mimosa was in fact making her way to the belvedere at this moment. It was 10.30 and that was the appointed time. She was eagerly looking forward to it, but she frowned as she heard the sound of voices in the gardens.

The high point of the evening was come. It was time for the appearance of The Cake. Nothing had been arranged for this all-important item when Auguste had been drawn in, and it had taken all his ingenuity and successful blandishments of Monsieur Nègre to produce the masterpiece.

The doors of the supper room were opened, and in came six footmen, carrying The Cake. What would Soyer say to this? Auguste proudly asked himself.

'Ah,' cried the Grand Duke excitedly. 'It is Misha! Oh, *ma chérie*, it is Misha!' And he so far forgot his grandducal dignity as to kiss the Grand Duchess full on the lips, before running round all sides of the cake.

It was a much magnified Misha, who in real life had been on the small size for a cat. Her replica was six foot high, made of spun meringue and sponge cake. A problem had been posed by the fact that Misha was mainly black, a colour not conducive to the confectioner's art. But Auguste had decided that this should be some angelic manifestation of Misha in white, with groups of crystallised flowers as eyes and lips. Misha's little white paws were differentiated by cream tinted pink.

'Ah,' cried the Grand Duke suddenly, 'how can we cut this? It is *Misha*!' The tears poured down his face as though the sad day when Misha fell prey to a passing carriage were but yesterday. Luckily his dilemma was solved. Nothing was to be required of him. For suddenly the entire house was plunged into pitch-black.

There were a few stifled screams, muttered oaths from Rose, then a shout: 'You there, Auguste?'

'It's this new-fangled electricity,' grumbled the Grand Duke. It had clearly happened before. 'Call for Higgins. He mended it last time.'

Auguste, not so confident as the Grand Duke that this was mere coincidence, managed to find his way to the garden where he extracted a candle and brought it back, supporting it on a supper table. The news had evidently reached Higgins, for his voice was heard outside, promising action. The faces of the guests, standing still, holding on to one another, were eerie in the candlelight. Impossible to see who they were, even had the masks not hidden identity. In the gardens the candles threw out limited avenues of light, figures moving up to the house in the blackness.

Ten minutes later the lights came up and Higgins appeared, toolbox in hand, looking pleased with himself. 'Done in a jiffy,' he said to Rose. 'Right as rain.'

The lights might have been but the jewels were not.

A gendarme ran in white-faced and clutched Fouchard by the arm, shouting, 'The ghost, *Monsieur l'Inspecteur.*'

'*Ghost?*'

'*Masque de Fer.* It was him. He has the jewels.'

Fouchard was racing upstairs, hotly followed by Rose, Auguste and the Grand Duke.

On the desk there was no sign of the chest. There was a bellow of rage from the Grand Duke, incapable of other speech as he stared transfixed at the empty desk. Then suddenly he turned and rushed out again.

'What's all this about a ghost?'

'Glowing, *Monsieur l'Inspecteur*, in the dark, all glowing, in the dark. Then he vanished.'

'He did not come down the drainpipe,' said the gendarme detailed for that duty.

'You stayed there all the time in these ten minutes while the lights were out?'

'I was outside, *monsieur*,' said the first gendarme. 'When the lights went out, I unlocked the door and ran in. It was then I saw it.' His voice faltered. 'And for a moment, *monsieur*, I felt fear and ran outside.'

Rose groaned. 'And our friend escaped down the drainpipe.'

'*Non, monsieur*. I would have seen a glowing ghost,' the gendarme from the garden said firmly.

'And no one ran past you in the room into the corridor?'

'No, *monsieur*, I would have seen him, would I not?'

'Never mind the bleeding jewels, look at me.' La Belle Mimosa stood on the threshold. She had lost all pretensions to ladylikeness as she clutched her ravaged bosom. The dress had been torn, and being low-necked she was able to hold it strategically just a little too low. 'This bleeding hand shot out in the belvedere and ripped it off.' This was not the treatment her bosom was accustomed to receiving and she had clearly taken it amiss. 'What are you going to do about it?'

Slowly Auguste looked out of the window to the belvedere. 'Inspector Rose,' he said fearfully. *'Where has the Grand Duke gone?'*

Rose went white. 'Cripes,' he said, and set off down the stairs.

'And where is Boris?' wondered Auguste grimly.

He sped down the staircase and into the ballroom. No Grand Duke. No Boris. Out into the gardens towards the belvedere. But when he got there, there was still no Boris. Only his corpse lying on its back, a knife plunged into its heart.

Chapter Ten

The candlelight flickered weirdly over the group looking down at the corpse, unable to believe that murder had once again crept up upon them and in such unlikely form. Through the most direct candlelit path from the house came a small phalanx, summoned by a gendarme. Inspector Chesnais led three of Cannes' five English doctors, the Russian doctor and a French doctor, the latter anxious to assert his claims to priority. Rather reluctantly, they all came to the same verdict: Boris was dead of a stab wound to the heart.

'Could it be by his own hand?' asked Auguste, stricken. Boris, that oafish man, his culinary catastrophes, his bullish energy; no more meatballs, no more of the *zakuski*, now silenced in death. Only an hour since he had thought Boris a murderer. Now he was dead.

'There are no signs of struggle.' An English doctor peered at the wound. 'If murdered, it must have been completely unexpected.'

'Unless he were left-handed, he could not have delivered such a blow himself,' offered another. 'He could not have given it the necessary force. Look at the angle of the knife. Suicides don't as a rule stab through clothing.'

There were general nods of agreement, as the medical fraternity looked at the blood-spattered overall.

'Would the murderer have signs of blood on him?' inquired Auguste hopefully. There was little to be seen here with the knife still in the wound.

A doctor shrugged. 'Very little, if any. If he had pulled the dagger out – it would be different.'

'Odd,' said Rose, frowning. 'Spur-of-the-moment murder, and yet he has time to do that.' He pointed. The corpse was lying neatly on its back, arms at its sides. 'That's suicide out.'

And Auguste's theory with it. If Boris were a murderer it was possible he'd commit suicide, if he felt they might be on his track. If for instance he'd overheard Auguste telling Rose of his theory, or his discomfiting exposition to the Grand Duke. But this formal arrangement of the body put paid to that idea.

'Why,' Auguste pondered, 'would a murderer spend the time to give such attention to his victim, when he could not know if the lights would go up again quickly, perhaps sending people flocking back to the belvedere? Or indeed he could not know if he might be visible from the house in the darkness. A spur-of-the-moment murder, taking advantage of the dark, of the knife so conveniently provided, and yet a murderer who is not overcome with the enormity of his crime, but one who stays to arrange the body.'

He was smarting with the added humiliation that he had been wrong. Boris was not a murderer, but a victim. I will find out who, *mon brave*, he silently promised, feeling an affection for the old rogue, his iniquities in the cause of cuisine forgotten.

Doctors suddenly scattered like confetti as the Grand Duke charged into their presence, aware that something was going on. No gendarmes were keeping him out of things. The robbery – perhaps they'd found something in the belvedere. He roared in and, aware of the atmosphere first, then the corpse, stopped short.

'Boris?' he breathed, turning ashen. 'Who'd want to do that to old Boris?' There was quite genuine emotion in his voice. 'And just now some damned fool' – he caught sight of Auguste – '*you* were telling me old Boris was out to murder me. That's what comes of letting cooks out of the kitchen.'

Auguste was silent in humiliation, but the Grand Duke did not dwell on the point.

'Do you think Boris had anything to do with the theft?' he asked abruptly. 'Perhaps he saw the thief?' There was a note of eagerness in his voice.

'Why should the thief come down to the belvedere?' asked Rose practically.

'Plenty of people seemed to,' the Grand Duke pointed out. 'Saw heads bobbing around all over the place between the candles in the gardens.'

'Who, sir? When?' Rose asked urgently.

'Couldn't see who. Why don't you ask them?'

'We shall, sir. No doubt of that.'

'You don't intend to search my guests, do you?' asked the Grand Duke uneasily. 'It wouldn't go down too well.'

Nor should murder, was Auguste's instant thought.

'If we allow the guests to go home,' pointed out Rose, 'your jewels may go with 'em.'

'Let them go,' the Grand Duke said quickly. 'Catch the murderer,' he went on. 'More important than jewels. That's two he's got now. Who'll be next?'

'It may not be the same murderer,' Auguste pointed out. 'Perhaps Boris knew something about the jewel thief, and Lord Westbourne was killed for some other reason. Especially if you were the intended victim.'

The Grand Duke glared. 'I've had enough of your ideas. I tell you this, sir. You're a better cook than detective—' On this pleasant note he departed with Fouchard and Chesnais for the villa, leaving Auguste and Rose with the corpse, and a gendarme and doctor guarding it.

'Eighteen years since someone had the bright idea of using fingerprints for identification; and still we're not using it. I tell you, Auguste, if we were we'd have our murderer, just like that,' Rose said vehemently. 'The Bertillon

201

identification system is all very well, but you've got to have a sighting of the villain first.'

Auguste was grateful that Egbert made no mention of his earlier theories about Boris. They were still together, a team. A team that now would discover the truth. Auguste's honour was at stake.

It took some time to organise the departure of the guests, and it was well into the small hours that investigations were complete. Inspector Chesnais's were long since over in fact. There was no doubt in his mind.

Chesnais had little time for the niceties of the story told by the gendarme guarding the jewels, which he attributed to the over-rich diet of Provence.

'You see,' he told Rose triumphantly, 'no sooner do I release the Comte de Bonifacio than another murder takes place *and* a theft. This is the fault of Scotland Yard. Fortunately I was here to arrest this monster.' He paused. 'I have made an arrest,' he announced, squeezing every ounce of drama out of the situation.

'You've found the murderer?' Rose asked doubtfully.

'I have found the thief and I have no doubt a murderer too.'

'But—'

'I have employed the methods of *le maître* Eugène Vidocq. It is simple.'

'Who is it?' asked Rose, dread in his heart.

'I have arrested the Comte de Bonifacio.'

'For *murder* again?' Their worst fears were realised.

'For theft. A charge of murder will no doubt follow.' Chesnais departed in a blaze of self-importance.

The theft had been committed by the Ghost of the Man in the Iron Mask. Bastide was dressed as the Man in the Iron Mask. The case was proved.

Wearily, after Rose had hastened away with Fouchard, Auguste went into the supper room to gauge the chaos there. Life must after all go on. He must drag in the servants who, unable to go to bed, were clustered in the kitchens, to clear this wreckage, now Fouchard had given permission. No sign must be left by tomorrow. Thank heavens *Maman* had departed early. Dispiritedly he looked at the uneaten *plats*, the unappetising dirty dishes, the suddenly uninspiring galantine, through a haze of four-o'clock-in-the-morning dejection. Here was Misha, his beloved *pièce montée*, mutilated but hardly touched. So much loving care, and how little it mattered. He rubbed his eyes. He was seeing things. Wasn't he? He was already dreaming. But he wasn't.

Between Misha's front paws lay an old wooden chest on its side. Spilling all around it, cascaded on to the floor, were the Romanov jewels. Her white angelic fur was brightened with flashes of brilliant green, red and turquoise.

But of the Petrov Diamond there was no sign.

Fouchard had resolutely tackled his task of establishing from over 400 people exactly who had visited the belvedere during the supper interval, while Chesnais buzzed around like one of Trepolov's angry bees brushed off his comb, eager only to enjoy the honey of his labours.

On the Monday a dispirited group gathered once more in the belvedere at the Villa Russe. It no longer contained a corpse; the candleholders and half-burnt candles were sufficient memory of the Saturday night. The Grand Duke was slumped in misery, looking like someone whom events had conspired to outwit. There was a faint air of bewilderment on his face, coupled with unease.

His gardens were full of old candles, the ballroom of straggling palms and dead flowers. Fouchard had said the place might be cleared, but there were no damn staff to do it, what with everyone being interviewed and re-interviewed. And no cook! They'd been forced to send out to the Faisan Doré for food; that cook they'd hired – no, he was a detective, wasn't he? – or was he some kind of cook in

London? – anyway, he didn't seem interested in cooking luncheon, and the guests were all leaving and returning to Paris as soon as possible. Tatiana had left. Didn't blame her either. Who wanted to stay in a place where your jewels weren't safe, or your life either come to that? The Sûreté, Scotland Yard, and the Cannes police, and not one of them could lay their hands either on a murderer or, he thought sullenly, a thief. He frowned. He was in a somewhat awkward position.

An uneasy group gathered in the summerhouse, not the least uneasy of them Auguste. Events were getting out of control; he needed a holiday, it seemed, from detection too. How badly had he been misled. His cooking had never before failed to produce the answer to a problem.

Inspector Chesnais had departed for Paris, with a defiant Bastide once more in tow. A thief in Cannes could be left to Fouchard and the Nice Sûreté, but it stood to reason that if the Comte were the thief, then he had – despite what Inspector Rose said – killed Lord Westbourne in order to carry out his dastardly crime. The case was proved.

True, this took no account of why the Comte had left behind most of the jewels, and only taken the Petrov Diamond and the Seventh Egg, but it was not hard for Chesnais to find the answer. 'Mon ami,' he had loftily told Rose, 'this was merely his cleverness to throw me off the scent. It would be difficult to escape my eye with the lesser jewels, but the diamond, and the egg, could be hidden in his *hat*!' He had waited for approving cries but none came.

Fouchard had agreed with Rose. The investigation should continue to find Boris's murderer. provided Rose continued it.

Emmeline had not yet realised Bastide's unavoidable absence.

'Where's Basty?' she demanded impatiently, twitching at her tennis skirt. Her hat lay at her side, in readiness for an hour of lawn tennis and gentle dalliance with Alfred. 'I thought all whose who were in the belvedere were going to be here.'

'I'm afraid he's been arrested again, miss,' Rose told her reluctantly.

'What?' screamed Emmeline, as Alfred moved closer in protection. 'But that's impossible. He was here with us. Wasn't he?' She appealed to her new hero.

Alfred looked somewhat shamefaced. The fight didn't seem so much fun in view of what had happened afterwards. 'Yes, we were – er – duelling,' he confessed.

'What? With swords?'

'No,' admitting to the onset of modern times, 'with fists.'

'Would this be before or after the lights went out?'

'Before,' they said in unison.

'Then Mrs Tucker came down,' said Emmeline offhandedly, averting her eyes from the lady '—and Mr Washington.'

Mr Washington, sitting obediently now by Lady Westbourne's side, was contemplating whether a younger unmarried lady, even if matrimony were the inevitable result, might on the whole be much less trouble than his present involvements.

'And then, *mademoiselle*?' Fouchard prompted.

'We all talked.' Her voice trailed off, and no one seemed disposed to add anything.

'So you were all there together when the lights went out?'

'No,' she admitted unhappily. 'Basty and I went back to the house and a little later the lights went out.'

'I don't think that's quite accurate,' said Rachel, smiling. 'If you recall, the Comte left somewhat before you, and you ran after him. We followed a little later.'

'Did you catch him, miss?'

Emmeline turned pink. 'No,' she whispered, 'but he was

there. I know. I nearly caught up with him at the house but when the lights went out I came back to find Alfred, because the candles were alight here.'

'Did you—?'

'I had gone in search of her,' admitted Alfred unhappily. Once he had got free of Phèdre's clutching hands, he thought crossly. 'But I took a wrong turn and found myself at the house, so I turned and came back.'

Rachel had never seemed less attractive to Alfred.

'You didn't come back,' she said lightly. 'I don't recall, do you, Harry?'

'Well, I was going to,' said Alfred belligerently. 'I was nearly there when I heard Lady Westbourne's voice, and it seemed to me that no gentleman should obtrude on such an argument,' he finished firmly, delivering blow for blow. No, indeed, much more fun to linger in the dark outside the light cast by the candles. It had been quite a conversation.

'Argument?' said Lady Westbourne with knitted brow. 'What can you mean, dear Mr Hathaway? Harry, Rachel and I are old friends. You didn't take seriously my words to Rachel, did you? My poor Alfred, we play these little scenes from time to time to give her practice in dramatic art. It's a game we play.'

'You said you'd kill her,' pointed out Alfred with relish.

'Kill Rachel? My poor boy. You have much to learn. In any case, I didn't, did I? Look, here she is today, as beautiful as ever.' She bestowed a sweet smile on Rachel, indicating that she herself had been the victor.

Rachel looked round for Cyril. Cyril was such a tower of strength. Dear Cyril.

'When did you all leave the belvedere?' Rose continued.

'Cyril and I left together,' said Rachel. Left was hardly the word. He'd almost had to drag her, Cyril recalled. 'We went straight back to the house.'

'In fact we took the longer path of the "4". We had things to discuss,' said Cyril, a trifle grimly.

'And Lady Westbourne, you and Mr Washington were in the belvedere when the lights went out?'

'No, Inspector, we were on our way back when they went out, with Count Trepolov, who had joined us by then.'

It seemed so cosy; it had not been. Really, Harry almost made it seem as if he were yielding his place to Nicolai again. She had soon scotched that.

Trepolov was sitting in misery. Tatiana had returned to Paris, saying no more of his proposal. He must follow her. Surely now she would return his suit? But he must go now, despite the fact that the new colony of bees should be arriving. But he would soon be back, and they could be married in July or August, the time when the bees swarm, time to make new homes and a new life, a fitting time for a honeymoon.

Now he was recalled by a start with the distasteful subject of Saturday night, when he had wandered in the gardens to the belvedere, consumed in misery about Tatiana. Fancy Dora thinking he would return to her. How foolish. How little he cared now that the slight had been delivered whether she had another lover or not. All that was past.

'And why did you go to the belvedere, Count Trepolov? To see Lady Westbourne?'

He hesitated. 'No, Inspector, I wished to be alone with my thoughts. I had just become betrothed in marriage to the Princess Tatiana Maniovskaya and wished to think over my happiness.'

'Congratulations, sir,' said Rose, then suddenly jolted: *Tatiana?* A Russian princess. He glanced at Auguste, whose face told him all he wished to know.

'I left with Lady Westbourne and Mr Washington,' Trepolov said, 'just as the dead cook arrived. He was not dead then, you understand. He was annoying us. He asked us to eat his *zakuski* while we wished to continue our discussion,' he said with dignity. 'So we left, walking round the avenues. The "8", I think it was. While we were there the lights went out, and we hurried back to the house.'

'And you passed no one going in the opposite direction?'

'Yes,' said Lady Westbourne, glowing with triumph. 'One *person* did pass us – I believe *person* is the word. That *person* was in bright yellow.'

'So our friend Mimosa – if Lady Westbourne's right – was in the belvedere while the lights were out. Or Alfred Hathaway or young Miss Vanderville. The others claim to be back in the villa or making their way there.'

'They could have returned,' Auguste pointed out, trying hard to concentrate on what Egbert was saying and not the pain that raged within him.

'They'd have been seen in the avenues by the candlelight.'

'Not if they walked on the far side of the avenue. There would be a dark area where the candlelight shadow ends. And the candles in the belvedere are so high they would not show anything going on beneath them to observers from the house.'

'I don't see why La Belle Mimosa should kill Boris.'

'Unless it were Boris grabbed at the egg.'

There was a pause. 'Perhaps we'd better go and see the good lady,' said Rose reluctantly.

La Belle Mimosa appeared delighted to see them. 'So both of you wish to be my lovers, hah!' she cried triumphantly.

'No, Miss Mimosa.' Rose was firm. 'We've come to see you about Saturday night, as you know full well.' He didn't need Auguste's presence, strictly speaking, but he certainly was not going alone.

She was wary, the glint in the tigerish eyes very noticeable.

'So you find my egg, huh?'

'Not yet. Now, I understand you were walking towards the belvedere round the avenue of "8" when the egg was stolen. Sure you weren't already at the belvedere?'

208

'*Non. Eh, Inspecteur, quel est ton prénom? Que tu es beau, toi.*' Her tones were liquid honey. 'I was walking towards the belvedere, it is true,' she conceded, brought back to Saturday by the look on his face, 'but never got there. Picture it. The lights go out in the house. I am in the avenue. I run back towards the house. *Mon Dieu*, what is happening, I ask myself. But as I do so, I hear a sound in the garden. "Come here," he growls. I am foolish. I do so and this hand grabs me. *Mon Dieu*, what is happening? My egg, it is gone.'

'And what were you going to the belvedere for?'

'I go to admire the stars, *chéri*. What else? You think I go there to stab some crazy old Russian, eh?' She laughed. '*Non, Inspecteur*, I see the so proud Lady Westbourne go, I see Harry Washington with Madame Tucker.' She minced round the room in neat mimicry of Rachel Tucker under the influence of the tragic muse.

'Did you not see who stole the egg?'

'He had a cloak and a big hat, and a mask. That is all I know,' she said carelessly. 'And it was not a ghost. A ghost does not stay to insult a lady by putting his hand down where he has not paid to touch,' she added bitterly.

'And what of the gendarme guarding you?'

'*Pouf*, he is no good that one. When the lights go out, he goes rushing towards the house,' she said scornfully.

'Could this man have been the Comte de Bonifacio?' inquired Auguste.

She turned her full attention on to him, a slow smile lighting her face. 'Eh, Auguste. All men are the same in the dark.'

'All right, Higgins, tell me. What's your story?'

Higgins jutted out his jaw. 'Yer mean, where was I, Inspector, during the 'anky-panky? You knows very well. I was mending the electricity. General 'andyman, I am. Lucky I was around,' he added virtuously.

'We do not know *you* mend the electricity,' pointed out Auguste, determined to restore his wounded confidence in his powers of detection. 'We see you *go* to mend it, and we see you later saying you *have* mended it, and *voilà*, the lights are back on once more. But we do not know that perhaps Muriel is not down there mending the electricity while you are in the belvedere.'

Higgins sighed. 'So it's murder now as well as theft. The trouble with you lot in Scotland Yard is that you think life's all Sherlock 'Olmes and Dr Watson. It ain't that complicated. The lights went out, and I fixed 'em. Ten to one, you'll find the bloke that murdered Westbourne and old Boris was just feeling in a nasty mood and stabbed the first person 'e came across.'

'I'll be in a nasty mood afore long, Higgins, if I don't find out what you're up to,' said Rose feelingly.

Rose was to find himself one step nearer very shortly. In police headquarters, he found Fouchard eyeing eagerly a bunch of telegrams from Scotland Yard, sent regardless of expense, though doubtless there would be words spoken once Rose had returned. Whilst on foreign soil, however, they felt duty-bound to support him.

Rose whistled in surprise as he regarded the contents of one of the telegrams, and handed it to Fouchard, eagerly reading over his shoulder.

'So much for gentleman cricketer Harry Washington.' Harry Washington, it had transpired, was the son of Bert Lincoln, cracksman and jewel thief, at present safely a guest of Her Majesty's prison service. 'Like father, like son perhaps.'

But the beauty of the day lay in another telegram. The long shot had hit target. It had taken the Yard somewhat longer to track this one down. James Higgins had no previous connection with the Grand Duke Igor. But Mrs Muriel Higgins had.

'Muriel's mum,' Rose told Auguste in Mrs Didier's parlour some time later, 'used to work for the Grand Duke as a seamstress. There's no sign of her having left under any cloud, no trouble while she was working there. Far from it. There were no robberies at all. And *that*'s interesting in itself. So interesting, I think another word with Mr Higgins might be in order. There's something odd there all right, whether or not it's connected with Boris's death. I can't see why he'd want to kill old Boris, or why anyone would, come to that. He must have been killed because of what he knew or saw. And that would suggest it must have been someone in the belvedere who saw him there or someone who saw him going there, or overheard you telling him to take his food down there, and dashed back after him.'

'La Belle Mimosa is the most likely.'

There was a pause. 'A clever lady she is,' said Rose.

'And a pretty one.'

'Going to add her to your conquests?' said Rose incautiously.

Auguste tried to laugh, and remembering belatedly the Princess Maniovskaya, Rose quickly changed the subject.

'Now Boris has been eliminated, it seems likely he knew more than he said about Westbourne. Whether he knew it or not, he was holding some clue.'

'I think perhaps he did not know it,' said Auguste, still smarting from the Grand Duke's rebuffs and little mollified that Egbert still seemed disposed to take his thoughts seriously.

'What's your reasoning?'

'Because he was not a man of intelligence, to put two and two together. If he saw two, he would talk of two, and of two again, not of four. If he had seen something he saw I think he would have told us.'

'Suppose he were blackmailing someone? That could be a reason for killing him.'

'I do not see Boris as a blackmailer.'

'Then the other way round. Suppose someone were blackmailing *him* into silence with bottles of vodka or whatever, but realised this couldn't go on for ever. That sooner or later Boris would talk.'

'The kitchenmaid said,' Auguste thought back, 'that he didn't see the Grand Duke come out because he was out milking the cow. But suppose he saw someone *then*. Saw someone entering a window, something not quite right.'

'Yet he said he saw nothing. He was clear enough for all the vodka to see the dagger on the table – and to recall he only saw me and the Grand Duke go into the study.'

'There is one other possibility,' said Auguste slowly. 'That he knew who he had seen but was protecting the person.'

'Why?'

'Perhaps because they were Russian – they are a close circle.'

'Not among the nobs and lower orders,' objected Rose.

'But Boris identified himself with the Romanovs, and with Russian honour. So just suppose he'd seen a *Russian* kill Lord Westbourne.'

'Trepolov?'

Auguste stiffened at the name. How could she contemplate it? If it had to be anyone, why *him*?

'Trepolov'd no motive for killing Lord Westbourne – or the Grand Duke. Ex-lover of Lady Westbourne is hardly a good reason, and ex-lover is what he was. Still, it's possible, I grant you.' He glanced at Auguste.

'It would give me great pleasure if Trepolov were the guilty man,' Auguste said quietly.

'Ah.'

'To think that such a man—' He broke off, with a swift look at Rose. 'It is insupportable.'

'Quite so, Auguste.'

'There's the Grand Duke and Duchess,' went on Auguste

with an effort. 'Boris would protect them, and it would tie in with his melancholy after the event. The Russian despondency of which Natalia has told me. *Toska* they call it.'

It was an obvious fill-up for something to say and eagerly snatched at by Rose.

'Spare me that, Auguste. Not our Igor.'

Auguste laughed somewhat awkwardly. 'I cannot see the Grand Duke Igor deciding to kill his cook. But of course there have been such abominations.' He went off on a sidetrack. 'There was the Earl Ferrers who killed his steward, of course, and—' He broke off and looked at Rose.

Rose nodded. 'I know. We're still forgetting all about our friend Higgins. And the lovely Muriel.'

At this moment Mrs Didier brought in apéritifs and appetisers of *moules* marinated in lemon, wine and herbs.

'Taste them, my friend,' Auguste advised. 'They are somewhat different to those on Southend Pier.'

'There's nothing wrong with a good whelk,' Rose proclaimed stoutly. 'Our friend Higgins does a grand line in them at The Seamen's Rest. He's tied in with this somehow.' He frowned. 'I don't see him as a murderer, though. Thief perhaps. Here to remove the swag, certainly. But do you see Higgins shinning up drainpipes like an ape? Or dressing up in fancy cloaks? Much too fat.'

'Muriel's not.'

Auguste was at the flower market early on the Tuesday morning. He would take some flowers to Kallinkova, who had been dancing at Monte Carlo the previous evening. She would await him this morning eager to know what was happening. In his wretchedness over Tatiana, he had unconsciously avoided Natalia, when she had been so good to him. He bought a huge bunch of camellias and, almost blinded by them, cannoned into someone.

'Pah. You are a bad omen,' said the old Cannois. 'Every

213

time I see you something bad happens. I get arrested, I see ghosts . . . My son, you bring trouble in your wake.'

Auguste stood still, his spirits at the lowest ebb he could remember. Tatiana gone, she loved another. Natalia was her own mistress, doubtless she too would soon go. His art lay in ruins, and as a detective he seemed as good as a fallen soufflé. Did he truly bring trouble in his wake? Murder had followed him from Kent to the Galaxy Theatre, from there to Plum's – and now to Cannes, his native town. He swallowed, and seeing this the old Cannois's eyes softened. He patted his shoulder comfortingly.

'*Alors, mon fils, courage.* You are a *peis d'Avril, peut-être.* A mackerel. The April fool that comes too quickly to the net. Reflect, my son, reflect.'

Chapter Eleven

Natalia buried her head in the camellias, a gesture Auguste recognised. He recalled just so had she bent that graceful neck in *The Awakening of Flora*. He also recalled that camellias had no perfume, and wondered of what she was thinking. Perhaps it was simply to hide irritation at being thus interrupted in the midst of practice. He looked at her unlovely blue practice clothes and thought inconsequentially that those baggy trousers might very well do for bicycling. He quickly reproached himself for thinking thus critically of her. How privileged he was that she had even consented to see him. Her goodness, her kindness, her beauty – just the sight of her assuaged the pain in his heart left by Tatiana, now gone from his life for ever, gone back to Paris, no doubt to prepare for her wedding. Why did they speak of pain in the *heart*? It rested, that ache, not in the heart, but the stomach, lying there as physically manifest as one of Soyer's heavier receipts indulged in late at night.

Natalia sighed. 'I shall be glad when this season is over. I dance only tonight, and Thursday – and then—' She snapped her fingers.

'And then where?' he asked with resignation.

'Vienna, *chéri*, but then,' looking thoughtfully at him, 'in Paris. You come to see me?'

'*Non*,' he said abruptly. Not Paris, with its memories.

'Then we shall meet again when the good God wishes. Or perhaps not, if He sends your lady to you in my place.'

'That is not possible,' he said stiffly. 'She is to be married.'

'Ah. *Mon pauvre Auguste,*' Natalia said gently. Then: '*Eh bien*, now you tell me what happened on Saturday night after the inspector made me leave.'

She had changed the subject after a look at Auguste's face, but to a subject which had obviously caused her much annoyance. She was still aggrieved that she had been dispatched like the other guests with no recognition given to her special status. She had merely been delegated as hostess to the Princess Tatiana Maniovskaya who was to leave for Paris early the next morning. That had been most enjoyable, but nevertheless she still smarted from being omitted from the scene of the crime.

'So, poor Boris Ivanovich. Who wanted to kill him? He was a blackmailer perhaps? And he had a meeting in the belvedere with his victim?' It was an excellent plot for a *Strand Magazine* shocker but even she conceded that Boris hardly fitted the pattern.

'*Non*, it was a spur-of-the-moment murder,' Auguste said. 'It was his own knife. Moreover it was no appointment, for I myself sent him there.'

'And did anyone hear you tell him to go to the belvedere?' she pressed.

Auguste considered. 'It is very possible. I' – he looked shamefaced now that Boris was dead – 'I had raised my voice,' he admitted. He had indeed – he could remember the surprised glances of the guests looking round. But who? Which guests? He ransacked his memory. Surely – the thought went as Natalia spoke:

'He was not killed in mistake? After all, the lights were out.'

'Not in the belvedere. The candles gave sufficient light. Whoever killed him knew it was Boris. The murderer was either present when he arrived, or saw him setting off down the gardens, or' – he admitted – 'he heard me ordering him to go.' That memory again.

'But nobody would be in the belvedere alone?' objected Natalia. 'They would go *with* someone.'

'Many people,' said Auguste gloomily, 'seem to have been in the belvedere, and by the time the lights went out most claim to have been back at the villa, either with other people or having gone back alone. Except,' he paused, 'for Mr Hathaway and La Belle Mimosa.'

'Pah,' said Natalia vigorously. 'Why should La Belle Mimosa kill Boris? She makes a fool of you, perhaps.'

The old Cannois – you are a *peis d'Avril*, my son, Auguste thought fleetingly.

'*Mais non*,' he said. 'One must not think that because she shouted to the world that she would kill Westbourne, that she *told* us she was walking to the belvedere when Boris was there, that she is *not* the person who committed these crimes. We are not playing games here.'

'Why should she wish to kill Boris?' Natalia demanded, still scornful.

'Because he knew who killed Lord Westbourne,' said Auguste simply. 'Because he knew who the thief was.'

'Knew who – Ah, *mon ami*. You have robberies on the brain, you and the good Inspector Rose. Now I tell you, Auguste. I said I would help you in this affair so I have been talking. I have talked to more ladies of society, and some not in society, in the last ten days than ever before, and I tell you, Auguste, much goes on. You know already that Lady Westbourne had a lover, that she now has another lover, but you do not know that the day before the cricket match Lord Westbourne had discovered this fact and said he was going to put an end to it. She was scared. She did not know what to do. Suppose she decided what to do? Much happened at the cricket match, and not all on the field. Suppose when Lord Westbourne stamped off to make his report, she went with him? Think back.'

Auguste thought. He remembered La Belle Mimosa shouting, he remembered Lord Westbourne, deep in discussions on Africa, disappearing to write his report, and an idea came to him. Just suppose— He was recalled abruptly

217

to the present by Natalia's voice finishing triumphantly: '. . . Trepolov.'

Auguste thought savagely of the pleasure it would give him to see Count Trepolov arrested. 'He was with Bastide,' Auguste muttered unwillingly. 'They went out to the field.'

'*Oui, c'est vrai*, but what did he do while Bastide was kissing the lovely Emmeline?'

Auguste brightened. 'Natalia, you are a pearl of great price. A white truffle in the midst of mere mushrooms.' Then his face clouded. '*Non.*' He heaved a sigh. 'It is not possible. Washington saw him in the gentlemen's cloakroom. We must go on thinking if we are to free Bastide—'

'Bastide? *Comment?* But he *is* released.' she cried in surprise.

'Inspector Chesnais arrested him again, this time for being the robber. He was dressed as the Man in the Iron Mask, and so the Great Detective believes that because the robbery was done by the Man in the Iron Mask, it must be Bastide. No matter that the thief glowed in the dark. The identification is complete. He would like to pin the murders too on Bastide but at the moment cannot prove this.'

'*C'est ridicule, ça*,' said Natalia slowly. 'Something must be done. *La pauvre Emmeline.*'

What would Mrs Rose say if she could see him now, driving along the Boulevard de la Croisette in the carriage filled with flowers, next to one of the world's leading ballerinas, and wearing a fashionable new boater he'd bought at Folkett-Browne's in the Rue d'Antibes at the urging of Miss Kallinkova. Egbert grinned at Auguste. What would she say about this French haircut, come to that? Yet underneath this fairy-tale life he was well aware of the darker side, the side that spoke of murder and passions. And how easy it was to forget that to keep all this going there was a whole army of poorly paid French servants, who barely scraped a living. He supposed it was no different anywhere else; it became more noticeable in a place where foreigners were the meringue and the native population only the sponge beneath. He smiled. Auguste had got him at it now – giving everything a cooking analogy.

The Cannes Battle of Flowers organised by the Fêtes Committee was a special event. The Croisette was jammed with carriages smothered under flowers, many people in fancy dress and people throwing flowers at each other with much merriment. Rose had drawn the line at fancy dress but Natalia had fastened round his neck a garland of jonquils. He hoped this did not get back to the Yard, that no one was around to record this fact for the social columns of the *Illustrated London News* or even the *Cannes Gazette*. Lord Westbourne's murderer still remained at large, the murder of Boris too was unsolved, and the thief still remained elusive. The Grand Duke and Duchess passed their carriage in the Delahaye. Apart from the absence of the horse, it was indistinguishable from a carriage, since the vehicle was almost buried in flowers, the Grand Duchess seated in their midst like a fountain arising from a pool.

'There's that police inspector,' said Rachel suddenly to Cyril and the dog – once more in favour as she found herself bereft of outside male attention.

'True, my dear.'

'Why's he still here?'

'They haven't solved the murders yet. He cannot return until Lord Westbourne's murder is solved.'

'But they had the murderer! That Count.' Rachel's voice almost squeaked in most unactresslike tones.

'Apparently not.'

'You don't think he'll go on investigating, do you? Not *us*?' Rachel asked carefully.

Cyril did not answer.

She did not persist but flung a piece of heliotrope, not at

Dora Westbourne's face, but at her hat, knocking it askew, which was far more devastating. In return she received a red rose in her lap. Not from dear Dora. From Harry Washington.

Was it *lèse majesté* to throw flowers at a Grand Duke during the Battle of the Flowers? thought Auguste hazily and decided it wasn't. Unfortunately the orange flowers caught the Duke behind the ear. Auguste hastily ducked. Only Kallinkova was looking Igor's way, and his eye met hers meaningfully. She laughed, and tossed a geranium in his direction.

Now Count Trepolov was passing them. How dare he? thought Auguste furiously. He was riding in the Battle of Flowers with another woman when he was betrothed to Tatiana. Auguste had hardly recognised him. He was dressed as a bee, his companion clearly representing honeysuckle (the only reason for her presence had Auguste but known).

'He has murderer written all over him,' Auguste said viciously to Rose. He flung a particularly solid sprig of orange-blossom at him, and had the pleasure of hitting his target. 'He looks so like a murderer,' he continued wistfully. 'He had much time to kill Lord Westbourne and—'

'Now, Auguste, Trepolov's out. You know that.'

I still think he's a villain, Auguste thought, mutinously. Tatiana, to think that anyone but he, Auguste, should marry Tatiana. This holiday was turning into misery . . . save for seeing dear *Maman* and *Papa*. Almost he wished to give up this detection, yet he knew he had to stay to the bitter end if Bastide were to stand any chance of freedom. Yet now he *knew* who the villain was despite his wistful leanings to Trepolov. And very shortly now he would tell Egbert and Natalia. He had had time to think.

*   *   *

The Prince of Wales already was a free spirit. Riding in the carriage of his American friends, the Goelets, he was enjoying pelting as many bosoms as he could manage under the pretext of his fancy dress costume of a masked Don Juan. He fooled nobody.

He was congratulating himself that he'd had the sense to bow out of Igor's masquerade ball. He went hot and cold at the thought he could have been involved in a *second* murder.

Emmeline sat next to Alfred, her parents facing them. Alfred was enjoying himself. He gaily pelted Rachel with a heliotrope as her carriage passed by, not noticing the look on her face that resulted. True, Emmeline had been just a little quiet since Bastide's abrupt reappearance and rearrest but nevertheless Alfred was happy. Her parents, clearly thinking a penniless English poet was one step up on a murderer and thief, were smiling on his suit. Oddly, Emmeline, once her parents had given their blessing, didn't seem quite so ardent when he kissed her, but she would come to herself again. Greatly daring, with her parents watching indulgently, he took her hand and was rewarded by a faint smile.

'You'd never think,' said Rose, amazed, looking at the flowers arcing through the air between carriages, 'that they were all suspects in a double murder case, would you?'

The day was sunny, the air was perfumed, all the glory of Cannes surrounded them, lulling them into its sensuous embrace.

'*Non*,' said Auguste absentmindedly. 'I would not.' He would not speak now. The dish required just a little more cooking before he presented it.

' 'Ello, Wales,' shouted a throaty voice to Don Juan. A true gentleman, he did not, like the occupants of many other carriages, ignore the greeting, crude though it was, but

221

cheerfully tossed a rose at the Chinese Empress. La Belle
Mimosa was riding in solitary state, her carriage smothered
in sweet-smelling mimosa. Her thoughts were not as sweet.

Save for the Prince of Wales, only Kallinkova bowed
towards her as their carriages passed. '*Bonjour, madame,*'
she greeted her. A grin crossed La Belle Mimosa's face as
she took in her companions.

'Eh, Natalia, you throw me a rose, huh? That one—' She
pointed to a red-faced Egbert.

From the beach, the old Cannois stood watching disgustedly. The Battle of the Flowers was for the *hiverneurs*
nowadays. Now in the old days it had really been something. It had been part of the old Cannes. It was part of the
old Provence. The Greeks had brought the floral games.
His eyes lit up. Races by naked girls. Now that had been
something . . . Not so long ago, only two hundred years or
so, in his great-great-grandfather's time, they'd still run
them in Grasse on every Thursday in Lent. Then the bishops
had put their foot down. He sighed. Spoilsports. No indi-
viduality anywhere any more. It had come to this –
hiverneurs throwing flowers at each other. He noticed
Auguste and shuffled forward purposefully to the carriage.
'It's Friday, *mon fils*,' he cackled. 'You'll be out tonight,
yes?'

'Why?' Auguste looked at him suspiciously.

'Good hunting, my son. I reckon he'll walk tonight, that
ghost of yours. He likes Fridays, he does. 'Specially this
one.'

'Don't you ever tell Edith about this,' said Rose forcefully
as, fortified by a feast of *Papa*'s *bourride* and *Maman*'s
Pond Pudding, they set out that evening. 'A whiff of a
suspicion about me going ghost-hunting and I'd never hear
the last of it.'

'And moreover it is the day of April fools,' Auguste

joked. 'Nevertheless, I think there is something deeper than a jest here.' He shivered. The evening was cool. There was not a soul about. This was not La Croisette where the grand hotels ensured a flow of people whatever the time of day; this was the old town where people went to bed early and rose early, and at night there was no distraction comparable with the pleasures of eating a meal behind closed shutters, and retiring replete to bed.

They walked out of the Rue du Barri and climbed into the Rue de Mont Chevalier, leading up to the church and the old fortress.

'It was here that he walked before, Egbert. Just there he vanished.'

'Into thin air? I don't believe in ghosts, Auguste. And I don't believe in this one. What I do believe is that if we track him down, it may help us persuade friend Chesnais to let that boy go.'

'I think,' said Auguste excitedly, 'that we can do that without a ghost, *mon ami*. I feel the truth stares us in the face, and we have ignored it.'

'What – cripes, look at that!'

Rose grabbed Auguste's arm, and pointed. High above them by the battlements of the old fortress was a shrouded figure, glowing dimly in the dark.

'It's him.'

'Well,' said Auguste grimly, 'if he's glowing he is our thief and no ghost. *Courage, mon ami*—' as much to convince himself as Egbert.

'Sure?' gulped Rose, as they ran up the slope of the pathway. Below the fortress the path divided, one way leading round to the far side, the other, the quicker way, to the postern-gate drawbridge leading into the Place de la Castre surrounded by the battlement wall.

'You go that way, it's easier,' panted Auguste, speeding round the far side and up the connecting steps. His heart was thumping by the time he arrived at the old fortress.

Pelting round to the front into the Place de la Castre, he joined Rose by the battlement wall overlooking the hillside.

'Nothing?'

'Nothing,' Rose confirmed.

'But there must be some sign. There's no other way he could have gone. The church?'

'Locked.'

'The old church?'

'Locked. And so's the tower.'

They gazed out over the dark Suquet hill, below them the Bay of Cannes, the Croisette and the new town glowing with lights.

'That was no ghost,' said Rose flatly. 'Was it?' he asked, suddenly uncertain.

They looked around them but neither the old disused twelfth-century church of St Anne behind them nor the new church of Notre Dame bore any sign of possible routes of escape for human ghosts.

'I tell you what, Auguste, this is an April fool and no mistake. If that was a ghost, I'll eat my new boater.'

'I think I can find you a dish more palatable than that, Egbert,' said Auguste thoughtfully. 'The dish that stares us in the face.'

'Let's hear it.'

'It seems to me that we all overlooked one thing,' said Auguste. Here in the cool air it seemed so clear, so obvious, he wondered at their blindness. 'Lord Westbourne announced he was going into the writing room to prepare his report for the Niger Conference. He never did so – he was murdered before he had written more than a few lines. Suppose that was the intention? Suppose someone wanted to stop his report?'

'Bastide?' said Rose doubtfully.

'No. Westbourne was a peacemaker. Had Bastide stopped to think – as he rarely does – he would realise that Westbourne was France's best hope – that's unless Bastide

224

actually wanted a war, of course,' said Auguste, side-tracked. 'In which case it does give him a motive if Westbourne was about to suggest a compromise. But others too perhaps. Now think, who would know Westbourne's views? Who is in the Colonial Office?'

'Cyril Tucker,' said Rose thoughtfully. 'Of course.'

'Suppose it was in his personal interests to stop Lord Westbourne's arranging a compromise? Just suppose. And he could have done it,' said Auguste eagerly, 'if he'd followed Westbourne out almost immediately.'

'I'll make inquiries,' said Rose. 'It's a thought. It's definitely a thought. I'm going to Paris tomorrow to see Chesnais and I'll go back to the Yard to see what I can find out. I'll let you know when I'll be back.' He paused. 'While we've a moment, Auguste, that Princess Tatiana – was she your Tatiana by any chance?' he asked awkwardly.

'Yes.' Auguste stared out over the bay, trying to stem the wave of misery that flowed over him.

'Did she know you were here?'

'She saw me when I took the menu to the Grand Duchess. She left and we did not speak.'

'Ah.' There was a silence, then: 'It's a funny old case, isn't it?' Rose tactfully changed the subject. 'Like that maze at Stockberry Towers. And that play of Shakespeare's.' An idea occurred to him, but before he had time to pursue it:

'Look!' Auguste hissed and pointed downwards. There in the gardens below them was a ghostly glowing figure, beckoning. 'This way. We watch him this time.' Auguste was already running.

Rose followed him through the postern and on to the pathway, but the ghost had already vanished.

'You take the top road, Egbert. I will go down the hill.'

Auguste ran down the pathway. This was ridiculous, he was thinking. He was in search of a ghost that wanted to be seen, that was clear. Was that it ahead? He turned the corner. The figure didn't seem to glow now, but there was

225

undoubtedly a misty shape in the gloom beyond the single gas light. A shape that had nothing to do with imagination. He ran towards it as it disappeared round the corner. No matter. He would catch it up, there was nowhere for it to go. No doors that might open for it provided Auguste was quick. Yet by the time he reached the old watchtower, misty and dank-smelling, the road held nothing but himself. He was alone.

'Here!' he heard Rose's voice shouting, high above, just as he himself shouted, 'Egbert! *A moi!*'

Impossible that the ghost could still be up there! Rose had made a mistake. Yet Auguste turned and panted back up the pathway. No human could have run quicker. By the time he reached Rose his breath was coming in uneven jolts.

'I nearly got him,' cursed Rose. 'Round there, going down to the old town behind the hill.'

'He wasn't,' said Auguste. 'He was my side of the hill, by the old watchtower.'

'No, *here* – look!' Rose pointed to the foot of the pathway leading off the hill, where a black-cloaked figure had halted, its hand briefly raised in farewell, before disappearing into the gloom.

'The fellow seems to fly. And he wasn't glowing either. There's no ghost. He's human, and using phosphorus. But it can only be on one side of the cloak. He turns it inside out. That's how he wasn't noticed going into the room by the gendarme. *Ghosts!* Rubbish. Our man went along the corridor or down the drainpipe and in his black and all the confusion wasn't seen.'

'Then why,' asked Auguste, not wholly convinced, 'did he bother with the phosphorus at all?'

'Had to persuade them he was a ghost, so as they would panic and run outside, and he could pinch the jewels.'

'But that—' Auguste stopped, then looked at Rose who nodded and completed the sentence.

'Meant the lights had to go off.'

'Higgins,' they both said in unison.

'*Maman*, it is too much. The Grand Duke must do without a cook—'

'Would you let the Grand Duke go without his Easter luncheon on the *jour de Pâques*?' Madame Didier cunningly pleaded.

'Then I will prepare it, *Maman*, and not you.' Thus resigned, on Saturday the 9th Auguste found himself once more in the kitchens of the Villa Russe.

It was strange without Boris rumbling around. The police were all gone now, and the villa was licking its wounds. But with no trace yet of the Petrov Diamond, and Boris's murder still not solved, there was a feeling of unease in the air. Tomorrow morning Egbert would return, and then perhaps all would be well once the murderer was arrested.

Meanwhile he had seen little of Natalia, and nothing of the Tuckers. The case was almost over, but why did he not feel the same sense of combined exultation and relief as he had before?

The Easter cake was ready for the morrow. How Boris would have approved. He offered up a silent apology for having suspected him of being a murderer and in propitiation had prepared the Russian Easter specialities of *kulitch* and *pascha* himself. He could do no more, barbarous though they seemed. Doughy, heavy and solid. Was this fare for Provence? True, the cardamon was an interesting touch. He had won the approval of the kitchen staff at any rate by the time he was ready to go. The *real* food, the lobster, the *faisan*, were as perfect as his professional eye could demand. *Voilà*, tomorrow he would meet Rose, and the case would be settled. *Then* he could enjoy his holiday.

He unlatched the gate of the tradesmen's exit and went out into the quiet velvet night. With a sudden lurch of horror he realised he was not alone in the chemin de

227

Montrouge. Dropping from the wall on to quiet feet not far in front of him was a familiar figure, cloak, hat and mask. This couldn't be a ghost. This was flesh and blood, and he intended to find out whose.

But startled at first, the other's reflexes were quicker, as he sped away on quicksilver feet. How so quietly? pondered Auguste even as he ran. Perhaps it was not a man, not a ghost, but a hallucination. Despite a nagging irrational fear that when he reached him his arms would enclose empty air, he ran on in pursuit, up towards the grounds of the Villa Nevada and the fir woods. Would he turn right towards the woods, seeking safety among the cypresses and pines? No, he was going into the grounds of the Villa Nevada. Auguste hauled himself up slowly over the high wall, but the other had the advantage and had disappeared by the time he got there. Breathing heavily, Auguste stood indecisive. Where now? He must not lose him again . . .

Bushes loomed dark at him in the night, trees rustled gently. Not a sign of human movement. Then he saw the folly, an English eccentricity of a summerhouse. He must be in there. He crept up to it, out of sight of the door, entering only to see his quarry disappearing through a window.

That settled it. No ghost! he thought grimly. Auguste ran out of the door and through the grounds like an eel, brushing past huge eucalyptus trees and palms. His prey was making for the far wall. Ten seconds later and he was over it.

Cursing, shins already barked from the last encounter with a wall, Auguste flung himself over, falling heavily on the other side. He picked himself up, to see just ahead of him his quarry, who had stayed for a moment to look back at his pursuer's mishap.

Staggering after him Auguste ran on, through the carpet of pine needles. Perhaps his own cuisine gave him strength, perhaps his quarry half-halted in indecision, but he gained on him, until he was but a hand's stretch beyond Auguste's grasp. A superhuman effort, and the cloak was in his hand.

A sudden lurch of terror lest nothing be beneath it, lest it were a ghost after all. Then throwing himself at his quarry's back he brought him to the ground, tumbling together until the wiry body lay struggling beneath him. With his last ounce of strength, he ripped off the mask.

It was Natalia Kallinkova.

Chapter Twelve

'*Alors, Auguste, ce n'est pas amusant, ça.*'

Natalia stalked round the room, a caged leopard, while Auguste watched grimly.

'You will tell me what you were doing. It was to protect Bastide, perhaps? And he is the real thief, not you?' he inquired, desperately wishing to give her the benefit of the doubt.

'*Non,*' she said scornfully. 'Yesterday, and the other evening, yes, to show Bastide could not be a thief. But the rest – Ah, you will never understand.'

'I understand very well,' Auguste said loftily. 'It is you who do not. *Ma mie*, I have no choice. I must hand you to Inspector Rose, who is bound to tell Inspector Fouchard, or even Chesnais.'

She sat down, folded her arms and glared. '*Naturellement*. You have no imagination, no *délicatesse*.'

'It is not delicate to be a thief,' he hurled at her. Then pleadingly: 'Natalia, there must be some *reason*. Please tell me.'

She glanced at the little clock on the mantelpiece and laughed, which infuriated him even more.

'*Non,*' she said simply.

'Then I stay with you here, until I can get word to Inspector Rose tomorrow morning.'

'You will not come to my room. I don't want people who don't trust me in my bed.'

'And I do not want you escaping from the window. You

231

are almost certainly a thief and perhaps a murderess.' They glared at each other, the small lithe figure in black, and the slim, tall cook.

'Ah, Auguste, you cannot believe that.' Tears filled her eyes. Were they genuine? Almost he relented.

'Of course I do not. I cannot. But when you refuse to give me an explanation, what else can I do?'

'Tomorrow morning all will become clear, Auguste. And now I go to bed. I am your prisoner. Very well, I will sleep in my bed. You shall lie across my threshold like the Imperial guards.'

Auguste felt his eyes closing, closing; he could not stay awake all night. She wouldn't try to escape, would she? She was his Natalia. How could such things be? It was a nightmare. 'Tomorrow,' she had said, but suppose in the morning she had vanished? He wrestled with the probability that his angel was nothing but a common thief, or rather an uncommon thief, with this ridiculous charade of a ghost. And perhaps a murderess too. No, that was impossible. He refused to believe it. Yet all night he tossed and turned restlessly on the sofa drawn across the entrance to her room. She, not he, had insisted on it, a glint in her eye.

It was not until one o'clock on Easter Day that Egbert Rose appeared in response to Auguste's summons on the telephone. The morning had passed in tense silence, and to a tired, worried Auguste the sight of Egbert was a shock, for despite the seriousness of the situation, the inspector was trying hard not to grin as he came in. Kallinkova, demurely clad in light blue, her hair dressed in girlish curls, bore little resemblance to the panther struggling in his arms last night, thought Auguste grimly. How was he going to persuade Rose that last night had really happened? But he didn't need to. Auguste's words hadn't made any sense at first to Egbert Rose. But a lot had happened since then, and now it did.

'Didn't I say, Auguste, that there was someone around throwing dust in our eyes like that Puck? I don't say I approve, but it's you, isn't it, Miss Kallinkova? You and those eggs . . .'

'Eggs?' echoed Auguste, an awful foreboding creeping over him.

Not long before, an interesting scene had taken place at the Villa Russe.

The day had not started well. In the absence of Boris, the Grand Duke had been reduced to painting the traditional red eggs for the table himself, and had covered himself in red dye, making himself look more like Sweeney Todd than a Grand Duke.

The red-painted egg labelled The Grand Duchess, left by the Grand Duke overnight on her breakfast table, proved hard to open. Very hard. And no wonder.

Deep in conversation about the political situation in Bulgaria, the Grand Duke peered round the enormous palm adorning the table as he heard his wife say, 'Igor!' in a strange voice. She was staring fascinated at her egg.

'Off, is it? It's that blasted police sergeant we've hired as a cook.'

'No, Igor. It's the Petrov Diamond.'

She raised her eyes, and gazed thoughtfully at her husband.

He turned brick-red. 'I didn't put it there,' he said inexplicably.

'I'm sure you did not, Igor. But is it not interesting that the thief returns not only all the jewels, but the diamond too? What an unusual thief. Especially since the Sûreté Générale tells us he is in their custody in Paris?'

The Grand Duchess remained thoughtful as, following the traditional custom of Easter Morning, they went into the gardens to watch the servants hunt for their Easter eggs in the grounds, which contained small gifts from the Grand

Duke and Duchess. This morning was to provide a most unusual surprise. Instead of the familiar rouble in a painted wooden egg, six lucky recipients found themselves blankly staring at a Fabergé Easter Egg, each of which contained a large ruby.

The Grand Duchess's face grew more thoughtful still, the Grand Duke's even redder, as his wife's accusing eyes fell on him. The six eggs were rounded up firmly but politely by the Grand Duchess, despite a noticeable desire by one small scullerymaid to hold on to this strange present, and offer of restitution quickly made. Collecting her trophies, the Grand Duchess sailed back to the villa, the Grand Duke trailing disconsolately behind. She spread them on a table and studied them carefully, especially the miniatures of her husband.

'These look to me, Igor, uncommonly like Fabergé eggs, and resemble that worn by a lady in yellow. Igor,' she paused, 'I feel there may be something about which I have been kept in ignorance. Do you not think the police should be summoned?'

Igor clearly did not, but the question had been merely rhetorical as she moved purposefully towards the telephone.

'Igor is a delightful, though mean grand duke, Inspector,' Natalia said soberly. 'He has no one to blame for his discomfiture but himself – though I am afraid he will not see it that way.' She sighed. 'I will try to cheer him up,' she added. 'He is generous to begin with, he hands out Fabergé eggs to his former loves, and tells his friends of his generosity. Then he makes a big mistake. He grows mean. There are too many ladies. So he gives not Fabergé eggs, but common copies with inferior rubies. Fakes. Then he makes a bigger mistake. He gives a fake to La Belle Mimosa. Imagine such foolishness! And,' she dimpled, 'he then makes a bigger mistake still: he gave a fake to me! To

234

me, Natalia Kallinkova, prima ballerina in St Petersburg, in Vienna, in London, *to me*!' Her eyes flashed at the indignity.

'But I knew La Belle Mimosa,' she continued, 'and I persuaded her not to face Igor with his *bêtise*, but to make a plan to humiliate him. His Imperial Majesty the Tsar helps – without knowing, naturally. He demands of Igor that he get the eggs back; no one but the Tsar shall give these gifts. So Igor asks me for my poor little fake back too, lest I or La Belle Mimosa should boast of having a Fabergé egg.' She looked scornful. 'So I worm the truth out of him, and, *voilà*, the plan is made. I will steal the eggs for him, I tell him, and give them to him back. All for the sake of the love we used to share. And he believed it! Such is the vanity of men! But once I give them to him, I plan to steal them back at the masque in order to expose him publicly for his meanness. So either all the ladies will get their eggs back or gifts to compensate them. And this is what I did.'

'And why this Man in the Iron Mask?' asked Auguste suspiciously.

Her eyes danced. 'It is fun, yes? When you are a woman, you cannot roam the streets alone at night. You are not supposed to know the freedom of breeches. It is not ladylike! Huh! But I like it, it is fun. And what better way to burgle than when people run away from you? So I take this way. I thought I would experiment, haunt the tower, take advantage of the old legend – and then I saw Auguste. Oh what fun to tease.'

Waves of fury vibrated in the air.

'If you are a ballet dancer, acrobatics are easy; to scale a wall quickly, to climb a tree, *pouf*, it is nothing. You are gone in a second – and so the ghost of the Man in the Iron Mask walks, in plenty of time to practise for the burglar. When people are afraid of ghosts, they expect to see them, even when they are not what they seem. The rumours were all round Cannes in plenty of time for the ball. I had a bedroom on the second floor to change in for the ball, where of course I change to Iron Mask, and as soon as the lights went out—'

'Helped by your accomplice,' said Rose grimly.

'*Précisement*. I made my way along the balconies to the Petite Bibliothèque, go in the window, change my cloak to the phosphorus-coated side, and when the gendarme comes in to see all is well, *pouf*, he is so scared, running out into the corridor again, I change the cloak round, take the box and simply walk along the corridor to my room.

'My *second* accomplice is waiting. I hand over the box and change at my leisure. The box is taken downstairs, the lights go up, and my accomplice removes the box in front of you all. Later I remove the eggs and the Petrov Diamond, and return the rest of the jewels to the supper room later. Ah, Auguste, your lovely Misha. She looked so pretty with the jewels.'

Auguste glared.

'This accomplice wouldn't happen to be Mr Higgins, miss?' asked Rose resignedly.

'But of course, Inspector. He is so very good with electricity.'

'And your second accomplice would be Muriel, I suppose.'

'Mrs Higgins. Just so. And that dear old man also. He was so helpful.'

'And why,' said Auguste quietly, 'were only *six* eggs found – I believe you said that, did you not, Egbert?' Rose nodded.

Natalia made a face. 'Ah, dear Mimosa. Not the best of accomplices. First, she chatters, and I believe it is through her that Lord Westbourne told you he had proof of my identity. And then she agrees to cooperate on her terms only. She does not trust the Grand Duke to give her a real egg or valuable jewels, so she insists that when I steal the eggs she has one of the real eggs in place of her fake, right

236

away. So I have to forge an invitation – not difficult – and poor Muriel Higgins must run to the belvedere, snatch the fake and give Mimosa a real egg, all in the dark. And how pleased Mimosa was, and what a performance she gave then. Igor must make it up to her generously now.'

'And the Petrov Diamond?' said Auguste still suspicious of her motives. 'What need of that?'

'Eh, Auguste, you think you are clever, huh? I make a better criminal than you detective. I want the Grand Duke to call in the police; if I just steal the eggs, who knows about it, eh? Igor will not tell. We need the police there, lots of them, so everyone knows when the eggs are found again.'

Rose looked grim.

'But *how* does everyone know?' asked Auguste. 'Only the servants at the Villa Russe—' he stopped, and nodded.

'Yes,' said Natalia. 'Mr and Mrs Higgins and the old Cannois will make sure the whole of Cannes knows – especially the ladies Westbourne and Tucker.' She chuckled.

'Do you realise the amount of public money Scotland Yard has spent on this?' said Rose grimly. 'Not to mention the Comte de Bonifacio being locked up? What's Chesnais going to say?'

'I could not have guessed how stupid Inspector Chesnais would be,' she said with a frown. 'I appeared as soon as I could to show that Bastide could not be the ghost of the Man in the Iron Mask.'

'Egbert, you will not tell Chesnais the whole story?' Auguste was horrified now all was clear. 'You cannot mean this? No harm has been done. The Grand Duke cannot complain as he in effect stole the eggs himself. And in Kallinkova, see what the world would lose if she went to prison.'

There was a terrible moment of silence. Then: 'You've a point,' said Rose. 'Chesnais would hardly want to arraign the Grand Duke . . .' He frowned. 'I've no authority here of course. All in all, provided the ladies are compensated, and provided we can get Bastide freed, I think it had better remain an unsolved crime.'

A relaxation, a sigh of relief from Auguste.

'But it wouldn't, mark you,' Rose went on, 'if it weren't for the fact we've got two murders to clear up.' He paused. 'It's done now, thanks to you, Auguste.'

'To me?' Auguste felt a glow; he had not failed. Rose's Paris trip had yielded fruit.

'You have discovered something about Mr Tucker?' he asked eagerly.

'You were quite right, Auguste. Not only has the gentleman very substantial holdings in the Royal Niger Company but it was quite difficult to establish the link since he was holding them under a false name. Obviously it wouldn't look too good for a gentleman in his position at the Colonial Office to have such a great personal interest in the Niger question, when he's supposed to be briefing the conference objectively. It all hinges on the interpretation of the international treaty of eighteen ninety. The British Government, no doubt partly through the mouth of Mr Tucker, claim the treaty gives them absolute powers in the hinterland west of the Niger and north of the ninth degree of Latitude, which is the area the French are disputing. But apparently this treaty is open to question, and Westbourne was inclined to compromise. Now if he'd found out about Tucker's interests and was threatening to reveal them—'

'Yes,' said Auguste, his reputation restored. 'Of course, that would explain what we heard Westbourne suggest.' He glowed.

'Chesnais is set on making an arrest this afternoon. He's none too sure, but is going to play along with it.' Rose glanced at the clock. 'Three o'clock at the Villa Russe. The last party.'

Except for Lady Westbourne and Mrs Tucker, Fouchard had had difficulty in persuading everyone of the importance of their attendance at the Villa Russe, and various gendarmes had been dispatched in pursuit of those who were enjoying the delights of a visit to the hermit on St Cassien hillside, or the Observatoire, and it was thus nearer four when the last of the group arrived at the salon in the Villa Russe.

Rose had filled in the time constructively. 'Well, Higgins?'

'Well, Inspector?' Higgins straightened up from the Delahaye to meet the coming Armageddon.

'You didn't keep perhaps one gem for yourself?'

'No, Inspector. Not that I know what you're talking about.'

'Caught us nicely by walking past with your toolbox. What did you do with the real one?'

'Muriel took it.'

'All right, Higgins. Explain.'

Higgins paused as if in admiration of his handiwork in polishing the horseless carriage.

'I take it you've no authority 'ere, Inspector?' he inquired politely.

'None,' said Rose cheerfully.

'E's a mean old sod,' said Higgins unexpectedly and unresentfully. 'That's what Muriel and me thinks. It all goes back to Muriel's mum. She works there for years and years, faithful service and all that stuff, 'onest as the day is Muriel's mum. So all the while, me and Muriel puts the word round London, hands orf the Grand Duke. No nicking, no cracks, no nothing, 'cos Muriel's mum thinks he's all right. Then Muriel's mum gets her eyes screwed up and she can't work no more. Thank you very much and 'ere's a copy of the Russian Bible. Mean old devil. So I promptly takes the word orf. 'Ave a go, lads, I said. Give it all you've got. But we 'ardly got started afore Miss Kallinkova comes to see me. Right suspicious I was at first – 'ow she got my name and all. But she's a lady all right. She talks me round to seeing this is more fun. *And* a bit of an 'oliday,' he said virtuously. 'Going straight makes a change – seeing you've no jurisdiction of course.'

It was almost like an afternoon at the Monte Carlo casino, waiting to see on whom the die would fall. But this casino was playing for high stakes. Auguste was almost glad that he knew the outcome and could prepare himself.

Sitting with Chesnais and Fouchard was a sulky Bastide, released in their charge pending confirmation of Rose's most satisfactory theory. Typical imperialists, dragging people in and out of prison. He had hardly had time to suffer. True, Emmeline seemed eager to see him, which was compensation, and not very eager to sit by Hathaway.

Auguste looked at Natalia, who was chatting to Rachel as though she had not a care in the world. She was beautiful, she was good, but she was not for him. She had been right. He had been forced to realise today that she lived in a different world, that she was not his Natalia, but someone who was his but for a fleeting time, and even then had a whole secret life of which he was not aware. It changed things. A squeeze of the hand, as they sat in the carriage, and without a word it was all acknowledged, leaving a vast emptiness in his heart.

Cyril Tucker was blandly talking to Alfred Hathaway. How self-effacing, how normal-looking. So Jack the Ripper must have looked in everyday life. Yet underneath torrents raged. A double murderer.

And Lady Westbourne, sitting apart from Washington. To think they had almost accused him of being the thief. Auguste smiled. The son of a jewel thief. How would the Gentlemen of England take to that if they knew? Lady Westbourne's eyes were resting thoughtfully on Alfred Hathaway. Come to that, Auguste noticed with indignation, so were Kallinkova's. Ah no, he must be imagining things. And there – he turned his glance away quickly – was Count Trepolov, sitting haughtily by the side of the

Grand Duke and Duchess. How could she? Oh, how could she?

There was a crash, as without waiting for a footman to open the door La Belle Mimosa entered, an Easter vision. 'Hey, Igor, look at my egg!' She held out her hand on which a Fabergé egg, complete with portrait of the Grand Duke Igor, rested. Igor shrank back. Lady Westbourne and Rachel Tucker glanced at each other with smiles of satisfaction. They had arrived early for their quiet discussion with Igor.

Once again the Grand Duchess swept into action. She rose composedly to her feet. 'Thank you, madame,' she said, as she swept the egg from the outstretched hand before La Belle Mimosa could withdraw it. 'The item will be returned to his Imperial Majesty the Tsar. I think you will find this sufficient compensation, madame,' she added before the scream of rage left Mimosa's throat.

La Belle Mimosa's eyes narrowed as a footman advanced with a small box on a salver. She opened it, looked at the gold necklace and speedily calculated its value. At least she wouldn't have to go about with that bloody great lump on her bosom any more. Gold necklace . . . she examined it carefully and bit it. She nodded. Then she swept a curtsy that would have done justice to the grandest debutante, giving the Grand Duchess an excellent view of her erstwhile rival's greatest asset. The Grand Duchess smiled sweetly. Her eye roved thoughtfully over three other ladies in the room, all of whom were smiling sweetly and innocently. But no more was said.

Inspector Chesnais took his moment of glory. By his investigation he had shown that the Comte de Bonifacio was innocent. He beamed. True, Scotland Yard had been of some slight assistance in revealing the true murderer of Lord Westbourne.

Dora gave a sob and Hathaway rose to sit by her in con-solation. After all, if Emmeline had decided that Corsican Napoleon was better than he, why should he not? Emmeline

in fact had discovered the joys of being eighteen years old.
Devotion was all very well, but so *boring*. There were so
many delightful young men in the world, who were neither
Corsican counts nor poets.

Egbert Rose began to speak.

'I've our friend Monsieur Didier to thank for leading me
to the solution.'

The Grand Duke's brow furrowed in annoyance.

Auguste's ego bounded to a new height. He could not
bear to look at the Tuckers.

'Following his suggestion, I went to Paris and London
and carried out some investigations with my friend here,
Inspector Chesnais. And what we found has led us to make
a positive identification of Lord Westbourne's murderer.'

There was a stir and a muffled shriek.

'Shall you make an arrest, Inspector?' boomed Rachel
tremulously. She did not look at her husband.

'No, ma'am. For one thing, I've no authority here, and,
secondly, the murderer is dead.'

Dead? Auguste stiffened, thunderstruck. Cyril Tucker
looked politely interested, no more, Rachel suddenly
relieved. *Dead?* What was this? Was this a trick of
Egbert's? It must be.

'Lord Westbourne was killed by the Grand Duke's cook,
Boris, just as you suggested, Mr Didier.'

The Grand Duke gave the first reaction. He spluttered.
'Nonsense!'

Auguste was tossed into a topsy-turvy world.

'There's no doubt, sir. Inspector Chesnais has discovered
that he became involved with the group of Nihilists who
were lying low in Paris and flushed out in the early 'nineties
– all but Boris. He was saved by working for you, which
made him above suspicion at the time. In London I've discovered he was a frequent visitor to the Autonomie Club
in Tottenham Court Road where all the Anarchists used to
go. Remember the bomb that exploded in Greenwich Park

and killed the man that was carrying it – a Frenchman, Bourdin? He was a habitué of the club and there's reason to think Boris knew him in Paris.'

He paused. 'Boris was not a clever man. He believed in two things: the honour of Mother Russia, and that one day the people would rise, though I doubt if he knew just what that meant until he met the Nihilists in Paris and they persuaded him it was his duty to kill you as an enemy of the people. But to him you upheld the honour of Russia so he simply ignored them. Then circumstances brought things to a head. At the match, sodden with drink, he decided you'd let Russia down, sir.'

The Grand Duke, beleaguered on all sides, sat deflated lacking even the will to protest that he had achieved a wonderful victory in avoiding defeat at the match.

'He saw you go into the study, turned away, perhaps to get you some milk – who knows? – and then it occurred to him. There was the dagger. He entered. Westbourne over his shoulder saw it was only a servant and went on writing. There was the blazered back. Short-sighted, seeing that and the glimpse of the beard, he stabbed him fatally. Then he went back to the kitchen, and collapsed – where you found him, Mr Didier.'

The Grand Duke's brows were still knitted in stupefaction. 'Do you mean to tell me that I've been paying a Nihilist to cook for me for eighteen years?' The Duke seemed to think Rose was to blame as the enormity of it smote him.

'Well, not eighteen – but a good part of that, sir. Yes.'

No less rigid with shock was Auguste. He had been right in his theories. But what of Tucker? Why had Egbert let him think Tucker was guilty? Why had he not taken him into his confidence? And above all, who—?

'There's one thing they all forgot to ask,' said Rose, eyeing Auguste thoughtfully as they departed. 'Who killed Boris?'

'Naturally, they were not interested,' murmured Auguste, still aggrieved. 'He was only a servant.'

'Don't take it amiss you were wrong,' said Rose, getting instantly to the bottom of Auguste's discontent. 'I couldn't tell you. Chesnais insisted on it.'

'Did Tucker kill Boris then?' asked Auguste, bewildered.

'You can forget about Tucker, Auguste.'

Auguste grunted, deflated.

'It's that dust in the eyes again,' said Rose. 'Firstly, we made the mistake of thinking that as there were two murders, they must be connected. They weren't. Not a bit.'

'But who would want to murder Boris apart from Westbourne's murderer?' Auguste asked, completely at sea.

'You can come with us to see. Chesnais's agreed. We're going to make the arrest now. We thought it too dangerous at the Villa Russe.'

They climbed into the police van with Chesnais, Fouchard and two gendarmes. As they arrived at the villa, Auguste was silent when he saw where he was, his heart churning with emotions.

The manservant opened the door. His master was in the garden he told them. At the far end of the garden was a tall uniformed figure, face unguarded, sword at his side. He was bent over a hive, opening it, singing loudly the while.

'One moment. I must just attend to my bees,' he cried.

The group halted abruptly as, annoyed at the noise and disruption, the bees swarmed angrily into the air and fastened on their nearest prey. With a cry of mingled ecstasy and pain, Count Trepolov lunged his sword into his body.

'Why?' said Auguste some time later, still visibly shaken. 'Why did you not warn me?'

'I couldn't, Auguste. I was sworn to secrecy. You need a drink, and no wonder,' Rose said compassionately. 'Didn't expect that to happen. Very nasty.' They sat down at a café on the Allées de la Liberté. 'Chesnais will place on record that he was mad, and there's no doubt he was in a way. He'll put forward that Boris had something on Trepolov; that Trepolov killed Boris, because he knew Boris had killed Lord Westbourne, or because he knew Boris was a Nihilist and so killed him before he could kill the Grand Duke. On account of the fact that he had a passion for the Romanovs.' Rose paused. The air was heavy under the velvet sky.

'Why did I not see?' asked Auguste helplessly.

'You said he looked like a murderer, but you were guessing. You got halfway and no further. Because you were blinded by this man, Auguste, because you thought he was going to marry your princess.'

Blindly Auguste set down his glass. '*Non* . . .'

'When I was in Paris,' said Rose carefully, staring out to the sea, 'I found out a lot about Boris, as I said, but I also paid another visit. You see, this case has been a mix-up from the beginning and it got worse as it went on. It got so you couldn't see the criminal – and not the victim either.'

'You mean Lord Westbourne and the Grand Duke?'

'No, I mean Boris. Boris was killed in mistake for someone else.'

'For whom?' Why did his hand tremble?

'For you, Auguste.'

A shiver, as Auguste looked at his friend. 'For me?' he whispered.

'I paid a call on a lady when I was in Paris. The Princess Tatiana. A very nice lady too, if I may say so,' Rose said carefully, not daring to look at Auguste. 'I had this idea floating around in my head. I asked her a question or two, and she answered quite straightforwardly. I asked her if she was going to marry Count Trepolov.'

'You—' Auguste began chokingly. 'Tatiana—'

'She told me no, so I started wondering why he'd said she was. It must have been pride, I thought. Had she definitely refused him? I asked. Oh yes, she said. And then she told me something else. She said she'd told him she was in love with another man, whom' – Rose steadied his voice – 'she could not marry, and therefore wouldn't ever marry anyone.'

'And who was this man?' asked Auguste carefully, trying to keep his voice neutral.

'She told him, she said, she was in love with the cook.'

Auguste was suffused with joy and sadness, incapable of speech or thought. He could not seem to concentrate on what Rose was saying. It made no sense.

'So I went on to reason,' Rose continued, 'that she was staying in the Villa Russe. She couldn't have meant *Boris* though. She hadn't seen him. She meant *you*. You'd seen her when you took the menu to the Grand Duchess. She must have assumed *you* were the cook there. But to Trepolov "the cook" meant Boris.'

Then Auguste remembered. He heard himself at the cricket match saying, '*Non, monsieur*, I am not the cook. There is the cook.' And he had pointed at Boris, and so signed his death warrant.

'So Trepolov decided if he couldn't have her, you weren't going to either. I think he saw the murder as some kind of duel, from the way he laid out the body.'

'Did he love her so much?' Auguste asked in a low voice.

'I don't think he did. Not for herself, anyway. I think he was mad and that's what she thinks. He was mad about two things: his bees and the Romanovs. He wanted Tatiana because she's related to the Romanovs, and you got in the way. A cook. It was an insult of the highest order.'

Auguste looked at the drink in front of him. 'Boris was killed for me.' He tried to take in the reality of the words.

'He'd have gone to the guillotine, anyway, Auguste. Don't go feeling sorry for him.'

Auguste gave a great sigh. Tatiana loved him. The air was warm, the enchantment of Cannes restored, but it was empty of Tatiana's presence. As was his life for ever. Yet she loved him, and he was alive, and there was always hope. He smiled and rose to his feet. 'Let us go, Egbert.'

They began to walk towards the Rue du Barri and the promise of Madame Didier's salmagundi for supper.

'You know, Auguste,' said Rose presently, judging the moment right, 'I always knew it couldn't be Tucker.'

'Why?' Auguste asked indignantly.

'No Englishman would kill another at a cricket match.'

Auguste forced a laugh and then, restored, laughed again. Things were right between himself and Egbert.

'What about Kallinkova?' asked Rose as they walked up the Rue St Antoine towards the Suquet Hill.

'She is a great and rare blossom, Egbert. But not for me. We pass our different ways. For me now always she will be the Man in the Iron Mask.'

Rose was silent for a few minutes as they climbed the steps to the pathway above the Rue du Barri. 'That reminds me,' he said suddenly, 'I'd been meaning to ask. What happened to the other one?'

'What other one?' asked Auguste blankly.

'The other night – we both shouted together. We both spotted the so-called ghost. Yet I was up there chasing – Kallinkova. You were down here going the other way. As soon as you joined me, we both saw Kallinkova on the far side of the hill. She was real enough. But what happened to the other one?'

They caught each other's eye. The eerie night air took on a sudden chill, and with one accord their footsteps broke into a run.

A selection of bestsellers from Headline

FICTION

STONE COLD	John Francome	£4.50 □
PRODIGAL SINS	Rosalind Miles	£4.99 □
MAGGIE OF MOSS STREET	Pamela Evans	£4.99 □
SHADOWFIRES	Dean R Koontz	£4.99 □
REASONABLE DOUBT	Philip Friedman	£4.99 □
THE OLD CONTEMPTIBLES	Martha Grimes	£4.99 □
THE ASSIZE OF THE DYING	Ellis Peters	£3.99 □
WATERSMEET	Philip Boast	£4.99 □
TREAD SOFTLY ON MY DREAMS	Gretta Curran Browne	£4.99 □
THE POWER	James Mills	£4.99 □
PURPOSE OF EVASION	Greg Dinallo	£4.99 □

NON-FICTION

THE ENTERPRISE YEARS	Lord Young	£5.99 □
A Businessman in the Cabinet		

SCIENCE FICTION AND FANTASY

SETI	Fred Fichman	£4.50 □
RITNYM'S DAUGHTER	Sheila Gilluly	£4.99 □
WOLFKING	Bridget Wood	£4.99 □
THE GOD KILLER	Simon R. Green	£3.99 □

All Headline books are available at your local bookshop or newsagent, or can be ordered direct from the publisher. Just tick the titles you want and fill in the form below. Prices and availability subject to change without notice.

Headline Book Publishing PLC, Cash Sales Department, PO Box 11, Falmouth, Cornwall, TR10 9EN, England.

Please enclose a cheque or postal order to the value of the cover price and allow the following for postage and packing:
UK: 80p for the first book and 20p for each additional book ordered up to a maximum charge of £2.00
BFPO: 80p for the first book and 20p for each additional book
OVERSEAS & EIRE: £1.50 for the first book, £1.00 for the second book and 30p for each subsequent book.

Name ....

Address ....

....

....